Sky Dog's eyes narrowed. "A wheel *inside*? A medicine wheel?"

Glupp shook his head, his brow furrowed. "No, not that kind of wheel. A wheel that works with a machine." The Lakota shaman frowned in annoyed confusion. Kane and Grant exchanged puzzled glances. Then Brigid spoke up: "A *cog* wheel?"

Glupp's eyes brightened and he threw her a fleeting, appreciative glance. "Yeah, that's it! A cog wheel!"

Sky Dog's scowl deepened. "What the hell is he talking about?"

Brigid smiled wryly, lifting three fingers one at a time as she enunciated the letters. "Cee-Oh-Gee. Continuity of Government. The Millennial Consortium has found a COG facility inside Medicine Mountain."

Other titles in this series:

James Axler
Outlanders®

CERBERUS
STORM

A GOLD EAGLE BOOK FROM
WORLDWIDE®

TORONTO • NEW YORK • LONDON
AMSTERDAM • PARIS • SYDNEY • HAMBURG
STOCKHOLM • ATHENS • TOKYO • MILAN
MADRID • WARSAW • BUDAPEST • AUCKLAND

First edition November 2005

ISBN 0-373-63848-5

CERBERUS STORM

Copyright © 2005 by Worldwide Library.

Special thanks to Mark Ellis for his contribution to
the Outlanders concept, developed for Gold Eagle.

Printed in U.S.A.

It is I who travel in the winds,
It is I who whisper in the night,
I shake the trees,
I shake the earth,
I trouble the waters on every land.
—Song of Towasi, the Owl Prophet

The Road to Outlands—
From Secret Government Files to the Future

Almost two hundred years after the global holocaust, Kane, a former Magistrate of Cobaltville, often thought the world had been lucky to survive at all after a nuclear device detonated in the Russian embassy in Washington, D.C. The aftermath—forever known as skydark—reshaped continents and turned civilization into ashes.

Nearly depopulated, America became the Deathlands—poisoned by radiation, home to chaos and mutated life forms. Feudal rule reappeared in the form of baronies, while remote outposts clung to a brutish existence.

What eventually helped shape this wasteland were the redoubts, the secret preholocaust military installations with stores of weapons, and the home of gateways, the locational matter-transfer facilities. Some of the redoubts hid clues that had once fed wild theories of government cover-ups and alien visitations.

Rearmed from redoubt stockpiles, the barons consolidated their power and reclaimed technology for the villes. Their power, supported by some invisible authority, extended beyond their fortified walls to what was now called the Outlands. It was here that the rootstock of humanity survived, living with hellzones and chemical storms, hounded by Magistrates.

In the villes, rigid laws were enforced—to atone for the sins of the past and prepare the way for a better future. That was the barons' public credo and their right-to-rule.

Kane, along with friend and fellow Magistrate Grant, had upheld that claim until a fateful Outlands expedition. A displaced piece of technology…a question to a keeper of the archives…a vague clue about alien masters—and their world shifted radically. Suddenly, Brigid Baptiste, the archivist, faced summary execution, and Grant a quick termination. For Kane there was forgiveness if he pledged his unquestioning allegiance to Baron Cobalt and his unknown masters and abandoned his friends.

But that allegiance would make him support a mysterious and alien power and deny loyalty and friends. Then what else was there?

Kane had been brought up solely to serve the ville. Brigid's only link with her family was her mother's red-gold hair, green eyes and supple form. Grant's clues to his lineage were his ebony skin and powerful physique. But Domi, she of the white hair, was an Outlander pressed into sexual servitude in Cobaltville. She at least knew her roots and was a reminder to the exiles that the outcasts belonged in the human family.

Parents, friends, community—the very rootedness of humanity was denied. With no continuity, there was no forward momentum to the future. And that was the crux—when Kane began to wonder if there *was* a future.

For Kane, it wouldn't do. So the only way was out—way, way out.

After their escape, they found shelter at the forgotten Cerberus redoubt headed by Lakesh, a scientist, Cobaltville's head archivist, and secret opponent of the barons.

With their past turned into a lie, their future threatened, only one thing was left to give meaning to the outcasts. The hunger for freedom, the will to resist the hostile influences. And perhaps, by opposing, end them.

Prologue

Though he couldn't see his pursuers, he sensed them tracking him in the darkness, sidling through the deeply shadowed forest just out of the range of his vision and hearing.

His name was Tuktel Tahea Yanka, which translated as Fleet Deer, and on this night he did his best to honor it. He ran through the shifting curtains of snow with the speed and agility of his totem animal.

The black gnarled branches of trees clutched at him as he sprinted among them. The scattered pines cast distorted, skeletal shadows over the white-flecked ground, and the wind whispered taunts to him. The rustling of air seemed to carry the distant voices of spirits, of Fleet Deer's forefathers, filling the mountain silences with an undercurrent of terror.

He refused to heed the whispers. Fleet Deer's young legs pumped steadily, the muscles as finely honed and strong as the best bowstrings woven by Lakota artisans. Still, he accepted with fatalistic certainty that he couldn't outdistance his pursuers. The Lynx Soldiers were familiar with the country and were expert trackers. Alone, unarmed, barefoot and naked except for a breechclout, Fleet Deer entertained no hope of standing them off until—or if—Sky Dog came in search of him.

Fleet Deer realized his only chance lay in eluding his enemies by reaching Lodge Grass Creek and concealing his trail and scent in its waters. But the creek was a long way off. He prayed his friend Chikala had fared better than him in confusing Catamount and Deathmaul. Both men had broken away from the Lynx Soldiers at the same time, running in opposite directions with the enraged shrieks of Catamount and the bewildered snarls of Deathmaul ringing in their ears.

Despite the cold, sweat sheened Fleet Deer's face and poured down his neck where the large veins pulsed from his exertions. He couldn't remember how long he had been running, but he knew he soon had to rest. Sprinting downhill over rough ground was almost as exhausting as running uphill. The frigid night air burned his throat and the soft tissues of his nasal passages.

Fleet Deer had grown to fifteen summers loving to run. He had trained himself to be the swiftest of foot of his people. He took pride in his graceful long-legged lope, his legs moving so fast and smoothly they blended into a blurred glide that spurned the rocky ground beneath his feet.

He knew better than to look back, so he kept his gaze focused only on what lay immediately ahead of him. Still, he couldn't help but wonder how far he raced down the face of Medicine Mountain. He guessed three or four miles at most, since the Moon had been in a different position when he broke free of the Lynx Soldiers. With a great mental effort, he put his pursuers out of his mind and tried to give himself up completely to the task of running.

His mind toyed with images of galloping horses, of thundering herds of buffalo. He thought of home, of his mother and of his uncle Sky Dog who had dispatched him, Long Nose, Buffalo's Ghost and Chikala on the spying mission. He resolutely ignored the pain that grew in his chest and the waves of dizziness assailing him, instead concentrating on his legs, commanding them to keep moving. He swallowed a mouthful of cold air, wincing as it burned his lungs. He jumped over a log, nearly stumbled on loose stone, regained his balance and forced himself on.

The young Lakota warrior wondered if his pursuers were only playing with him as they had with Long Nose and Buffalo's Ghost, taking an evil delight in running him, harrying him like prey until he collapsed and begged for death. Fleet Deer felt he had to look back, just a quick glance. He knew his body couldn't tolerate much more punishment without rest. He was afraid his muscles would seize, his legs lock up and freeze. The poison of fatigue was spreading through his system. He cast a glance over his right shoulder, squinting through his long black hair streaming out at the back of his head. He saw nothing, but the light in the forest was tricky. Patches of deep gloom alternated with pallidly lit glades where the Moon managed to shine its lambent light down through the interwoven boughs.

Fleet Deer slowed his pace but didn't come to an immediate stop for he feared that his muscles would stiffen in the cold. By degrees, he carefully shortened his stride and relaxed his pace until he was trotting. He found a tree against which to lean. He inhaled deeply, air rasping in and out of his straining lungs, then held his breath for a few seconds, listening intently. He heard only silence, except for the pounding of his heart.

Slowly he exhaled and after a few moments his respiration was no longer as labored. Gusts of wind began to whip the tree limbs, flakes of snow dancing in the shafts of moonlight. He massaged his stiff knees, noting apprehensively the numbness of his toes. Thrusting his hands into his armpits to keep the fingers warm, he realized that to assume he had made his escape was optimistic to the point of naiveté, but still, he experienced a surge of hopeful giddiness. He had run the best race of his life and was proud of himself. Then he heard the noises.

A stealthy rustling sounded behind him, as of a large body moving through the brush. There were other noises approaching him, too—not quickly, not loudly, but not pausing, either. Things crept through the darkness toward him on two and four legs, and he knew they possessed fangs, claws and a thirst for blood.

Pushing away from the tree, Fleet Deer gulped air,

balancing himself on the balls of his feet, flexing the tendons. He knew he had to keep running. He refused to consider what would happen if he was recaptured.

He began running again, but with less speed than before. The arch of his right foot cramped and every time it impacted with the ground, needles of pain shot up through his leg into his hip.

Fleet Deer breathed in strangulated gasps, heedless of the noise he made. He knew his pursuers could see him or smell him so keeping quiet was far less critical than continuing to run. Apparently, those who chased him felt the same way. He heard them clearly, closer behind him, despite the wail of the wind that caught up the snow and whirled it around him like miniature cyclones. Soft running footsteps kept pace with his own, and animal pantings came from behind him.

The strength of the wind increased and the bare tree limbs shook with it, dried pine needles showering him. Fleet Deer tasted a warm salty tang on his lips. It took him a few seconds to realize that his mouth, chin and even his upper chest were covered with blood. It rivered from his nostrils, his body's silent protest against the punishment it was taking.

He knew they were very close behind him now, and the skin between his shoulder blades crawled in anticipation of receiving a lance head or a hurled tomahawk there. The rest of his body tensed, expecting the impact of clawed paws and the tearing agony of razor-sharp fangs.

He caught a brief, almost subliminal glimpse of a figure flitting from a patch of moonlight into a wedge of
murk. The impression he received was of an animal, feline head. The gloom suddenly seemed to be populated
by silent stalkers all around him.

With blood-chilling suddenness, a screeching yowl
pierced the darkness, full of malign triumph. Fleet Deer
choked back a sob of helplessness, of hopelessness.
The chase was almost over.

Bursting through a row of elms, Fleet Deer nearly
pitched into empty space. He dug in his heels and
rocked to a clumsy stop, panting loudly. Directly in
front of him the lip of a gully sloped precipitously
downward. The drop was about twenty feet into the
rushing, ice-edged waters of Lodge Grass Creek, trib-
utary of the Powder River. The surface glittered with
highlights cast by the Moon and the stars.

Fleet Deer didn't hesitate. He jumped, arms and legs
flailing the air. He splashed feetfirst into shockingly
cold water. The icy temperature nearly made him empty
his lungs in a gasp. Clamping his lips tight, he swam
beneath the surface, stroking furiously. The creek, fed
by melted snow spilled down from the Bighorns, was
only a degree or two above freezing. He knew if he
stayed in the water too long, he might never get out of
it.

Swept along by the current, Fleet Deer kept beneath
the surface until the pounding of blood in his temples
and the frigid bite of the water became intolerable. He

kicked upward and his head broke a thin layer of ice filming the shallows and he fought the impulse to cough and gasp. Tree roots, looking like gnarled fingers, twisted down toward the creek from the bank.

Raking his long hair from his eyes, clenching his jaw muscles to keep his teeth from chattering, Fleet Deer tilted his head up and back, scanning the indigo sky and mountainside beneath it. He saw nothing but the Moon and a frosty scattering of stars above the tree line, somewhat veiled by the snow flurries. There was no sign of his pursuers and though he wanted to believe he had lost them, he couldn't convince himself.

He stroked for the far side, and using roots as hand- and footholds, the young Lakota clambered his way up the muddy bank until he reached the top of the bluff. He felt more than justified in lying down and catching his breath.

He couldn't lie for very long. He knew he had to keep moving or the low temperatures would do what claws and fangs had not. Despite that realization, Fleet Deer didn't rise. He continued to lie there, noting how pleasantly warm his limbs began to feel. The spreading warmth stung him into a floundering rush to his hands and knees. Horror surged through him. He was freezing to death.

Staggering erect, he forced himself to start running once more, his every footfall jarring his entire body and blurring his vision. He swerved to avoid the trees looming in his path and searched for a clear path so he could achieve his full speed.

Fleet Deer heard a splashing from the creek behind him, a faint, husky grunt and involuntarily he cast a glance over a shoulder. He didn't turn away from another tree fast enough. His left foot plunged into a hollow formed by two thick roots and pain seared through his ankle. As he fell, he heard the faint crunch of cartilage.

Repressing a groan of frustration and pain, Fleet Deer extricated his foot and pushed himself to his feet again. He achieved three shambling steps before agony flashed through his leg, from foot to thigh, and he fell again. He didn't know if his ankle was broken or sprained, but he knew he wasn't going to run any farther.

Raising himself on his elbows, he dragged himself back to the trunk of the tree that had cost him his mobility. He twisted to a sitting position and waited, composing his angular face into an expression of calm, fearless acceptance. When he heard the snuffling sound in the darkness, his lips twitched in fear but he quickly clenched his teeth, baring them in a defiant grimace. With a slight shaking of leaves, the brush parted.

As he expected, he saw Deathmaul first, padding among the trees on huge paws. The young man's throat constricted at the sight of the heavy muscled, tawny cougar, the moonlight dappling through the branches shining on its glossy coat. The cat's mouth was open as it panted, saliva dripping from the long yellow fangs, the beige fur dark and wet from crossing the creek.

Fleet Deer guessed twelve feet stretched from his bewhiskered snout to the black tip of his tail, and he probably weighed about two hundred pounds.

When the creature caught sight of him, he didn't
snarl or hiss. He growled, a very low rising and falling
note, almost like signal, and regarded the young man
with calculating, faintly luminous green-gold eyes.
Fleet Deer did not move, forcing himself to meet the animal's stare. He received a brief, almost subliminal impression of intelligence glinting in the cougar's eyes.

The great cat was a hunter of men not by instinct but
by conscious choice, driven by devotion to his master
and the simple lust of death dealing. Fleet Deer numbly remembered tales of Deathmaul's horrific ferocity.

Then he heard the swift rustling of running feet and
six Lynx Soldiers materialized out of the gloom, spreading around him in a semicircle. They were all young
lithe women, and all were dressed in pelts of panthers
and bobcats that left their copper-colored limbs bare except for bands of colorfully beaded fur. Their jet-black
hair hung loose, framing faces painted with brightly colored geometric designs to symbolize their warrior society and spirit power. They were armed with
long-bladed knives and tomahawks. Two of them cradled single-shot rifles in their arms, brass cartridges affixed to the wooden stocks to allow for swift reloading.

The Lynx Soldiers didn't approach him but eyed him
from a distance with the same kind of passionless calculation as Deathmaul. Fleet Deer knew they awaited

the arrival of their chief. A few seconds passed before Catamount stalked out of the shadows and strode toward him, moving with a feline grace of her totem, her muscles undulating beneath bronzed flesh. The suffuse moonlight gleamed in satiny highlights on the curves of her bosom, the sleek thighs and long muscular legs.

Catamount wore the hollowed-out head of a panther like a hood. Its golden-brown pelt draped her shoulders and back like a cloak. From underneath the pelt fell two thick braids of black hair, barely covering her high, round breasts. A brief kilt of cougar skin was twisted about her loins, and wet boot moccasins encased her feet to midcalf.

Fleet Deer couldn't help but stare at her, both in fear and admiration. Catamount was a strong, long-limbed woman, nearly six feet tall. Her big eyes were like chips of anthracite and set wide apart in a face of coldly chiseled loveliness. The set of her lips, the angle of her chin suggested the austerity of a goddess.

He had heard tales of the chief of the Lynx Soldiers for years, a savage warrior, a renegade whose strange dark beauty haunted men's dreams. Rumor also had it she was a witch, and she cast spells over male enemies who then swore they would die for her—and, it was whispered, had indeed died after a spending a night or two in her lodge.

In her right hand she gripped a long lance, its wooden haft decorated with feathers and sixteen coups—the scalps of Catamount's enemies slain by her in combat.

The trophies marked her as perhaps the most deadly warrior of all the Lakota people.

The cougar lumbered toward her, lowering its head to be petted. She fondled it roughly behind the ears, then slapped it absently on the haunch. The beast sat, staring piercingly at Fleet Deer.

Catamount stepped up to within a few feet of the young man and gazed down at him silently, contemptuously. Lowering her lance, she prodded his swollen left ankle with its point. Fleet Deer didn't react despite the pain flaring up and down his leg. Catamount smiled slightly, approving of his stoicism.

In the Lakota tongue, she said, "You have run far this night." Her tone of voice held a bell-like contralto, vibrant and imperious. "Sky Dog named you well. But the totem of the puma is a far more powerful totem than a deer. Did he not tell you that?"

"My uncle told me many things," Fleet Deer retorted, a bit surprised by how steady his voice sounded. "He told me how you were exiled from our band because you did not put the welfare of all the people ahead of your own soldier society."

She didn't appear to be offended, intoning quietly, "There is Sky Dog's truth and there is my truth."

Angrily, Fleet Deer retorted, "I have seen you take orders from the white dirt-diggers with my own eyes! That is *my* truth!"

"All these truths cannot be braided into one rope. But you are here with me, so it is my truth that matters this night. If you live to speak with Sky Dog again, you will learn whose truth has more power…his or mine."

Fleet Deer couldn't suppress the note of suspicion in his voice. "You will let me go?"

Catamount moved her head forward slightly. "You will return to Sky Dog and give him a message. Tell him that the *tai-me* will soon be found. He will not send any more spies or warriors against me, the Lynx Soldiers or the Millennialists. We will seek him out when we are ready."

Fleet Deer couldn't feel relief. Taking a deep breath and slowly releasing it, he asked, "What about my friend? Where is Chikala?"

Catamount shook her head as if annoyed. She half turned and gestured imperiously with her lance. A Lynx Soldier stepped close, dragging a length of rope. It was attached to a cruel yoke made of two tied-together saplings. The yoke formed pincers around the neck of a young naked man, his wrists bound tightly to either end of it.

Cold nausea surged in Fleet Deer's belly. Chikala swayed, his blood-streaked face bruised and battered beyond almost all recognition. His name meant Little One, an obvious joke since he was very tall and burly for his age. His mouth sagged open and his eyelids drooped. Behind his friend's eyes, Fleet Deer saw only exhaustion and pain.

"I suppose you want me to free him, too," Catamount stated with a forced exasperation. "You really are taking advantage of my merciful nature."

Fleet Deer refused to be baited. He swallowed hard, not trusting himself to speak.

"But," Catamount continued, "since he provided me and my soldiers with a few moments of sport I'll give him a chance. If he can run one hundred feet without Deathmaul catching him, I'll let you both go free."

The Lynx Soldier detached the rope from the yoke and spoke sharply to Chikala. He didn't appear to understand or even hear, but he suddenly lunged forward, shouldering the woman aside. She screeched in anger, snatching at him. The young Lakota had taken barely three steps when, with a single spring-steel legged bound, Deathmaul leaped atop him.

The yoke of wood splintered and snapped, the thongs giving away like wet cobwebs. A swipe of curving, unsheathed claws flayed almost all the flesh from Chikala's back. He went down amid flying ribbons of blood and uttered a single, brief outcry.

"That's a shame," Catamount said blandly.

As Fleet Deer watched in sick horror, the giant cat gutted Chikala with a single slash of a hind paw. Loops of blue-pink intestines spilled onto the ground. Huge jaws closed over the back of the young man's head, the fangs sinking into the bone with a crunch, shearing through the skull.

Catamount called to the cougar and almost immediately the animal released its prey, backing away from the flesh-stripped, eviscerated body, its muzzle and bared fangs glistening with fresh blood.

She stepped over the coils of viscera lying on the barren ground, a knife blade gleaming in her hand. Propping her lance up against a tree, Catamount bent over Chikala and moving with the skill of long practice, inserted the point of the knife beneath the mangled flesh at the youth's hairline. She made two swift incisions and ripped away his scalp. It separated from the skull with a sticky smack.

Marching over to Fleet Deer, she thrust the scalp toward him. "I'm afraid your friend was a disappointment both to me and Deathmaul. You will have to make your journey alone. You can take this part of him with you, if you like."

Fleet Deer spit at the woman but didn't score a hit. Lips curling over her teeth in a silent snarl, Catamount bent and wiped the bloody scalp of Chikala upon his face and chest. Restraining his mad urge to grab her by the throat caused his limbs to tremble.

Catamount stepped away from him, eyes glaring from the shadow cast by the cowl formed by the panther's snout. Her full breasts heaved in fury, her nipples, distended either by the cold or arousal pushing aside the braids of hair. Sheathing her knife, she reached down to her wet moccasins and withdrew a long thong of rawhide. Quickly, she tied three small, hard side-by-side knots in it. As she did so, she spoke curtly to her warriors. A pair of Lynx Soldiers stepped forward and hauled Fleet Deer to his feet, paying no heed to his barely repressed groan of pain.

They securely tied his wrists behind him with plaits of leather.

Catamount looped the wet rawhide thong around the young Lakota's throat, centering the knots at the windpipe. "Now," she said softly, her voice a seductive croon, "you have perhaps three hours to get back to your nest of spies before the sun rises, the rawhide dries and strangles you. So, if I were you, I would run as fast as I could away from this mountain."

With that, she spun Fleet Deer and prodded him none too gently in the backside with the point of her lance. He leaped forward, then limped hastily into the darkness.

A woman with white tufts of beaded fur dangling from either side of her head murmured, "He will not make the camp of Sky Dog before he dies."

Catamount shrugged dismissively and turned away, stretching out her hand toward Deathmaul. The beast arose, bumping her hand with its head, purring loudly. "Even so, Snow Leopard, he will still deliver the message. A dead man can oftentimes speak far more eloquently than a live one."

Chapter 1

Like snails inching across a vast expanse of white sugar, the convoy crawled over the barren snowfields of the Bighorn Basin. Engines laboring, the five heavily loaded carriers crept up the grade, spumes of frozen powder arcing from beneath the huge knobby tires. Suspensions creaked loudly and the axles groaned as the trucks rolled one by one over the crest.

The vehicles jounced and swayed along the old road. The passage of years and assaults of the elements had raked it into a rugged hellway. The security men assigned to each of the big vehicles gripped the edges of the wooden guard boxes erected atop the cargo compartments of the trucks.

Roughly clothed, the keen-eyed men kept constant watch on the far-reaching vista of the white wastes, searching for anything out of place. The five men cradled black, spindly M-4 A-1 Colt carbines in their arms. Wind-whipped flurries of snow made it impossible for them to see for any great distance. Fortunately, clouds veiled the face of the early-morning sun, so the snowfield didn't reflect dazzling light.

Each of the cargo trucks was a converted twenty-four-foot moving van from the years preceding pre-dark. The logo EZ Haul was still visible despite rusty and repainted bodywork. The logos were accompanied by big-eyed cartoon images of nauseatingly cute bright green baby elephants pulling houses with their trunks.

For nearly a decade the fleet of trucks and their owner, Oliver Wendell Kimball, had operated under exclusive contract to Cobaltville. Kimball had journeyed far into Outland regions, trading, haggling and sometimes even stealing any items he thought might be of value to the fearsome Baron Cobalt. Of course he had never seen the baron, but he assumed he was fearsome nevertheless.

But all the contracts, exclusive or otherwise, came to an abrupt end when Cobaltville fell and the baron himself vanished. Not long afterward, people began leaving the ville—first in a sporadic trickle from the ghetto of the Tartarus Pits, then in a steady stream of refugees even from the Enclaves, the high-caste residential towers. Lowborn and high, they shared a desire to build new lives for themselves far from the deadly anarchy that had overwhelmed not just Cobaltville but all of the nine baronies in the continent-spanning network.

Kimball knew of a thriving settlement in Wyoming known as Sweetwater Station, built along the banks of the river of the same name. He let it be known the station was actively seeking able-bodied settlers. He was surprised by the enthusiastic response he and a couple of other men in his line of work received from the former citizens of Cobaltville.

Kimball was only too happy to turn his trading fleet into a relocation service, the profession that the trucks had originally practiced, as long as the people paid for his services and protection. Ville scrip no longer held any worth except as tinder or tissue, so he took out his fee in trade. Many of the refugees from Cobaltville had looted as much as they were able to carry when they fled the barony and were possession rich, despite the fact many of the items did not, on the face of it, seem to have any practical value, like computer software.

Riding in the cab of the lead freighter, Kimball considered that, examining several CD-ROMs in their plastic jewel cases. Although he had no idea of what Turbotax 2000 was supposed to be, he hoped somebody at Sweetwater Station would. The truck hit a rut and he dropped one of the cases onto the floorboard.

As he groped for it between his booted feet, he cast a sour glance over at Tubb, the wheelman. "Next time, see if you can't just drive us off a cliff and save us a whole lot of time, why don't you."

The man paid no attention to either the words or the sarcastic tone in which they had been delivered. Tubb handled the big truck with a casualness that bordered on the careless, but the man had been Kimball's top driver for more than five years and none of the trucks he had driven had suffered so much as a flat tire.

A thin and wiry man, Kimball's leathery face was

deeply seamed. He had long, thick iron-gray hair and a down-sweeping leonine mustache of a similar hue. His clothes—denim pants, chambray shirt and fringed leather jacket—were so old and worn that he resembled an elderly scarecrow. But the dark eyes beneath his grizzled brows were bright and alert.

By contrast, Tubb was a big, red-faced man with a paunch. He spoke only when necessary. He rarely saw a reason to employ words with more than two syllables, so as a raconteur, he was decidedly substandard.

Rather than try to engage the wheelman in conversation, Kimball put on a headset and monitored the quarterly security check-in of the convoy guards over his comm. After all five of the men reported in, he announced, "No sign of trouble yet."

Kimball's voice carried above the rumbling of the tires and the roar of the truck's engine. Tubb didn't respond verbally, but he tightened his big hands around the steering wheel and pursed his lips thoughtfully.

"I know," Kimball said impatiently. "I ain't forgettin', either. The last train through these parts never made it. Four wags and eighteen people all disappeared, includin' Hogarth himself."

Tubb frowned and shook his head slightly as if in exasperation.

"Hell, I know Hogarth and his crew was good," Kimball snapped defensively. "But he wasn't expectin' trouble and he was underarmed. He was takin' folks to Sweetwater Station just like us, but we ain't gonna get

blindsided by no Hell Hounds or whatever the fuck
they're called."

Tubb shrugged, signifying his contribution to the
discussion, if it could be called that, was over. Sighing,
Kimball assured himself the pump-action shotgun
clamped to a dashboard bracket was properly loaded,
then looked through the windshield at the foothills of
the Bighorn Mountains rising from the white horizon.
The convoy still had to cross through the South Pass before it was within the Sweetwater territory, and the pass
was at least another full day's travel, providing the
weather held and the frames of the trucks survived the
terrain. He hoped the patience of the passengers would
hold up, as well.

Hitching around in his seat, Kimball slid open the ob
port to the makeshift passenger compartment and
looked in at the six passengers, four men and two
women. "How you folks doing?"

The people raised their eyes to him and murmured a
variety of complaints or noncommittal responses. The
one window was sealed tightly, and the interior smelled
of unwashed bodies and liberal dashes of cheap scent
to conceal the reek. Kimball figured the passengers had
to choose between the stink and freezing to death and
for the moment, they chose the stink.

Two of the men and one of the women looked like
typical ex-Tartarans to him—gaunt, dirty, shabbily
dressed and exuding a sour, almost animal odor that no
amount of perfume could disguise. The men were ob-

viously former slagjackers, furtive of expression and breath redolent of home-distilled whiskey. They had given their names as Bo and Luke. Every so often, Luke removed a metal-walled flask from a coat pocket and took a sip from it.

The woman jammed between them called herself Hannie, but no matter what name she gave, Kimball recognized her as a gaudy slut—or a former one. What comeliness she might once have had was long gone. Her dark blond hayrick hair fell over her face, locks of it stirring as she snored in a drunken stupor. Although Bo and Luke claimed to be farmers, Kimball was fairly certain they acted as Hannie's pimps. More than likely they intended to establish a gaudy house, the first bordello in Sweetwater Station.

The second woman passenger was about as different from Hannie as it was possible to imagine. She was a kind of female Kimball had only rarely glimpsed but never expected to see in one of his convoys traveling into the Outlands.

A tall woman with taut, long legs, she looked to be several years younger than Hannie, but again it was hard to be certain. Her roses-and-milk complexion was lightly dusted with freckles across her nose and cheeks. Her big feline-slanted eyes weren't just green—they were a deep, clear emerald.

A mane of red-gold hair fell in loose waves almost to her waist. Her manner of dress—black leather jacket, skintight jeans and calf-high black boots—didn't de-

tract from her femininity, since the ensemble showed off
her willowy figure to full advantage. She had signed the
passenger roster as B. Baptiste.

Luke extended a flask toward her. "How about a nip
to keep off the chill?"

Kimball wasn't surprised when B. Baptiste flipped
a right hand in a terse, silent rejection of the offer.

"Just trying to be friendly," Luke said, flashing cav-
ity-speckled teeth in an insincere smile. "Thought we
might talk about a business opportunity I could put you
into once we're at Sweetwater."

B. Baptiste didn't respond, but regarded him stonily.
Shrugging, Luke put the flask to his lips, swallowed a
mouthful and stowed it inside a coat pocket.

"Young man, your choice of liquid nourishment
smells like a toxic chemical spill," commented another
male passenger. He spoke with a lilting, almost singsong
accent which Kimball couldn't identify but was pleasant
to the ear. "I would be grateful if you restrained yourself
from imbibing it again until we're out in the fresh air."

Kimball had been unable to decipher the name the
man had written on the ledger and so he thought of him
as "Swami." He was of medium height with a dark face,
prominent nose and bright blue eyes that contrasted
starkly with his deep olive complexion. On his head he
wore a white turban with a small silver brooch pinned
to the front of it. The black frock coat buttoned up to
his neck would have made him look like an undertaker
except for its satiny sheen and fur-trimmed cuffs.

Luke glowered at him. "Don't recall askin' your opinion, towel-head."

The turbaned man only folded his arms over his chest, smiling at him patronizingly, with no fear in his eyes or bearing.

The sixth passenger said quietly, "That's a coincidence… I don't recall asking *your* opinion about the towel-head's opinion."

Luke shifted his eyes toward the man who had spoken. His glower became an intimidating glare, then almost immediately dissolved to an inoffensive, almost fearful gaze. Kimball didn't blame him much.

The man wore faded road leathers, a battered brown jacket and cracked leggings tucked into high-topped jump boots. The soles were in suspiciously good condition, but Kimball knew that good footgear often meant the difference between living and dying in the Outlands.

Tall, long-limbed and rangy, the man was built with the stripped-down economy of a timber wolf, with most of his muscle mass contained in his upper body. A wolf's cold stare glittered in his pale blue-gray eyes.

Beneath thick dark hair, the man's high-planed face was set in a grim mask. A faint hairline scar showed like a white thread against the sun-bronzed skin of his left cheek. His chin and jawline bristled with a couple days' worth of whiskers.

When asked his name for the ledger, he had suggested Kimball sign him in as Alias Smith. The convoy master wondered if his friends, assuming he had any, called him Al. He didn't need to see the guns beneath the leather jacket to know they were there. Alias Smith looked like a seasoned killer, but not a man who made much of an issue about it. He didn't need to. Despite the rules prohibiting carrying firearms in the passenger compartments, Kimball didn't feel the time was proper to raise the issue.

"Easy, folks," Kimball said soothingly. "No need to get on the prod. We'll be stopping as soon we get the bottom of the grade so you can have a bite of breakfast and stretch your legs."

The heavyset man named Bo said scornfully, "And mebbe get 'em cut out from underneath us by the Hell Hounds."

Kimball repressed the urge to shush the man. He had hoped this group of pilgrims hadn't heard of the ruthless attacks by the legion of faceless killers called the Hell Hounds. They had made the Bighorn Basin a place of danger and terror for months ever since the fall of the baronies. He wondered if the other passengers in the other trucks were as tense and anxious as Bo seemed to be.

When he thought about the big black man and small albino girl riding in the rear vehicle he experienced a surge of anxiety himself. For a reason he couldn't identify, those two seemed to be kin to Swami, B. Baptiste and Alias Smith even though he hadn't seen them exchange so much as a nod during the past two days.

Kimball shut the ob port and turned back around, a frown on his stern face. "Stop us whenever you can," he instructed Tubb. "Our passengers are getting antsy and at least one of them is heeled."

Tubb raised questioning eyebrows, then glanced meaningfully at the shotgun but Kimball shook his head. "He ain't the type to turn over his blasters, and I can't take 'em…not without gettin' myself kilt or wounded. And I don't feel like gettin' kilt or travelin' with no wound."

Within a few minutes, Tubb eased the truck to a halt, brakes squealing, in the center of a small cup formed by three sloping bluffs and a dry creek bed. To the south stood a grove of poplar trees, running raggedly toward the distant foothills of the snowcapped Big Horn Mountains. Over the trans-comm, Kimball told the drivers of the other trucks to make the announcement of a ten-minute rest stop to their passengers. The carriers rolled into a loose crescent formation between two of the knolls.

Kimball climbed out of the cab, wincing at the stiffness of his legs. The air was cold, the temperature probably no higher than thirty degrees but very refreshing after the close confines of the truck. He surveyed the twenty-five or so people disembarking from the cargo compartments of the vans, noting absently how similar many of them seemed to one another in garb and bearing but also how different a few others looked, too.

Squinting toward the vehicle at the rear of the convoy, Kimball watched the big black man step down from the truck, followed a moment later by a small figure wrapped up in a hooded poncho. He didn't help her down—she jumped out, landing very gracefully beside him. She was very small, barely five feet.

The man towered above her, massive through the shoulders and chest, standing at least four inches over six feet. Much of his coffee-brown face was cast into shadow by the broad brim of an old felt fedora. Gray threads showed at his temples. A gunfighter's mustache curved fiercely around his lips, and the ends drooped halfway to his chin. He was dressed in patched denim jeans and a leather hip jacket over a khaki shirt. High-laced jump boots, almost identical to those worn by Alias Smith, rose nearly to his knees.

Kimball felt suspicion rise in him. He didn't believe in coincidence, just as he didn't believe that the prior convoys had been attacked at random. He knew the raiders had been supplied with intel, probably by confederates posing as passengers.

The diminutive, poncho-wrapped figure tugged down the hood of her garment, revealing a hollow-cheeked face the color of bone. Her eyes shone with the bright hue of polished rubies and her short-cut hair circled her head with a spike-tipped white crown. One of the genetic quirks of the nukecaust aftermath was a rise in the albino population, particularly down south in bayou country. Albinos weren't exactly rare anywhere else, but they were hardly commonplace, so she made an eye-catching sight.

A wisp of a memory ghosted through Kimball's mind, a vague recollection of hearing about a big black man in the company of an albino girl. He remembered they were associated with a sunset-haired woman and a pale-eyed man. He couldn't put those memories in any kind of context, but he suddenly decided there was something ominously familiar about the four people.

The transceiver of the headset filled Kimball's ear with static, and then Jack Crabb's tense voice, from the guard post atop the third truck, blurted, "Somebody or somethin' comin', boss. Off to the east about half a klick."

Oliver Wendell Kimball swept the white wastes with narrowed eyes, peering through the plumes of his breath. Far away little snow puffs rose above the horizon, with a number of dark specks beneath them. As he watched, the specks grew larger, mingling together in a wedge. Very faintly he heard the throb of multiple engines.

"Comin' on steady, a-riding too fast for folks what ain't aimin' to make trouble," Crabb said.

"Right," Kimball said distractedly. "It looks like we're in for a storm."

"We're ready with a storm of our own."

The man calling himself Alias Smith had spoken from directly behind his left shoulder. Kimball jumped and swore, then realized Smith wasn't looking at him but gazing at the approaching objects through the ruby-coated lenses of compact binoculars. They looked disconcertingly new.

"What do you mean, Smith?" Kimball demanded. "What kind of storm?"

Lowering the binoculars, Kane favored the smaller man with a cold, predatory smile. "A Cerberus storm."

Chapter 2

Heeling away from Kimball, Kane reached up behind his right ear and activated the Commtact attached to the mastoid bone. "Grant, we're about to have company."

"Acknowledged," came the unruffled response. Grant's voice sounded like a lion's, waking up grumpy from a nap. "I'll start unpacking our welcome baskets."

Eyebrows knitting at the bridge of his nose, Kimball asked, "Who the hell are you talkin' to, Smith? My name ain't Grant."

"No," Kane replied, pointing over his shoulder. "But his is."

Following the extended finger, Kimball stared at the big black man unlatching the door to the side cargo compartment of the truck. "Hey," he protested. "That's against the rules—"

Kane saw the comprehension rushing through him, forcing his eyes and mouth to open wide. Kimball gazed at Grant, then turned to gape up slack-jawed at him. In a voice barely above a hoarse whisper, he exclaimed, "Grant? Know who you and your friends are now—Kane."

"Then don't interfere with us and you just might get your convoy to Sweetwater Station in one piece…or halfway intact."

"Yes, sir!" Kimball sounded jubilant, if not over-joyed by the prospect of the carnage to come. "Hell Hounds against the baron blasters! No contest!"

Kane turned toward Brigid Baptiste and Lakesh, giv-ing vent to an unhappy sigh. He had enjoyed the rela-tive anonymity of Alias Smith while it lasted. He wasn't too pleased by having the term "baron blasters" applied to him and his friends once again, either.

The appellation was nearly a hundred years old, de-riving from the warriors who staged a violent resistance against the introduction of the program of unification. Neither Kane nor Grant enjoyed being referred to as a baron blaster—their ville upbringing still lurked close to the surface. They had been taught that the so-called baron blasters were worse than outlaws; they were agents of chaos, terrorists incarnate.

However, the reputations of Grant, Domi, Kane, Brigid and the Cerberus warriors had grown too awe-some to be contained by the inadequate term. Everybody who lived in any of baronies had heard tales of Kane and Grant, the two rogue Magistrates who had continually escaped and outwitted all the traps laid for them by var-ious barons of different villes. No two men over the past two hundred years had reputations to equal theirs, even if it was unclear how many of the stories were based in truth and how many of them were overblown fable.

"The bait has been taken," he announced to Lakesh and Brigid.

Mohandas Lakesh Singh nodded sagely. "As I knew it would."

Brigid cast him a slightly annoyed glance. "We still don't know who's supplying the inside information to the raiders."

Kane peered through the eyepieces of the binoculars again. "Whoever it is will give themselves away in pretty short order."

The distant collection of black specks reminded him of ink spots on a linen table cloth. He adjusted the focus and the specks resolved into more distinct figures. The Hell Hounds looked black because they wore Magistrate body armor, just as the Roamer reports to Cerberus had described. He counted between twelve and fifteen of them astride motorcycles. Judging by the faint but deep-throated throb, he guessed the machines were powered by 80 cid engines.

The riders disappeared into a shallow coulee then a moment later reappeared, topping the hummock one after another as though they were performing a close-order drill. They braked to a halt more or less simultaneously, engines idling.

Kane assumed the motorcycles had been appropriated from the Cobaltville armory. He had never heard of motorized bikes being part of the ordnance there, but he doubted a full inventory had ever been made available to Baron Cobalt—Overlord Marduk now, he corrected himself.

Although motorcycles weren't a completely unknown mode of transportation in the Outlands, they weren't commonly used, either. Even the best roads were in serious states of disrepair and lone cyclists were too exposed, too vulnerable to the weather or snipers. The few motorcycles he had ever seen in use were wired-together rattletraps, although he retained fond memories of a BSA Lightning he had ridden during a mission to the British Isles.

"Looks like we're dealing with fourteen, maybe fifteen ex-Mag slaggers on bikes," he declared.

"That's it?" Brigid asked, a note of incredulity underscoring her tone. "Only fourteen or fifteen?"

Kane lowered the binoculars. "What did you expect?"

"Something a little more formidable than a biker gang, ex-Magistrates or no ex-Magistrates. From the reports we've received, at least two convoys disappeared without a trace out here. A crew of disenfranchised Mags on motorcycles doesn't seem up to the task."

Kane found himself in reluctant agreement with her. Before he could reply, a panicky female voice screeched, *"Look!"*

The woman named Hannie stabbed a frantic finger toward the approaching figures. The other passengers turned to look, murmuring in apprehension and bewilderment.

"It's the Hell Hounds!" she shrieked. "O merciful God, save us!"

Her delivery struck Kane as just a bit too rehearsed, but he was in no mood to play drama critic, not when Bo joined her and made an exaggerated show of gazing in the direction of her finger, shading his eyes with both hands.

"The Hell Hounds!" he choked out loudly. "Heard of them, but I didn't believe there was such an outfit."

The passengers of the trucks uttered cries of fear and milled around uncertainly. They turned toward Oliver Wendall Kimball, shouting terrified questions at him.

Luke stepped up to the convoy master, gesturing grandly: "Our only chance is to surrender and hope they spare the womenfolk!"

Observing the melodramatic performance, Lakesh commented dryly, "I think the spies have just given themselves away."

Kimball cast an imploring look toward Kane. "What should I do? Make a fight of it?"

"Of course," Kane answered calmly. He nodded toward Grant and Domi, who were hastily unloading two drab, military-green plastic cases. One was several feet longer than the other. "We may not have them outnumbered, but we have them outgunned."

Bo speared Kane with a venomous stare and grabbed a handful of Kimball's coat. "Don't listen to him! Take a vote!"

Even as Bo bit out the words, Grant raised the lid of a crate and removed the hollow cylinder of a LAW 80 rocket launcher. He hefted it expertly in his arms.

Bo's eyes flew wide. He sputtered, "How—? Who in the—? Wait a second, you can't—"

Brigid interrupted his stammering diatribe. "Mr. Kimball, I imagine if you search those three you'll find some sort of comm."

Luke stiffened and his right hand streaked inside of his coat. Before he could withdraw it, Kane crossed his arms over his chest and whipped out twin dull gray Bren Ten autopistols from shoulder holsters. He centered the sights of the right-hand pistol on the man's left eye and covered Bo and Hannie with the other. Luke froze in midmotion, gazing into the dark hollow bore. He swallowed hard.

"No, go ahead and pull it," Kane instructed him quietly. "Then drop it."

As Luke carefully complied, Kane knew he didn't have to divide his attention between him and his companions. Out of the corner of his eye, he glimpsed Brigid Baptiste holding her TP-9 pistol in a double-handed grip, sweeping the barrel in short left-to-right arcs between Bo and Hannie.

Kane felt a quiver of surprise when he realized Luke hadn't reached for a weapon. He held a small trans-comm unit in his hand, a molded rectangle of black plastic and metal. He wasn't surprised when he recognized it as standard Magistrate issue. Its range was limited, but in clear weather and relatively open country, reception and transmission could be stretched to a couple of miles.

"Still want me to drop it?" he asked, his voice trembling.

"No," answered Kane. "Give it to towel-head here."

Lakesh stepped forward to take the comm from the man's grimy fingers, muttering, "How very politically incorrect, friend Kane."

Not understanding Lakesh's cryptic comment, Kane didn't respond to it. Pressing the bore of the pistol against Luke's deeply seamed forehead, he demanded, "Who are you signaling with it?"

Luke squeezed his eyes shut, lips writhing over discolored teeth. "An ex-Mag from Cobaltville. One-eyed man. Calls himself Carthew. He's the leader of the Hell Hounds."

The name struck a faint chord of recognition, but Kane wasn't inclined to examine the tone of familiarity too closely at the moment. "Does he expect to hear from you before the attack?"

Luke hesitated and Kane twisted the pistol bore harder into his flesh. In a half-gasped burst, he said, "Yeah! I'm to signal him if the convoy is gonna surrender!"

Stepping back, Kane nodded for Lakesh to hand over the comm to the man. "Tell Carthew we're surrendering."

With shaking fingers, Luke flipped up the cover of the comm and pressed a key to open a channel. As he placed it against his ear, Kane exchanged a swift look with Brigid. She arched a quizzical eyebrow but said nothing. She didn't need to, since Kane knew they shared the same thoughts. They had no idea if Luke was expected to speak code words. If he didn't, then the tactic of trying to lure the raiders in would only tip them off.

"Yeah," Luke said into the comm. "It's me. Come on in. It's safe."

Luke frowned, listening intently. "Okay. Okay. Yeah. Him, too."

Kane felt the cold prickles of suspicion at his nape. Then Luke extended the trans-comm toward him, keeping his eyes cast downward. "He wants to talk to you."

Kane's eyebrows rose toward his hairline. "Me?"

"Your name's Kane, ain't it?"

Knowing he did a poor job of disguising the astonishment that widened his eyes and opened his mouth, he holstered the Bren Ten and numbly took the comm from Luke. He didn't put it to his ear until he had recovered a bit of his emotional equilibrium.

"This is Kane," he said in a studiedly neutral tone.

The response was so long in coming, he nearly repeated the question. Then a man's voice, surprisingly youthful but shot through with static, filtered into his ear. "I couldn't be sure it really was you until I heard your voice. Kane, you son of a bitch bastard, what the hell are you doing out here?"

"I might ask you the same question," he retorted, ransacking his memory for a face to put to the voice.

"And I'll bet that big son of a bitch bastard in the hat is Grant."

"Who the hell are you?" Kane demanded, squinting toward the motorcyclists assembled atop the bluff.

"You don't remember me?"

Kane raised the binoculars to his eyes again. "This slagger says your name is Carthew but I don't recall meeting a one-eyed man by that—"

Kane bit back the rest of his words. Full recollection came to him in a rush, the faint chord of recognition the name had struck earlier now sounding like the bass register of a piano struck by a sledgehammer.

He swept his gaze over the men on the distant ridge. All of them wore black polycarbonate body armor, lightweight exoskeletons that fit snugly over undersheathings made of Kevlar weave. Small, disk-shaped badges of office were emblazoned on the arching left pectoral, depicting a stylized, balanced scales of justice superimposed over nine-spoked wheels. The badges symbolized the Magistrate's oath to keep the wheels of justice turning in the nine villes.

Like the armor, their helmets were made of black polycarbonate and fitted over the upper half and back of the head, leaving only a portion of the mouth and chin exposed. The red-tinted visors were composed of electrochemical polymers and connected to a passive night-sight that intensified ambient light to permit one-color night vision.

One of the armored men, his legs aspraddle on ei-

ther side of his motorcycle, peered at him intently
through a set of binoculars that looked like a twin of his
own. He waved with one gauntleted hand.

"Let me see your face," Kane said.

A short, contemptuous laugh filled Kane's ear. "Sure,
why not? It's not like you can report me to Salvo or to
the baron, is it?"

Lakesh stepped to Kane's side, brow furrowed.
"What is going on?"

Kane didn't answer, watching as the man in Mag
black let the binoculars dangle from a strap around his
neck while he tugged his helmet up and off his head.
Although he hadn't known Carthew very well back
when he served with him in the Cobaltville Magistrate
Division, Kane knew him by sight. His strongest memory of the young man was still imprinted on his face—
an ugly, livid scar that wealed down from the left side
of his forehead, disappearing beneath a black patch
over his right eye and emerging from its bottom edge.

"Remember the night I got this?" Carthew asked,
tracing the scar with a forefinger while speaking into a
trans-comm held in his other hand.

"Very clearly," replied Kane. "The raid on Mesa
Verde Canyon, about three years ago. You took a .50-
cal ricochet in the visor."

Carthew flashed him a boyish grin, made macabre by
his disfigurement. "After I was rehabilitated, I got stuck
in the Intel section, getting calluses on my ass and pushing paper from one desk to another." He paused and the

grin disappeared. "A hell of a lot of that paper had to do with you and Grant and that traitor archivist you escaped the barony with—what was her name, Baptist or something?"

"Baptiste," Kane corrected automatically.

"What?" Brigid asked.

Kane gave her a never-mind gesture with one hand. "That's getting to be a long time ago, Carthew. We're all in new lines of business now."

In truth, the Magistrate incursion into Mesa Verde Canyon felt like far longer than a mere three years ago. To Kane, it seemed almost as if the events had happened to someone else, on another plane of existence entirely.

"Us Mags in the Cobaltville Division anyhow," Carthew shot back, his tone acquiring a flinty, challenging edge. "What the hell are you doing out here, Kane?"

"Talking with your pal Luke," replied Kane. "Finding out all sorts of things about the Hell Hounds…except why you're called that."

Carthew chuckled. "My idea. I thought it sounded a little more dramatic than 'Gang of ex-Mags on motorsickles.' What else did he tell you?"

"Not too much, so far," Kane admitted. "But I don't imagine I'll have to get much more persuasive with him before he becomes downright loquacious."

"I agree," Carthew said. "That's why he doesn't know too much."

The far-off report of a rifle came like the crack of a

breaking stick. Crying out, Luke staggered forward, grabbing for Kane as the high-velocity slug caught him between the shoulder blades. For a few seconds, he clung to Kane by handfuls of jacket sleeves, his mouth opening and closing like that of a landed fish. Then strings of scarlet spilled out over his lips and he dropped first to his knees then fell facedown in the snow. A dark wet stain spread slowly between his shoulder blades. He lay there, his feet kicking feebly in post mortem spasms.

People dropped flat to the ground, shouting in fear and wonder. Kane stayed upright, glimpsing one of the Mags lowering a rifle outfitted with a telescopic sight. He growled into the trans-comm, "You just said he didn't know too much."

"That's true," Carthew responded. "But he knew enough."

Suddenly Kane heard the steady drone of an engine and the clanking clatter of metal treads. The blocky form of a Sandcat hove into view, topping the crown of the furthermost bluff.

"Just like you do," Carthew continued coldly. "And that's more than sufficient to get you and everybody in the convoy very dead. Nice talking to you again, Kane."

Chapter 3

Grant looked in the direction of the familiar engine growl, the echo of the rifle shot still ringing in the air. The vehicle topping the ridge line was known by assorted names: Fast Attack Vehicle, All-Terrain Armored Personnel Carrier or simply a wag, but was most often referred to as a Sandcat.

A pair of flat, retractable tracks supported the Sandcat's low-slung, blunt-lined chassis. The armored topside gun turret usually enclosed a pair of USMG-73 heavy machine guns, but the snout of what appeared to be a 30 mm cannon protruded from this particular half dome.

The Cat's armor was composed of a ceramic-armaglass bond, which offered protection from both intense and ambient radiation. Like most everything else used by the Magistrate Divisions, the Sandcat was based on the existing predark framework of an M113 APC, built to participate in a ground war that was never fought.

"We're hip-deep in it," Kane's voice said flatly.

He had subvocalized so no one around him heard his

bleak assessment of the situation other than his companions outfitted with Commtacts. The little comms fit tightly against the mastoid bones behind the right ear, attached to implanted steel pintels. The unit slid through the flesh and made contact with tiny input ports. Its sensor circuitry incorporated an analog-to-digital voice encoder that was subcutaneously embedded in the bone.

Once the device made full cranial contact, transmissions were picked up by the auditory canals. The dermal sensors transmitted the electronic signals directly through the skull casing. Even if someone went deaf, as long as they wore a Commtact, they would still have a form of hearing.

"What else is new," Grant retorted gruffly, gaze fixed on the distant figure of Carthew. He had listened in on the conversation between he and Kane, transmitted by the Commtact. He vividly remembered the night in Mesa Verde Canyon, since it was such a flash point in his life. The ripple effect of the events there had swept him and Kane into Brigid, then into Domi and finally to Lakesh and new, far more dangerous lives as Cerberus warriors.

"It's not going to be easy taking out the Cat," Kane replied.

"There's a way," Grant stated matter-of-factly.

"Maybe," Kane conceded. "But what we're seeing could just be the proverbial iceberg's tip of the ordnance the bastards looted from the Cobaltville armory."

Every one of the nine villes had possessed huge arsenals locked away behind massive vanadium alloy sec doors, filled with enough death-dealing matériel to outfit a midsized army.

The armories contained rack after rack of assorted weaponry, everything from rifles and shotguns to pistols, mortars and rocket launchers. Crates of ammunition were stacked to the ceiling. Armored assault vehicles were also parked there, the Hussar Hotspurs and the Hummers, not to mention disassembled Deathbirds, the black choppers that had been the only form of air travel to make any kind of wide comeback since the nukecaust.

Almost all of the items were original issue, dating from right before skydark, the onset of the generation-long nuclear winter. The planners of the old COG—Continuity of Government—programs had prudently recognized that unlike food, medicine and clothing, technology, particularly weapons, if kept sheltered, could endure the test of time, and last generation after generation. Arms and equipment of every sort had been placed in deep-storage locations all over the United States, within vaults filled with nitrogen gas to maintain below-freezing temperatures.

"We can only do what we can do," Grant said, pulling out the two sections of the rocket launcher to their full extension. As he unfolded the reflex collinator sight he said brusquely, "Rounds."

Domi's ruby eyes flashed in mild, momentary annoyance at his tone, but she gingerly removed a projectile from the crate. There were six of them, each one resembling a cylinder tipped by a blunt-nosed cone. "You didn't say 'please.'"

Before the final word passed her lips, the dark bore of the cannon protruding from the Sandcat's gun turret spouted a puff of gray smoke. It was followed instantly by a loud crack. A few yards from the farther truck, a fireball ballooned up from the ground. Clots of frozen earth rattled against the chassis. People screamed in fear, running toward the trucks, crawling frantically beneath them. Neither Domi nor Grant moved.

"Finding the range," Domi pointed out unnecessarily, her high, almost childlike voice unperturbed. "They're using high-ex warheads."

Grant nodded. "So are we. Load me up." He paused and added, "Please."

As Domi inserted the rocket into rear of the launch tube, Grant studied the barrel of the cannon and said aloud, for the benefit of Kane, Brigid and Lakesh, "My guess it's a Rearden gun...designed for accuracy, not speed. It's recoilless, but the rate of fire is pretty slow, no more than ninety rounds per minute."

No one asked him how such arcane information was useful. The four people had worked together long enough to respect one another's field of expertise. Grant's happened to be weapons, and they knew if anyone could take advantage of the cannon's rate of fire, he would find a way.

The band of black armored men began guiding their

motorcycles down the face of the bluff, engines roaring. Long before they drew within range, the carbines of the guards atop the trucks started cracking and spurting flame. Little geysers of snow erupted well ahead of the lead biker.

Grant shouted angrily, "Lay off, stupes! You're just wasting ammo!"

"They don't have much experience," Domi said.

She spoke the truth. Few people born after the establishment of the Program of Unification nearly a century before could boast skill with firearms among their abilities. Although hordes of exceptionally well-armed people once rampaged across the length and breadth of the Outlands, one of the fundamental agreements of the unification program was that the people had to be disarmed.

Of course, to institute this action, the barons and their security forces not only had to be better armed than the Outland hordes, but they also had to know the locations of the stockpiles wherein weapons could be found. The nine barons participating in the program were provided with both, and far more.

Even people who had been born in the Outlands could expect only limited experience with firearms. Although books and diagrams survived the disarmament sweeps, self-styled gunsmiths continued to forge weapons, although weapons more complicated than single-shot black-powder muzzle loaders was beyond their capacities.

The carbines in the hands of Kimball's sec men were in good condition and had obviously been safeguarded in a barony's armory until recently. But the men wielding them had little or no practice in bringing down moving targets. At the moment Grant's concern and attention were fixed on the Sandcat.

A plume of smoke spouted from the cannon's bore. Grant barely had enough time to shout "Down!" and shove Domi groundward before the shell impacted explosively near the rear of a truck. It had fallen short, but still the concussion shook the ground and gouted turf, snow and gravel in all directions.

A couple of the sec men, unnerved by the explosion, leaped from their posts, sprawling awkwardly on the ground. The other three stayed in their boxes but fired blindly through the billowing haze of smoke and dust.

Grant heard Kane shouting for the people to retreat, and not to seek cover within the trucks. Turning his head, he saw Kimball and the heavyset man he knew as Tubb dragging people out of the cargo carriers. The stratagem was sound. One high-explosive round from the Sandcat's cannon could ignite the fuel tank of a truck and touch off a chain reaction. Hauling Domi to her feet, Grant shouldered the LAW and bit out, "Let's move back."

Almost as soon as the final word left his mouth, the Sandcat's cannon barked again. Trailing smoke, the sleek 30 mm shell streaked over the heads of the Hell Hounds then struck the farthest truck. The warhead detonated, followed a fraction of a second later by an ear-splitting, eye-dazzling explosion of flame. The vehicle leaped over sideways, tilting up on two tires, the cargo compartment bursting open and strewing the ground with boxed items and personal possessions. Grant felt a blast of withering heat as fire spewed in a torrent from the fuel tank.

A rain of debris filled the air, jagged pieces of metal banging and clattering all around him and Domi. He crouched, shielding her diminutive form with his own, and waited until the echoes of the explosion faded and the clank and clatter of falling wreckage became a series sporadic thumps and thuds.

Grant figured the gunner aboard the Sandcat was either a terrible range finder or had deliberately sacrificed one truck strictly for psychological effect. He decided the latter possibility was the most probable, since the target had been the only truck not parked in cheek-to-jowl proximity with the others.

Impatiently, Domi wriggled out from under the shelter of Grant's body, declaring, "Let's put some distance twixt us and that cannon!"

Carrying the two cases, Grant and Domi backed swiftly away from the inferno of the truck, elbowing and shouldering their way through the milling, terrified crowd. They joined Kane as he shouted at Kimball, "Get your people under control or we won't be able to protect them!"

His mustached face ashen under its weather-beaten

tan, Kimball stomped among the frightened passengers, yelling profanity-seasoned instructions, grabbing people as they tried to scuttle beneath the trucks. "Move out!" he bawled. "You're puttin' yourselfs in worse danger by hidin' under the wags!"

When the people seemed reluctant to obey, Brigid said loudly and matter-of-factly, "Get out of the killzone. The raiders want the trucks, first and foremost. They won't pay much attention to you if you don't get in their way. They'll be too busy with us to care in which direction you go."

She pointed to the mouth of a brush-bordered dry creek bed a score of yards away. "Get in there and wait it out."

Her terse, well-educated tone of voice had a more persuasive effect than Kimball's yelling. They began running for the mouth of the draw, but a quintet of men and women didn't follow their fellow passengers.

"We want to help," one of the women declared. She was middle-aged, iron-haired, coarse of feature but with direct brown eyes and a forthright manner. "My name is Betsy."

"Good," Kane said, kneeling beside the smaller of the two plastic crates. As he pried open the lid, he added, "I don't have guns for you, but these might do."

Nestled securely within hollowed-out foam rubber pockets were over a dozen grenades, ranging from small round V-60s to canister-shaped flash-bangs. Quickly he began removing them and handing them up to the people who eyed the objects uncertainly. "Anybody have any experience with grens?" he inquired.

When he received murmured negatives and head shakes all around, he swiftly demonstrated with a small smoker. "You hold the gren in the same hand you use to throw it, with the safety lever between the first and second joints of the thumb."

Hooking the index finger of his left hand through the trigger ring, he continued, "Pull the cotter pin—not with your teeth—and throw the gren overhanded at your target, then drop or take cover. Keep in mind that even the largest grens have only a few ounces of high explosive. When compared to those artillery shells the Sandcat is firing, these grens are pretty puny. But at least I don't have any fraggers, so you won't have worry about staying out of the way of shrapnel."

Kimball revolved a grenade between thumb and forefinger like a farmer examining an egg and said sourly, "You just want us to make a diversion, is that it?"

Kane stood up, grinning crookedly. "Pretty much, yeah. But I'd prefer you didn't get killed while you're going about your diverting, though."

He cast a glance toward Lakesh and Brigid. "Either one of you want a gren?"

Brigid hefted her TP-9. "I'll stick with this, thank you."

Lakesh withdrew a 1911 Army Colt pistol from a coat pocket, handling it gingerly as if it were as unstable as an unpinned grenade. "And I have my old standby."

Both Grant and Kane eyed him dubiously, but they didn't put into words their thoughts: Mohandas Lakesh Singh was a genius, courageous and cunning, but he was also an academic. The few times he had gone out into the field did not have salubrious results. The only reason he was along on this op was that they had gotten tired of trying to argue him out of it and indulged his whim.

Domi stepped up beside Lakesh, unholstering her Detonics Combat Master from beneath her poncho. Checking the action of the .45-caliber autopistol, she said cheerfully, "I'll watch out for him, keep the important parts of him from bein' too shot up."

No one voiced an objection. As agile as a panther, Domi was accustomed to mayhem of all kinds, from hand-to-hand combat to down-and-dirty medleys with knives. A combat knife with a nine-inch-long serrated blade was scabbarded somewhere under her poncho. The razor-keen edge bore bloodstains from many kills, animal and human alike.

Autofire suddenly hammered outside the perimeter. The windshield of a truck shattered. One of the guards who had leaped from his post atop a truck returned the fire with his carbine, shooting through the smoke pouring from the gutted vehicle. He stood out in the open, weapon at his shoulder.

Return fire sounded and the man staggered, dropping his carbine. A bullet shattered his right arm, another slug caught him in the left leg and a third punched straight through his chest. He went down, sprawling in the snow, cursing the pain and his own carelessness.

A guard who had stayed inside the box mounted on top of a truck bellowed, "Franz! Get up!"

The man tried to comply, hitching himself around on his hands and knees. A Hell Hound wielding a Sin Eater burst out of the pall of smoke, crouched behind the handlebars of his motorcycle. The wounded guard froze, gaping at the mounted apparition. As the bike roared past him, the black-armored man took careful aim and shot the guard squarely between the eyes. Blood, bone and brain matter sprayed out in a gelid mass from the back of his head.

Because of the smoke, the rider didn't immediately see the group of people clustered around the open crates. When he did, he turned his bike toward them, leveling his Sin Eater in their direction in the same motion. Unhurriedly, Kane stretched out his arm and squeezed off a single 10 mm round from his Bren Ten. The slug caught the Hell Hound in the chin and snapped his head back. His body contorted into a crazed backward somersault out of the saddle and the motorcycle crashed onto its side. The engine stalled out and died.

Grant placed the LAW on his right shoulder. "Let's get ready." His voice sounded casual, almost bored. He strode between a pair of trucks. "I'll see how close I can get to the Cat."

Watching him go, Kimball chewed one end of his drooping mustache. "He don't sound too worried about it."

"At least we know what we're up against," Kane retorted. "That's an advantage we don't usually have—right, Baptiste?"

Brigid raised her eyebrows at him in exaggerated exasperation, but she didn't disagree with him. She had already assessed the threat presented by the Hell Hounds with the skills she had honed during dozens of firefights she had shared with Grant, Kane and Domi.

"Right?" Kane pressed.

"I don't know if we have it this time, either," Brigid retorted.

Then, amid the growl of many engines, Hell Hounds came barreling out of the smoke.

Chapter 4

The motorcycles raced and whirled around the trucks, circling and feinting at the defenders, then veering away. The tires flung up great clouds of snow, mixing with dirt so it hung heavily in the air like curtains of filthy lace.

Crouching, Brigid brought up the TP-9 in a double-handed grip and aimed at a pair of Hell Hounds riding shoulder-to-shoulder. She achieved target acquisition on the man who rode slightly in the lead and depressed the trigger. The pistol jerked in her hands and spit out a stream of 9 mm rounds that chopped into the man's armored torso. The polycarbonate absorbed and redistributed the kinetic shock, but the multiple impacts still sent man and machine teetering sideways, slamming into the other motorcycle with a screech of metal grinding against metal.

The bike flipped, turning end over end, catapulting the rider from the saddle, limbs waving like a rag doll's. The other Hell Hound tried to avoid the same outcome as his partner and steered sharply to the left, putting himself directly in front of the bore of Kane's autopistol.

Kane squeezed off one round. The steel-jacketed bullet struck the molded left pectoral of the Mag armor, puncturing the red duty badge, punching a hole through the hub of the nine-spoked-wheel insignia.

The Hell Hound's arms flailed as the impact pounded him backward from the saddle, almost as if he had been jerked by an invisible cable attached to his belt. He hit the ground heavily, a little geyser of bright arterial blood squirting up through the perforation in his badge.

The riderless motorcycle lunged forward a few feet. Before Brigid quite realized what he was going to do, Kane made a flying leap to the side of the bike, ran alongside of it for three strides, grasping it by the handlebars, then swung smoothly into the saddle.

Squeezing the throttle, working the clutch, he whirled the bike around and fired off three rounds at an approaching Hell Hound. Only one bullet found a target, a glancing blow to his right shoulder. Still, the armored man reeled, the bike wobbling dangerously, but he recovered and steered away. Kane upshifted into a pursuit.

The snarl of an engine filled her ears, and Brigid spared a swift glance behind her before she threw herself forward, shoulder-rolled and got to her knees. The front tire of the motorcycle bearing down on her missed her by a fractional margin, but she fired off the rest of the TP-9's clip at the Hell Hound, stitching the armored back with a zipper of slugs. A couple of ricochets sparked off the machine's bodywork.

She heard the man cry out in pain and anger, but he managed to keep the motorcycle under control. Swerving expertly, the ex-Mag lifted his bike onto its rear wheel and brought it around without the front tire touching the ground. Throttling up, he swooped at Brigid again.

Moving with calm deliberation, she thumbed the autopistol's magazine release, ejecting the empty, and slammed home a fresh clip. She chambered the first round and sighted down its length, just as she had been taught by Grant and Kane on the firing range at the Cerberus redoubt.

She glimpsed a small dark object arcing through the air from her right. A fireball bloomed right in front of the motorcycle, hurling up a cloud of dirt and snow. The Hell Hound reacted reflexively to the grenade's detonation, swerving to the left, the rear tire fishtailing. As he tried to regain control of the machine, a guard's carbine cracked in a staccato rhythm. Two rounds caught the motorcycle's engine block and three more struck the rider. Both man and bike then went down.

Brigid raised her gaze and waved her gun in a salute to the man atop the truck—and watched as he reeled under a hail of full-auto rounds fired from the Sin Eater clenched in the hand of a Hell Hound who roared past. The bullets tore through the man's lower body, climbing upward, shattering his knees and smashing into his hips and belly. Before Brigid could track the Hell Hound, his bike swept him out of sight between two of the vehicles.

Biting back a profanity, she surveyed the battle zone. The rushing circle of motorcycles had slowed, their movements more deliberate now that their riders realized they had incurred casualties. She didn't see Grant, but Domi and Lakesh were crouched under the rear wheel well of the nearest cargo carrier, both of them alert and watchful. They had stowed the crates beneath the truck.

"Grenade!" she called, extending a hand.

Domi blinked in momentary surprise, then tossed a round V-60 mini to her underhanded. Brigid snatched it out of the air and sprinted to the narrow aisle formed by the two parked trucks. Peering around the van bodies, she saw the Hell Hound, still astride his motorcycle, hand tight on the brake lever and gunning the engine in preparation for another dramatic charge.

Looking at the man, Brigid realized again how the design of the Magistrate armor was as much symbolic as it was functional. The figure mounted on the motorcycle looked somehow strong, implacable, almost invincible. When a man concealed his face and body beneath the Magistrate black, he became a fearsome figure, the anonymity adding to the mystique. His body was only partially exposed so Brigid targeted the man's polycarbonate-shod right shoulder. She squeezed the trigger once and the 9 mm bullet hit the man where she had aimed and nearly knocked him off his bike. He involuntarily released the brake and the motorcycle plunged forward on the rear wheel, heading directly for her.

Brigid unpinned the grenade and instead of throwing it, rolled it across the ground toward him. The rider dropped his front tire and the tread struck the metal-shelled egg. It instantly exploded and enveloped him and his bike in a ballooning ball of flame. The gas tank detonated, and the concussion slammed Brigid violently against the side of the vehicle, the shock wave nearly shoving her off her feet.

She caught only a glimpse of the Hell Hound's fire-wreathed body hurtling through the air. Shaken by the bone-jarring impacts of the unexpected double explosions, Brigid backed away, telling herself she had only evened the scales by killing the man who had killed her rescuer. Although she had long ago accepted the inevitability of taking lives in the course of her work with Cerberus, she had never been able to desensitize her conscience.

Kane's voice, tight with anxiety, suddenly blared through the Commtact. "Baptiste! Eleven o'clock!"

Brigid spun as two of the Hell Hounds vectored in on her, motorcycle engines roaring like rampaging beasts. The barrels of both Sin Eaters were trained on her. Instinctively she opened up with the TP-9, keeping the trigger depressed. The bullets struck the Mag armor and bounced away with keening whines and the two bikes came on.

Realizing that to stand and hold her ground would only get her shot or run down, Brigid turned and ran as fast as she could, her long legs pumping. Flames strobed from the bores of the Sin Eaters, and the bullets thumped the air over her head.

The ground suddenly shuddered beneath her pounding feet, and she heard the crumping detonation of a hand grenade, sounding like the handclap of a giant. She spared one glance over her shoulder as fire bloomed up between the two motorcycles. The explosion sent both bikes crashing onto their sides, strewing the ground with machine parts. The riders rolled gracelessly across the ground. One slammed headfirst into the wheel rim of a truck tire. The other man picked himself up, glanced over at his motionless partner, then began a shambling, stumbling run out of the zone, cradling an injured arm.

He had taken only a few steps before Oliver Wendell Kimball stepped into his path, a pump-action shotgun at his shoulder. He fired into the center of the black armor. The double-aught buckshot staggered the Hell Hound but he didn't fall, the polycarbonate scored by a multitude of shallow dimples.

Kimball marched toward him, squeezing and pumping through two more quick rounds, placing the first at the man's legs, then riding the weapon's recoil up to the ex-Mag's head. The blast of buckshot at knee level bowled the man over. He fell almost onto the shotgun's barrel. The second blizzard of buckshot pounded into his face, shattering his helmet's visor in a spray of scarlet liquid and red-tinted plastic shards.

Breathing hard, Brigid panted, "Much obliged. You've got a good arm."

Kimball nodded to her, a smug smile creasing his face. "My pleasure, ma'am, but I didn't chuck the gren." He hooked a thumb over his shoulder toward the brown-eyed Betsy.

Brigid waved to her and Betsy returned it with a right hand holding a canister-shaped flash-bang. Kane pulled up on his appropriated motorcycle, lurching to a halt so close to her that the side of the front tire brushed the toes of her boots.

Face drawn in a scowl, he demanded, "Haven't you heard of taking cover?"

Before she could respond angrily, Domi's worried voice filled her head. "Where's Grant?"

"Trying to get in position to take out the Cat," Grant rumbled in reply. "I'm not having much luck with the old soft underbelly routine."

"Hang on," Kane retorted. "Luck is on the way."

He gestured for Brigid to mount the saddle behind him. "Let's go."

Eyeing the machine hesitantly, she asked, "Why?"

"You're probably safer with me."

After a thoughtful pause, Brigid swung her legs over the saddle, planting her feet firmly on the pegs. Kane moved out, revving the engine. The remaining Hell Hounds were in full retreat, probably never having incurred such losses during their prior raids. They rolled up the face of the distant bluff, grouping around the Sandcat. The FAV still crouched on the crest, like a prehistoric beast of prey.

Grant knelt behind a snow-coated collection of rocks in a declivity in the terrain, peering down the LAW's length. As Kane guided the motorcycle toward him, the bore of the Cat's cannon belched flame and with a prolonged ripping sound, the shell arced over their heads and impacted less than three yards away from the rear bumper of a truck.

Lakesh's breathless voice husked into their heads over the Commtact. "That, as the bromide goes, was *too* close."

"Get everybody away from there," Brigid replied.

"Complying."

Kane braked the motorcycle to a halt behind Grant. Brigid swiftly dismounted, dropping into a crouch beside him. Kane stayed astride the bike, saying in disgust, "I don't think the bastards are interested in the cargo anymore."

Grant turned his head toward him. "I don't, either. But they're not going to let the convoy go on its way."

"Why not?" Brigid asked.

"Bad for business," Grant replied brusquely. "If word gets out the Hell Hounds had their asses kicked, they're finished."

Brigid squinted toward the Sandcat, and the men on motorcycles clustered around it. She was reminded of spoiled, upset children seeking solace and protection from a parent. "You mean they'll destroy the trucks and kill everybody just to protect their reputations?"

Kane nodded grimly. "Out here, your life is worth

only as much as your rep. The only way to keep other slaggers from taking over your valley is to stay the meanest son of bitch in the valley. It's worth the loss of the cargo to maintain their image."

The cannon fired again. Kane ducked instinctively, even though the shell came nowhere near him. It exploded almost beneath a cargo tank. Tires blew and two of the defenders were slapped off their feet, but the fuel tank remained intact. Because of the wafting smoke, Kane couldn't see who had been knocked down or the extent of the damage.

"Shit," Grant growled. "I can't get a clean shot at the Cat's vulnerable spot from here. Carthew can just sit up and shoot off his cannon at us all day and all night."

Kane nodded sagely. Reaching inside his jacket, he withdrew a pair of dark-lensed glasses. "I'll see if I can change that."

"How?" Brigid demanded, lines of worry appearing on her forehead.

Kane smiled wolfishly, slipping on the glasses with a flourish. He revved the engine, released the brake and popped the clutch. The bike leaped forward in a wheel stand. The torque came on in a roaring rush as snow, dirt and gravel spewed from beneath the rear tire. Easing up on the throttle, the front wheel dropped and Kane rode at an oblique angle toward the Sandcat, bouncing over ruts and rocks.

Brigid knew better than to call after him, but she

couldn't repress a sigh of exasperation. She could tell by the muscles bunching in Grant's jaw he wasn't enthusiastic about the tactic either, but he said nothing. It was difficult for Brigid to keep in mind that Grant and Kane had spent their entire adult lives as killers—superbly trained and conditioned Magistrates, not only bearing the legal license to deal death, but the spiritual sanction, as well. Both men had been through the dehumanizing cruelty of Magistrate training yet had somehow, almost miraculously, managed to retain their humanity. But vestiges of their Mag years still lurked close to the surface, particularly in threatening situations. In those instances, their destructive ruthlessness could be frightening.

Crouching over the fuel tank, Kane roared across the open ground between the Sandcat and the collection of trucks. A volley of gunfire snapped from the Hell Hounds arrayed around the FAV, but none of the rounds came very close. He leaned to his right and left, swinging his body like a pendulum, controlling the mechanical steed beneath him. The motorcycle zigged in one direction and zagged in the other.

Kane slewed the bike around in an *S* slide and cut a few doughnuts and figure eights to attract the attention of the Cat's gunner. Throttling up, he retraced his path. The cannon boomed, and a geyser of snow and dirt erupted ahead of him and to his left. Without slowing he rolled through a sifting blanket of grit. He casually waved the particles away from his face, glad he had chosen to put on the sunglasses. Puckering up, he blew a kiss toward the Sandcat's turret.

Another 30 mm round detonated a score of feet to his right, and the force almost knocked the motorcycle over. Throwing out a foot, Kane shoved the bike back upright as the tires found traction again.

With the V-twin engine thrumming purposefully, Kane rode the bike back and forth, lofting easily around potholes and ruts. Thumping explosions compressed his ears and the speeding machine shuddered from the jolt of the concussive shock waves. The artillery shells punched smoking cavities in the ground all around him. The vibrations of the multiple detonations were passed to him through the motorcycle, blurring his vision, numbing his senses. Dirt rained down over his back and shoulders.

After the sixth near miss, Grant snarled over the Commtact, "How long do you think you can keep up that kind of suicidal stupidity?"

By way of an answer, Kane screwed the machine's throttle down and leaned forward, belly tight against the gas tank. The bike lunged ahead at full revs, tearing through the planes of smoke and dust floating through the air. Hearing a mechanical clank and clatter, he glanced up toward the Sandcat and saw the vehicle shifting position on its treaded tracks, the turret—enclosed cannon barrel swiveling to follow him. Apparently the gunner was becoming frustrated by his inability to hit him.

"How's that angle work for you?" Kane asked over the Commtact.

"Not bad," Grant conceded. "Now if you wouldn't mind getting the hell out of my way, I might be able to get in one clean shot—"

Fire and smoke bloomed from the cannon's bore. The loud report pressed painfully against Kane's ears. A shaved sliver of a second later, the ground split in a blaze of light less than six feet ahead of the bike's front tire.

The motorcycle reared up like a terrified horse, and a bucketful of cold slush and hot grit scoured Kane's face. If not for his sunglasses, he would have been blinded. He slammed against the ground on his back with breath-robbing force. Instantly, he threw himself into a sideways roll, trying to avoid being crushed by the motorcycle as it tipped up and over on its rear wheel. It crashed down scarcely six inches from his head.

He stayed where he was, the motorcycle providing a little cover. The haze of smoke and grit that rose from the crater obscured him from the Cat crew's vision. Over the ringing in his ears, he heard hooting cries of malicious triumph from the Hell Hounds, and then the rattle of gunfire as they directed shots toward him. A few rounds struck the heavy metal chassis of the bike with semimusical clangs and little flaring sparks. Puffs of snow mushroomed around it.

Voice tight with repressing the pain lancing through his upper back, Kane asked, "Does this angle work better?"

Grant didn't respond in words. Barely audible over the cacophony of gunfire, Kane heard a ripping sound, as of a stiff piece of canvas tearing in two. A flaming projectile, seemingly propelled by a wavery banner of smoke, skimmed over him, following a course less than ten feet above the ground. Kane hitched over on his side to watch its progress. Small fins popped open on the tail of the rocket as it rotated, snaking upward in arc.

The HEAT warhead exploded in the flaring fireball on the underside of the Sandcat's prow, precisely in an area no larger than the span of a man's hand, between two sections of reactive armor. A lurid flower of flame spread over the ob ports and the turret. The 94 mm hollow charge punched a deep cavity up through the bow of the Cat. The incendiary compounds of the warhead turned the metal molten. From the undercarriage boiled a mixture of white, gray and black smoke.

The Hell Hounds clustered around the vehicle for protection kicked their bikes into motion only a few seconds before various flammables within the FAV ignited. Within seconds, tongues of fire lapped from every port, weld and seam of the Sandcat. Then the 30 mm cannon shells detonated.

With a series of eardrum-compressing explosions, the vehicle burst open from within, like an engorged tick, the gull-wing doors flying open. Instead of blood, a tidal wave of orange-yellow flame and concussive force poured out, expanding outward like a dinner plate and engulfing everything within a twenty-foot radius.

The Hell Hounds astride their idling motorcycles were bowled over like stalks of wheat blasted by hurricane-force winds.

A ball of flame streaked straight up, and spark-shot columns of acrid smoke spiraled from the splits in the hull. The metal treads of the tracks sheared away from the rollers. The thick odor of scorched motor oil and seared human flesh floated into the air.

A quartet of armored men, half-blinded by smoke and stunned by the shock wave, wrestled their motorcycles up and rode off like panicked deer. The hilltop became screaming, bloody chaos, with men shrieking and shouting contradictory orders and slapping at the flames licking along their polycarbonate exoskeletons. Through a part in the roiling vapors, Kane saw at least three Hell Hounds, or pieces of them, lying motionless on the ground mixed in with smoldering and slagged debris.

Kane resisted the urge to whistle in approving admiration. During his many years as a Magistrate, Grant had often dumbfounded his colleagues with his long-distance shots, almost always uncannily accurate, regardless of the size of the target. He had won a number of contests, competing with his fellow Mags and always outshooting any self-styled marksmen that the academy produced. Kane always placed his bets on Grant, and he always won.

Grant's voice said into Kane's ear, "I think that angle is just fine. Does it work for you?"

Slowly, Kane climbed first to his knees then to his feet, wincing at the red-hot needles of strained ligaments stabbing into his upper back. "Works for me. How about everybody else?"

"It doesn't work for Lakesh," came Domi's tense voice. "You need to get back down here."

Chapter 5

Plumes of smoke still rose from the body of the shelled truck, but the wind thinned them out and carried them away. Casualties were light—two dead and two wounded. Luke wasn't included as a loss. Hannie had suffered a cranial injury from a ricocheting bullet and lay on the ground, her bloody head cradled in Bo's lap. She moaned softly as he dabbed at her scalp wound with a dirty bandanna. Tears ran down his face and as Betsy stalked past him, he blubbered, "Help her, please."

Betsy stopped short of spitting on him, but the glare she directed at both people held only disgust. She continued on her way without a backward glance or speaking a word. The other passengers had left the cover of the gully and busied themselves seeing what could be salvaged from the destroyed truck and preparing the dead for burial.

Lakesh leaned against the front bumper of a truck, his coat unbuttoned and his sweater pulled up. He cupped his right rib cage with his left hand, liquid ribbons of scarlet seeping between his fingers. Although his lips were pale, his expression was composed, his blue eyes reflecting no pain. Domi knelt beside him, pawing through an open medical kit.

He glanced up at the approach of Brigid, Grant and Kane, intoning dolefully, "I fear I did not move with my characteristic alacrity."

Brigid sank down beside him, saying with mock severity, "I should lecture you about being so accident prone, but it would be classic example of the pot calling the kettle black."

Lakesh smiled slightly at the reference to the numerous injuries she had suffered since joining Cerberus. The most serious had been a head injury that had laid her scalp open to the bone and put her in a coma for several days. Now the only visible sign of the wound was a faintly red, horizontal line on her right temple that disappeared into the roots of her hair.

"What happened?" Grant asked tersely, the rocket launcher dangling from his right hand.

As Brigid pulled away Lakesh's hand so she could examine the wound, he answered, "I'm not really sure, friend Grant. I recall the cannon shell exploding beside the truck—"

"You pushed me ahead of you," Domi interrupted sternly. "Like I'm the one who runs like a pregnant turtle. As *if*. Then you—"

She broke off, eyes widening at the sight of the raw, blood-pulsing wound in Lakesh's midriff just beneath his right rib cage. Uttering a wordless cry of dismay, Brigid glanced around, then snatched the smoke-and-dirt-stained turban from his head, revealing his gray-streaked black hair.

"Hey," he protested feebly. "Do you know long it took me to make that?"

"You didn't make it," Domi stated crisply. "I did."

"Yes, but I designed—" The protest turned into a groan as Brigid folded the fabric into a double thickness and jammed it firmly over the gash, covering the edges of the wound and holding it in place with both hands.

"I need a pressure bandage," she snapped to Domi. "Stat."

Despite the circumstances, Kane couldn't completely repress a smile. Both Brigid and Domi had undergone training in field medicine by Reba DeFore, the resident medic of Cerberus. Brigid's imitation of the physician's brusque manner bordered on the uncanny.

"We'll have to hold this here until the bleeding stops or tapers off," Brigid continued.

"If it doesn't?" Kane asked, struggling to keep the pain from his bruised back muscles from registering on his face.

"I don't think a major blood vessel has been severed," she answered, "but the transverse abdominal muscles are definitely hemorrhaging."

She paused and smiled reassuringly into Lakesh's worried face. "That sounds worse than it really is."

"I was wondering when you were going to let me know," he retorted wryly.

Domi found the two-inch-thick gauze-covered pad

in the medical kit and waited for Brigid to pull away the blood-soaked turban. She did so carefully, and Kane grimaced at the sight of the blue-black bruise surrounding a triangle of ragged flesh. However, blood no longer pumped copiously from it.

Domi laid the pressure bandage over the gash, affixing the adhesive to his flesh, giving it a little squeeze to bring the antibiotic gel to the surface. Lakesh showed no pain, but he eyed his ruined headgear sorrowfully. "It took me two days to make that."

Brigid examined the bandage, saying, "It was just a disguise, Lakesh, not an article of clothing with sentimental value…except for this, maybe." She held up the silver brooch between thumb and forefinger.

Lakesh shrugged at the sight of it. "Sky Dog gave it to me months ago. He found it in a streambed." He pursed his lips thoughtfully and added, "Perhaps I should start wearing a turban as a statement of my ethnic identity. My family were Sikhs, after all."

"How's the Swami?" Kimball asked loudly, tramping over to them.

Lakesh cast the man a sour glance, murmuring, "On second thought…"

"I can't say for sure," Brigid said to the convoy master. "He's not going to die, but he's not going anywhere under his own power for a few days, either."

Kimball nodded, tugging at his mustache. "Lost two of my sec boys and a truck. Coulda been worse if not for you folks."

"A *lot* worse," Domi interjected.

Forcing a smile, Kimball nodded in agreement. "That's for sure, young missy. We can't stay here. Soon as we bury our dead and fix the tires, we got to get under way again."

"What's the hurry?" Grant asked.

Kimball regarded him with incredulous eyes. "Ain't you heard? This here is Sioux land. Ain't seen much of 'em lately, but that don't mean they don't know we're around. They put up with us crossing their territory, but they sure don't care for anybody who lingers."

Kane smiled knowingly. "If they show up, we can deal with them."

If Kimball found Kane's comment cryptic, he gave no indication. Since the nukecaust, many of the American Indian tribes had reasserted their ancient claims over lands stolen from them by the predark government. Although the hostilities between the tribes and non-Native peoples weren't as bloody as only a hundred years earlier, travelers crossed Indian lands holding tight to their topknots.

"The Hell Hounds got along with 'em, seems like," Kimball agreed dourly.

"Mebbe," said Domi. "But you ask me, the whole Hell Hounds routine makes no sense."

"Why not?" Lakesh asked, obviously seeking anything to divert his attention from the pain of his wound.

Domi shrugged, gesturing to the white waste all around. "They steal all the cargo and maybe kidnap the people. Where do they take 'em? There's no place to sell anything out here, is there, no slave markets?"

Lakesh raised his eyebrows. "Very astute, darlingest one." Inclining his head toward Bo and Hannie, he commented, "Perhaps that star-crossed couple can provide some intelligence that may shed light on the mystery."

Kane glanced over at the two people, noting that the wound on Hannie's scalp, although bleeding profusely, didn't look critical. Turning toward Domi, he extended a hand. "Give me the medical kit."

Domi scowled first at him then over at Bo and Hannie. "Hell with 'em. Get information out of 'em *my* way."

Reaching inside her poncho, she whipped out her long knife, her memento of her months of servitude as a sex slave in Cobaltville. She had freed herself by using the knife to cut the throat of her self-appointed master. "Carve what we need out of them turncoat sacks of shit."

In her anger, Domi reverted to her clipped, abbreviated mode of Outlands speech. Lakesh patted her shoulder. "Kane's impulse is sound. The tried-and-true method of attracting more flies with honey than vinegar."

Domi blinked at him, perplexed by the bromide. "What does that mean?"

Born in the midtwentieth century, Lakesh often employed dictums and phrases that held little meaning to anyone birthed after the global holocaust of 2001, much less those born one hundred or more years after that date.

"It means," rumbled Grant, a trace of impatience in his voice, "that they may be more inclined to cooperate if we help them."

Domi's lips worked, her porcelain features twisting in disgust, but rather than spitting she pushed the medical kit into Kane's waiting hand. He and Grant walked over to where Bo ministered to Hannie. Holding her tight, he stared up at the two men with the cringing ferality of a cornered rat.

"Let me take a look at her," Kane said, lowering himself one knee beside the woman.

The fear turned to almost pathetic gratitude in Bo's eyes, and he propped up Hannie's head so Kane could cleanse the scalp wound with liquid antiseptic. As he did so, he remarked, "Your Hell Hound pals seemed to think you, Luke and Hannie were a little on the expendable side."

Bo bared his teeth in what was meant to be a ferocious snarl, but it came off more as a pathetic parody. "That fuckin' Carthew…shoulda known better than to trust a fuckin' Cobaltville Mag to keep a deal."

Grant clenched a fist but kept a response to himself. Kane no longer felt much of an emotional reaction to aspersions cast on the honor of the Magistrate Division the two men had once so faithfully served. Over the past three years, they had learned that most of the aspersions were well-deserved.

For most of their adult lives, Kane and Grant had enforced ville laws and Baron Cobalt's edicts, legally and spiritually sanctioned to act as judges, juries and executioners.

The Magistrates were formed as a complex police machine that demanded instant obedience to its edicts and to which there was no possible protest. Over the past ninety years, both the oligarchy of barons and the Mags who served them had taken on a fearful, almost legendary aspect. Kane and Grant had been part of that legend, cogs in a merciless machine.

All Magistrates followed a patrilineal tradition, assuming the duties and positions of their fathers before them. They didn't have given names, each taking the surname of the father, as though the first Magistrate to bear the name were the same man as the last.

As Magistrates, the courses their lives followed had been charted before their births. They were destined to live, fight and die, usually violently, as they fulfilled their oaths to impose order upon chaos. Now, for the past three years, the two men had done their very best to not just dismantle the machine, but to utterly destroy it and scatter the pieces to the four corners of the world. They had very nearly succeeded. By a strict definition, Grant and Kane had betrayed their oaths, but as Lakesh was wont to say, "There's no sin in betraying a betrayer."

The bromide was easy enough to utter, but to live with the knowledge was another struggle entirely. When they broke their lifetimes of conditioning, the inner agony was almost impossible to endure. The peeling away of their Mag identities had been a gradual process, but now, when Kane thought of his years as a Magistrate, it brought only an ache, a sense of remorse over wasted years.

But old Magistrate habits died very hard, particularly because of the rigorous discipline to which they had submitted themselves. Casting aside their identities as Mags and accepting new roles as rebels and exiles hadn't been easy for either Kane or Grant. Although they never admitted it to each other, both men sometimes yearned to return to the regimentation and routine of their former lives. If nothing else, the world had made more sense back then.

The legions of black-armored Magistrates made certain everything made sense, according to the edicts of the Program of Unification. After skydark, the wastelands of America were up for grabs and as usual, power was the key. Pioneers who tried to rebuild found themselves either shoved off their lands or facing bandits who killed with no pretense of ethical or moral right.

The alternatives were few; one could live the life of a nomad or join the marauding wolf packs or set up robber baronages. Whatever option was chosen, lives tended to be brutal and short. The blood that had splattered the pages of America's frontier history was a mere sprinkling compared to the crimson tide that flooded postnuke America. It had taken the nine barons and the unified villes to clean it up the only way it could be cleaned up—with an iron-fist rule.

The barons claimed they were practicing a new form of social engineering based entirely on the thesis that humans were too intrinsically destructive to be allowed free will any longer. The ruined planet was mute, utterly damning testimony to the philosophy of individual choice and freedom. The old predark system of smoldering desperation and unchecked societal chaos that was consumed in a final nuclear conflagration was inferior in every way to the society the barons built.

Kane and Grant learned painfully they had spent most of their adult lives supporting a system that was nothing more than old-fashioned fascism with a new face. It was institutionalized and standardized despotism.

Outlanders, or anyone who chose to live outside baronial society or had that fate chosen for them, were a different sort from those bred within the walls of the nine villes. Born into a raw, wild world, they were accustomed to living on the edge of death. Grim necessity had taught them the skills to survive, even thrive, in the postnuke environment. They may have been the great-great-great-grandchildren of civilized men and women, but they had no choice but to embrace lives of semibarbarism.

Bo and Hannie were of that breed, but their animal cunning had turned to furtive skulking wherein they viewed their own kind as prey. Kane didn't think the two people were worth much, but as he was no longer a Magistrate he tried not to sit in judgment of anyone shaped by their environment. He didn't succeed at it very often, but he did try.

"So that's what you had going with Carthew?" Grant inquired. "A deal to set up convoys for him and his Hell Hounds to loot?"

Bo nodded. "And we got a percentage. It was only business."

Grant uttered a sound like a malicious chuckle. "You got a hundred percent screwed this time."

Tears glinted in Bo's eyes. "Don't I know it."

"What are your plans now?" Kane asked, carefully swabbing at the inflamed edges of the woman's head wound. He didn't see the gleam of cranial bone so he didn't think a skull fracture was likely. Still, he knew head traumas were tricky and not easy to diagnose or treat.

Bo squinted at him in puzzlement. "Plans? What do you mean?"

"He means," growled Grant, "what are you and that used-up gaudy slut of yours going to do?"

"Do?" Bo echoed vacantly.

"How are you going to get out of here?" Kane asked impatiently. "The whole scheme was for you, Luke and Hannie to ride out with Carthew and the plunder, right?"

Bo nodded reluctantly.

"That's not going to happen now," Grant stated matter-of-factly. "You'll be damn lucky if the folks here don't shoot both you and your slut in the heads and leave you here so you can fatten up the buzzards."

Bo swallowed hard, face screwing up in mounting terror. "They can't do that—"

"Can and will," Kane declared flatly, applying a gauze patch to Hannie's cut. "Unless you give us a reason not to let them…like telling us where the Hell Hounds are headquartered and what they do with the people and matériel they steal. Do they have buyers or what?"

Bo hesitated, his tongue tapping a nervous ditty against his bottom lip. "It's worth my life if I tell you anything."

Grant snorted in derision. "And it's worth it if you don't. If you talk, you'll at least be buying yourselves a few days."

Hannie spoke for the first time, a barely audible whisper. "Tell 'em, Bo. The riders shot down Luke like an old dog. We don't owe them nothin' now."

The fear in Bo's eyes slowly changed to sly calculation. "What do we get out of it? I mean, just leavin' us here for the red-bellies to find is worse than shootin' us dead."

"What do you what?" Kane asked, winding a strip of bandage around Hannie's head, trying to avoid where blood had clotted in her hair.

Bo nodded toward a truck. "Transportation to Sweetwater Station. Safe transportation."

Kane couldn't help but utter a scoffing sound. "I

don't think the citizens of Sweetwater Station will exactly roll out the welcome mat for you, just like I don't think any of Kimball's passengers will want to share a coach with you."

Bo ignored the observation. "Just want to get there. We'll ride outside, on the guard boxes if we have to. Deal?"

Grant and Kane exchanged a swift, questioning glance, both knowing they would have to inveigh heavily on Kimball to agree to safeguard the pair of treacherous slaggers for over a hundred miles.

"That depends on what you give us," Grant said, folding his arms over his broad chest.

Bo nodded, his head bobbing up and down on his scrawny neck like a puppet's with a nervous disorder. "There's a big mining operation over in the Bighorns…lots of men and machines. Carthew was supplyin' the excavatin' outfit with labor and materials."

"What outfit?" Kane asked suspiciously.

"A goddamn big one." Carthew turned the lapel of his jacket inside out, revealing a small brass button pinned to it. The inscribed image was a stylized representation of a standing, featureless man holding a cornucopia, a horn of plenty in his left hand and a sword in his right, both crossed over his chest. No words were imprinted on it, but none were necessary. Belly turning a cold flip-flop, Kane recognized it.

He arched a meaningful eyebrow at Grant and said quietly, "The Millennial Consortium."

Chapter 6

Bo's eyes darted from Kane to Grant and back again. "You've heard of 'em?"

They had. A few months before during a mission to Ragnarville in Minnesota, the two men had run across the name and Kane had been forced to kill one of the consortium's representatives.

At the time, Kane and Grant had assumed the Millennial Consortium was a group of organized traders who plied their trade selling predark relics to the various villes. In the Outlands, it was actually the oldest profession. The baronies hired their own traders, who in turn controlled the supply routes and made big profits that they plowed back into expanding or finding new caches of goods.

Looting the abandoned ruins of predark villes was less a vocation than it was an Outland tradition. Entire generations of families had made careers from ferreting out and plundering the secret stockpiles the predark government had hidden in anticipation of a nation-wide catastrophe.

After the world burned in nuclear flames, enough debris settled into the lower atmosphere to very nearly create another ice age. The remnants of humankind had waited until Earth got a little warmer to venture forth again. Most of the early survivors had been scavengers. They really had no choice. They banded together, found predark wags and recruited men and women strong enough to defend those armored vehicles. They raided villes of the dead where the radiation had finally ebbed enough to allow limited access. They traded among the settlements, swapping equipment for supplies, supplies for gas, gas for ammo, and the ammo was used to blast the hell out of whatever muties or competitors stood in the way of their scavenging.

Finding an occasional well-stocked redoubt, one of the many underground military installations seemingly scattered all over the nuke-ravaged face of America, assured a trader of wealth and security, presupposing he or she didn't intersect with the trajectory of a bullet that had his or her name on it. Most of the redoubts had been found and raided decades ago, but occasionally one hitherto untouched would be located.

As the stockpiles became fewer, so did the independent salvaging and trading organizations. Various trader groups had been combining resources for the past couple of years, forming consortiums and absorbing the independent operators. The consortiums employed and fed people in the Outlands, giving them a sense of security that had once been the sole province of the barons. There were some critics who compared the trader consortiums to the barons and talked of them with just as much ill-favor.

Since first hearing of the Millennial Consortium, scraps of intel floating into Cerberus from various sources in the Outlands indicated the organization was deeply involved in activities other than seeking out stockpiles, salvaging and trading. They were far-flung but apparently well managed.

Kane said to Bo, "Last I heard, the consortium was operating in Minnesota, in a place called Carver's Cave. I was told a man named Benedict Snow honchoed that particular outfit."

"Same bastard," Bo declared. "A real coldheart."

Kane resisted the urge to comment, "Look who's talking." He asked, "What are they doing up in the Bighorns?"

Bo shook his head. "I don't know, never saw their base...but it's got somethin' to do with Injuns."

Grant knuckled his chin contemplatively. "So Carthew goes out robbing and kidnapping to supply the consortium's operation?"

"Seems like it," Bo answered. "Goods an' a free work force."

Kane rose to his feet. "Makes a certain amount of sense. Is there a pickup point?"

"On the Powder River, that's where they rendezvous with the consortium boys. They load up a couple of riverboats and move on down." Bo's forehead furrowed in thought. "I couldn't tell you how to get there from here."

Kane believed him. He handed a few pentazocine tablets to Hannie. "Take these with water, not that nasty 'shine you favor."

The woman didn't look happy about the warning. "Okay. Thanks."

"We got us a deal, then?" Bo asked hopefully.

Kane shrugged. "All I can do is ask Kimball to take you along. They're his trucks."

Bo raised his voice in a strident challenge. "But you promised—"

"I promised you *nothing,*" Kane broke in, his voice a harsh rasp of angry contempt. "You set these people up to be robbed, killed, abducted and enslaved. They were just commodities to you, a business deal, right? Why should I treat you any different?"

Bo struggled to come up with a response. Neither Kane nor Grant felt inclined to wait so they returned to where Lakesh was being treated by Domi and Brigid. While Domi held the edges of his wound together, Brigid hooked little butterfly sutures into the top layer of epidermis keep the gash closed.

"Did your sugar catch any flies?" Domi demanded peevishly.

"In the case of Bo and Hannie," retorted Grant, "more like leeches. But, yeah, we now have an idea what was behind this. The Millennial Consortium."

Brigid's brow acquired a line of consternation as she applied the field dressing to Lakesh's stomach. "That's very interesting. What are they doing out here?"

Tersely, Kane repeated what Bo had said.

Lakesh pursed his lips meditatively. "Has to do with Indians, does it?"

Grant shrugged. "Sounds like."

Placing his hands over his bandaged belly, Lakesh said, "I have a vague recollection of some sort of religious significance between American Indians and the Bighorn Mountains but—"

"Medicine Mountain, part of northern Wyoming's Bighorn Range," Brigid announced, pointing to a distant snowcapped peak. "On a ridge near the summit is the so-called Medicine Wheel, a circular arrangement of stones measuring eighty feet across with twenty-eight rows of stones that radiate from a central cairn to an encircling stone rim. Placed around the periphery of the wheel are five smaller stone circles.

"The Medicine Wheel's function and builders remain a mystery. However, there is general agreement that it was built approximately three hundred years ago by indigenous Native Americans, and that its twenty-eight spokes may symbolize the days in a lunar month. To Native Americans, it was a sacred ceremonial site."

No one gaped at Brigid in astonishment, but Kane regarded her with a frown of annoyance. She was a trained historian, having spent over half of her thirty years as an archivist in the Cobaltville Historical Division, but there was more to her storehouse of knowledge than simple training.

Almost everyone who worked in the ville divisions

kept secrets, whether they were infractions of the law, unrealized ambitions or deviant sexual predilections. Brigid Baptiste's secret was more arcane than the commission of petty crimes or manipulating the baronial system of government for personal aggrandizement.

Her secret was the ability to produce eidetic images. Centuries ago, it had been called a photographic memory. She could, after viewing an object or scanning a document, retain exceptionally vivid and detailed visual memories. When she was growing up, she feared she was a psi-mutie, but she later learned that the ability was relatively common among children, and usually disappeared by adolescence. It was supposedly very rare among adults, but Brigid was one of the exceptions.

Since her forced exile, she had taken full advantage of the Cerberus redoubt's vast database, and as an intellectual omnivore she grazed in all fields. Coupled with her eidetic memory, her profound knowledge of an extensive and eclectic number of topics made her something of an ambulatory encyclopedia. This trait often irritated Kane, but just as often it had tipped the scales between life and death, so he couldn't in good conscience become too annoyed with her.

"Very enlightening," Kane commented dryly. "But what interest would that have for a trading consortium?"

She stood up, wiping her blood-streaked fingers on Lakesh's turban. "I couldn't say. However, you told me that the millennialists were digging in Carver's Cave in

Minnesota a few months ago. The connection can't be a coincidence."

"What connection?" Grant demanded.

"Carver's Cave is another Native American religious site," she declared. "Before they moved westward, the Sioux in that region called it Waken Tipi or 'House of the Spirits.' Quite a number of prehistoric drawings and carvings were found there."

"That's why it's called Carver's Cave?" asked Domi. "'Cause of the carvings?"

Brigid smiled. "Hardly...in the mid-1700s, Captain Jonathan Carver, a fur trader, came to the area. He was the first white man to explore the cave and so of course that's why his name was applied to it."

Kane gestured in almost but not quite mock exasperation. "Of course. I would have suggested it was named after a man, but—"

"So," Brigid continued with a studied tone of serene detachment she knew was sure to provoke Kane to even greater heights of annoyance, "it's patently obvious that the Millennial Consortium is engaged in a program of exploration or excavation of American Indian mystical sites."

"That may be," Grant remarked. "But so what?"

Lakesh squinted up at him. "Aren't you the slightest bit curious as to their motives?"

Grant shrugged negligently. "Not especially. We came out here to stop the Hell Hounds." He nodded in the direction of the smoking hulk of the Sandcat and the black-carapaced bodies scattered around it. "I'd say that mission has been accomplished." He paused and added flatly, "Most thoroughly."

Lakesh shifted position, grimacing a little. "Quite true, friend Grant. But if the Millennial Consortium has established a precedent for rewarding rapine, then there will be others only too willing to take the place of Carthew and his group."

"I agree," said Brigid. "We have to cut off the source of the funding."

"Not to mention," Domi put in, "the Indians hereabouts might not be too happy to hear about white men digging around in their holy sites. They could take it out on everybody."

No one refuted her. As far as most Native Americans were concerned, the nukecaust had been a blessing, the "purification" of ancient prophecy. The white man's government had dissolved in a twinkling, and though the world wasn't as rich and beautiful as it had been when the tribes raced wild and free across the plains and the mountains, it was still better than the living hell of life on a reservation.

Kane sucked a tooth reflectively. "We're talking a hell of a lot of territory to cover, Baptiste. Dark territory. What makes you think we can find the millennialists out here?"

She waved toward the hilltop. "A few Hell Hounds escaped. We can follow their tire tracks on the bikes they left behind."

Kane smiled crookedly. "Since when have you wanted to be a biker babe?"

She cast him frosty stare. "I'm a quick study, remember?"

Lakesh chuckled. "Capital idea! I've always been attracted to the dream of being an easy rider."

He made a motion to rise, then his face contorted in pain and he sank down again, clutching at the pressure bandage. He husked out, "Or in my case, a *queasy* rider."

"See?" Domi snapped. "Told you to stay put."

Lakesh nodded. "So you did, darlingest one, so you did. I tend to forget the limitations of my age."

"Don't trot out that line for me," Domi replied unsympathetically. "You're still on the high side of three hundred."

Lakesh had been born back before skydark, the nuclear winter that had cloaked the world in two decades of night. As a youthful genius he had been recruited and finally indoctrinated into the complex web of technology and treachery known as the Totality Concept.

His fields of quantum physics and cybernetics had eventually placed him as overseer of Project Cerberus, the division of the Totality Concept that dealt with matter transmission via hyperdimensional travel. His research and successes had been responsible for the final design of the mat-trans units, colloquially known as gateways.

Lakesh had seen Earth before it had disappeared

under scorching mushroom clouds, and retained vivid memories of times well before the nukecaust. He'd slept in cryonic stasis in the Anthill, the master Continuity of Government center located within and beneath Mount Rushmore, for more than a century.

In order to keep the Anthill complex operation viable following the atomic megacull of 2001 and the nuclear winter, operations were performed on the Anthill personnel who hadn't been placed in stasis. Making use of the new techniques in organ transplants and medical technology, as well as in cybernetics, everyone living inside Mount Rushmore was turned into a cyborg, hybridizations of human and machine.

Radiation-burned flesh was replaced by synthetic skin, while limbs with cancerous marrows were changed out for ones made of plastic, Dacron and Teflon. With less energy to expend on maintaining the body, the cyborganized subjects ate less and therefore extended the stockpile of foodstuffs by several years.

Fifty some years before, upon Lakesh's resurrection, many of his major organs were replaced, including his eyes, heart and lungs and even knee joints. He was restored to a semblance of health in order to further the plans of the unification program and the nine barons.

However, everything he'd seen and lived through since that time, everything he remembered from the past, had served to alter Lakesh's alliances. Instead of remaining a conspirator with the Program of Unification's aims and goals, he had become its most dangerous adversary.

Not quite a year and a half before, he had been an old man who could barely walk a hundred feet without pausing to catch his breath. That changed on a fateful day in China when the entity known as Sam had restored his youth and vitality by the introduction of cell-repair nanites into his body. Then Lakesh had felt he was living in the dream world of all old men—restored youth, vitality and enhanced sex drive, as Domi could attest.

However, the nanites in his body became inert after a time. He and DeFore feared that without the influence of the nanomachines, he would begin to age, but at an accelerated rate. But so far, that gloomy diagnosis had not come to pass. True, he was sporting new gray hairs and he noticed the return of old aches and pains, but so far the aging process seemed normal. He was cautiously optimistic that he would not reprise the fate of the protagonist of *The Picture of Dorian Gray*.

But the nanites could not miraculously repair incapacitating injuries, as he was finding out the hard way.

"I suppose I'll have to sit this campaign out," Lakesh said resignedly.

"Sit out what campaign?" Grant argued. "We're not soldiers."

"You didn't object to going after the Hell Hounds," Brigid reminded him.

"No, I didn't," the big man agreed. "And there's a

reason for that. Since the fall of the baronies, settlers have been moving into the Outlands for the first time in nearly a century, trying to rebuild the country and make new lives independent of the villes. That effort will crash to a halt if slaggers like Carthew and his bunch aren't stopped in their tracks. Word has to spread that there are people who'll put the brakes on that kind of scum. Making examples of the Hell Hounds is a matter of policy. I'm all for that."

"Then what are you against?" Kane inquired. "We can't leave some to seed, can we? That's a matter of bad policy. We didn't even do that when we were Mags."

"We've got some of the Roamer bands on our side now," Grant countered. "We could get word to them, let them go after the survivors."

For the most part, Roamer bands were nomadic outlaws who used resistance to baronial authority as a justification for their raids. But since there was no longer any baronial authority against which to resist, Cerberus had managed to turn several of the groups into allies.

Brigid made a sound of disdain. "Oh, come on, Grant. Trying to sic Roamers onto Hell Hounds is like trying to get foxes to make sure weasels behave around a henhouse. One is just as untrustworthy as the other. Passing the buck to Roamers isn't a logical solution."

Grant thrust out his jaw pugnaciously. "We've got bigger enemies to deal with now—remember Enlil and the other overlords? What isn't logical is to devote our attention to pissant punks like Carthew."

Kane suspected Grant's reluctance to go on such a mission had little to do with buck-passing or logic but he didn't put his suspicions into words. "I shouldn't have to remind you," he ventured, "that as long as Enlil and the overlords stay in the Mideast and on the African subcontinent—and we don't go over there—they're not our immediate concern. We're bound by a pact of non-interference for the time being."

Grant swept his gaze over Kane's and Brigid's faces, then threw his hands up in frustration. "All right. I'm outvoted. We'll trail the damn Hell Hounds."

Glancing down at Domi and Lakesh, he asked, "What about you two?"

Lakesh said, "I'm sure Mr. Kimball will allow us to continue on to Sweetwater Station. There I can recuperate and wait for your return. And if you take too long, I can get word to Cerberus. Perhaps someone there can come fetch us."

"Us?" Grant echoed, angling questioning eyebrows at Domi. "You want to go with him or us?"

The little albino woman nibbled at her underlip for a thoughtful moment. "I'll go where the need is the greatest. Lakesh is hurt, out here with strangers. He'll need someone to look after and doctor him." A rueful smile tugged at the corners of her mouth. "And if there's one thing I've learned since we all hooked up…ain't nothin' on Earth or off it you three can't handle, is there?"

Chapter 7

"Except for a fucking motorcycle," Grant growled, wrestling with the brake and gearshift levers as the bike inscribed a slow circle on the hilltop.

He rode around the smoldering wreckage of the Sandcat, sorting out the gears. He changed through them from bottom to top, then back down again. The machine was heavy, but it responded smoothly.

Finding travel-worthy motorcycles among the lot left behind by the Hell Hounds wasn't a problem. Sturdy machines, most of the damaged inflicted upon them was cosmetic, not mechanical. Brigid Baptiste had little problem working out the intricacies of the bike she chose. Grant, an experienced pilot of both helicopters and transatmospheric planes, required more time than either of his friends to get the feel of his motorcycle. The extra time did nothing to relieve his surly mood.

Finally, twenty minutes shy of high noon, the three people prepared to follow the narrow tracks in the snow left by their quarry. They distributed the equipment they had brought from Cerberus among them. Grant lashed the LAW case and rockets to the handlebars, Kane carried the box of grenades and extra ammunition while Brigid tied their survival stores onto her motorcycle's saddle.

All three of them carried Copperheads attached to clips beneath their coats. Chopped-down subguns, they were little under two feet in length. The extended magazines held thirty rounds of 4.85 mm steel-jacketed rounds, which could be fired at a rate of 700 per minute.

Even with their optical image intensifiers and laser autotarget scopes, the Copperheads weighed less than eight pounds. Gas operated, the grip and trigger unit were placed in front of the breech in the bullpup design, allowing for one-handed use. Their low recoil allowed the Copperheads to be fired in long, devastating, full-auto bursts.

Grant glanced down the face of the slope at the convoy, which Kimball was prepping to get under way again. The mustached man had reluctantly and profanely agreed to transport Bo and Hannie to Sweetwater Station, under the condition they kept to themselves in the back of the most packed truck and did not exchange words with any of the other passengers, least of all him.

Grant spied Domi helping Lakesh hobble toward the open cargo compartment of one of the converted moving vans. Clasping his stomach with one hand, the older man leaned into her, obviously grateful for her help and presence. Grant felt a pinch of shame that he had never let the young woman know, either by word or deed, how much he had appreciated her help and presence over the years.

But his heart was pledged to Shizuka, despite her responsibilities to the people of the island kingdom of New Edo. They were still determined to spend a couple of days together a month, despite their respective duties that kept them apart most of the time. Until a few months ago, it had been Grant's intent to leave Cerberus altogether and live in the little island monarchy of New Edo with Shizuka, particularly after the arrival of the Manitius base personnel. He felt—or had hoped—the new recruits would alter the balance of the struggle against the barons.

But after being captured and tortured by the sadistic Baroness Beausoliel, Grant realized the struggle remained essentially the same; there were just new players on the field. The war itself would go on and would never end, unless he took an active hand in it, regardless of his love for Shizuka.

Suddenly, as if she picked up his ruminations, Domi's head turned toward him. Although the distance was too great for him to see her eyes, he received the unmistakable impression she gazed expectantly into his face. Hesitantly, Grant lifted his right hand, then his entire arm and waved. The albino returned the gesture and returned her concentration to helping a bent-over Lakesh clamber up into the cargo compartment.

Studying the tire tracks, Grant noted how they dwindled in the distance, stretching like dark threads on a white sheet toward the snow-covered peaks of the Bighorns, many miles distant. The sun, climbing toward its zenith, tinted the hills and slopes with various subtle shades of violet and orange.

Kane twisted the throttle controls of his motorcycle, revving the engine so as to catch his attention. Grant frowned at him, then nodded. "Hi yo."

Brigid took the lead and the three of them rode at a moderate speed along the crest of the ridge and down into a shallow coulee, the noises of the engines sounding almost obscenely loud in the wilderness. Grant wasn't much concerned about the aesthetics—he was more worried about their approach being heard for miles, giving their quarry plenty of time to set up an ambush.

Of course, he reflected sourly, it wouldn't be the first time they'd deliberately put their heads between the jaws of a trap.

Sometimes it seemed that all he and his friends did was avoid, outwit, dodge, duck and even let themselves be caught by numerous traps set by their enemies. It had been part and parcel of the war they had waged for the past three years against the tyranny of the nine barons. They had devoted themselves to the work of Cerberus— and then unexpectedly, the entire dynamic of the struggle against the baronial tyranny changed.

The Cerberus warriors learned that the fragile hybrid barons, despite being nearly a century old, were only in a larval or chrysalis stage of their development. Overnight, the barons changed. When that happened, the war against the baronies seemed to be over, but a new one began.

The baronies had not fallen in the conventional sense through attrition, war or coups. No organized revolts had been raised to usurp the hybrid lords from the seats of power; insurrectionists had not met in cellars to conspire against them.

The barons had simply walked away from their villes, their territories, their subjects. When they reached the final stage in their development, they saw no need for the trappings of semidivinity, nor were they content to rule such minor kingdoms. When they evolved into their true forms, incarnations of ancient Annunaki overlords, their avaricious scope expanded to encompass the entire world and every thinking creature on it.

The Cerberus warriors had hoped the overweening ambition and ego of the reborn overlords would spark bloody internecine struggles, but in the eight months since their advent, no intelligence indicating such actions had reached them.

Of course, the overlords were engaged in reclaiming their ancient ancestral kingdoms in Mesopotamia. They had yet to cast their covetous gaze back to the North American continent, but it was only a matter of time.

Before that occurred, Cerberus was determined to build some sort of unified resistance against them, but the undertaking proved far more difficult and frustrat-

ing than even the cynical Kane or the impatient Grant
had imagined. Even months after the disappearance of
the barons, the villes were still in states of anarchy, of
utter chaos with various factions warring for control on
a daily basis.

Men like Carthew were not unique. Many former
Magistrates grabbed what they could carry from the
ville armories and plunged into the Outland territories
to carve out their own fiefdoms or empires, limited only
by resources and their imaginations.

As the journey continued, the temperature hovered
a few degrees above freezing. Grant, Kane and Brigid
were not uncomfortable by the cold due to features of
the one-piece garments they wore under their clothes.
Kane had christened the black, skintight garments
shadow suits, and though they didn't appear as if they
could offer protection from a mosquito bite, they were
impervious to most wavelengths of radiation. The suits
were climate controlled for environments up to highs
of 150 degrees and as cold as minus ten degrees Fahren-
heit. A network of microfilaments controlled the internal temperature.

The long shadows of afternoon began stretching over
the terrain and the Bighorn Range rose steadily above
the horizon. Gullies and ravines broke up the monotonous flatness of the plain, and here and there were
stands of aspen and cottonwoods. The three people kept
on a straight course for the Bighorns, so far in the dis-

tance it seemed they couldn't possibly reach them by the end of the month much less the day.

The vast stretch between the basin and the Bighorn foothills was probably one of the least explored regions of the Outlands. Even before the nukecaust, it had been sparsely populated. In the eighteenth and nineteenth centuries, the territory had been the shared hunting grounds of the Crow, the Bannock, the Cheyenne and the Sioux.

Gradually, the snowy plains gave way to rockier terrain but the trail was still visible, angling away from the foothills. In the afternoon glow, they climbed a hillside covered with pine and gray rock. At the top they looked ahead to the range of mountains rising to a white-capped peak.

Below them the trail wound down to a valley bare of trees and carpeted with brown grass. Kane pointed out the black fan shapes of vultures wheeling and circling above a high outcrop of granite.

Her voice transmitted clearly through the Commtact, Brigid commented, "A couple of the Hell Hounds were wounded. Maybe they expired."

"Yeah," Kane said, but he didn't sound as if he believed it. "Let's check it out."

The tire tracks they followed curved in the direction of the vultures. The descent was difficult, holding the heavy machines on low gear and riding the brakes. The engine noises startled a white-tailed deer grazing on the scrubby grass and it bounded away.

Within a few minutes, they rolled into a gloomy, stone-littered swale overlooked by a rocky buttress rising ominously fifty feet above them. It formed a giant headstone for the bullet-riddled corpse of a dead Indian and a pinto pony. The three people turned off the motorcycle engines but stayed in the saddles, studying the scene.

Judging by the consistency of the blood glistening on the ground, man and horse had been killed within the past hour. The carrion birds squawked resentfully and flapped away, reluctant to leave their banquet of flesh, viscera and bone.

Kane read the whole story quickly, without even dismounting. The dead Indian was a young brave who had apparently attacked the Hell Hounds wielding only a lance. It lay nearby, the wooden shaft splintered by automatic fire. Whether he had wounded one of the ex-Mags was a strictly a matter of conjecture, but at least three streams of 9 mm autofire dropped him and his war pony dead. His bullet-perforated rawhide shield bore the red-and-yellow cross-within-the-diamond symbol of the Lakota.

"Think we should give him a burial?" Brigid asked, her voice pitched low.

"The ground is frozen solid," Grant replied flatly. "And rocky as hell, too. It would take us the rest of the day to dig a grave."

Brigid nodded, her green eyes clouded with sadness. "It just seems sort of disrespectful to leave him here."

"It's more respectful to catch his killers," Kane said, planting his foot firmly on the kick starter of his motorcycle.

The ugly whine of a bullet played a discordant note as it ricocheted from a rock less than an inch from his left foot. The cracking report of a rifle echoed half an instant later.

Kane reacted instinctively, jarred by the unexpected sound. He leaped from the motorcycle's saddle, allowing it to tip over and crash to the ground, unlimbering his Copperhead in the same motion, questing for targets. He found half a dozen.

Sitting on ponies atop the granite rim above the swale, he saw men with their coppery faces distorted by red-and-yellow paint, their eyes glittering with naked hatred. They wore fringed deerskin shirts and leggings. Feathers adorned their long black hair.

The Sioux mounted in the center braced the butt of a Winchester against his shoulder, sighting down its length. He screamed one word and it was one of the few in the Lakota language Kane understood.

The warrior shrieked, *"Te-wichakte!"*

It meant "murderer."

Chapter 8

The horizon disgorged the sun, the snow-filtered light rays turning the gray sky a flaming red-orange. Sky Dog squinted against the glare, but he forced himself to watch the ascent of the fiery orb that lent the harsh earth warmth and life, even in winter. Behind him, mounted in single file, were twelve Kit Fox warriors from his Bitterroot band of Lakota.

Even though they were on a scouting mission, Sky Dog couldn't repress a twinge of pride when he thought of the fearsome sight the mounted warriors presented. The tails of the ponies weren't tied up for war and the men's faces weren't painted, but the magnificence of the Sioux warriors was beyond dispute.

The Kit Foxes held the greatest seniority of the many Sioux warrior societies. It was of great antiquity, dating back to long before their ancestors' first encounter with the *wasicun,* the white man. The Kit Fox society had a fourfold function. It was a social club for distinguished members of the tribe. The warriors preserved order in the camps and on organized hunts, punished offenders against the public welfare and cultivated a military spirit among the youths of the tribe.

Sky Dog, as the official tribal shaman and unofficial ambassador to anyone not of their people, felt the most uncomfortable with that aspect of the Kit Fox warrior's duty. Over the past few months, particularly since a number of their warriors had been slain, murdered by cowardly white marauders to hear Bear in the Woods tell it, their militance had become a little disquieting.

Bear in the Woods maintained that war was what the Lakota did best, but there had been few opportunities to straightforwardly engage an enemy lately, even among other bands. Although the Brulé, the Osage, even the Sans Arc were as much Lakota as Sky Dog's band, there was sometimes a fierce and deadly rivalry among the various soldier societies. The Kit Foxes were so anxious for conflict of some sort, Sky Dog feared they would cheerfully attack an ally, like the Absaroke whom they had recently befriended.

Already Sky Dog had been forced to discipline three of his warriors who wanted to go in search of Chikala and Fleet Deer. Although a shaman, not a war chief, his commands were to be obeyed until the council issued a formal declaration of war. A veteran of many battles, he knew it was pointless to make plans until an enemy's strength had been revealed.

The column of Lakota rode at right angles to the foothills, the sunrise on their faces. The hooves of their ponies made uninterrupted swishing sounds as they passed through the sparse, brown winter grass. The wind gusting over the Bighorn Basin was cold, but if the warriors found it uncomfortable, they showed no sign. The Kit Foxes wore antelope tunics trimmed with fox fur and fringed deerskin leggings.

Sky Dog's ruddy face was flat boned, with anthracite-black eyes set widely to either side of a thin, sharp nose. Shiny black hair plaited in two braids framed his face and fell almost to his waist. Behind his right ear a single white feather dangled. He was dressed in tanned buckskins, and the sleeves of his shirt bore the beaded geometric symbol of the Lakota.

Bear in the Woods was a man of similar age and build but he was dressed for battle in all but the face paint. Two eagle feathers fluttered in his loosely flowing hair, and his muscular torso was covered by a breastplate of red-dyed porcupine quills. A choker of wolf-and-fox teeth encircled the base of his neck, and an armlet made of silver bound his right bicep.

The man heeled his pony up beside Sky Dog and murmured, "Your nephew is long overdue."

Sky Dog didn't react, as if the leader of the Kit Fox society hadn't spoken. From his parfleche he removed a compact set of binoculars, a gift from Unktomi Shunkaha. Peering through the eyepieces, he fixed his gaze fixed on the distant gray-green face of Medicine Mountain.

"Fleet Deer, Long Nose, Buffalo's Ghost and Chikala are brave," Bear continued, "but they are only boys. We should go in search of them up the mountain."

Tersely, unemotionally, Sky Dog stated, "We agreed on a plan of action before we left the village. We will wait for word."

Bear in the Woods sighed, hitching around on his pony's saddle blanket to look at the men riding behind him. "There may not be word, my friend. The Kit Foxes fear that if indeed the Lynx Soldiers are allies of these white defilers—"

Sky Dog stiffened on his pony's back, rising slightly, binoculars still held to his eyes. Bear stopped speaking, squinting in the same direction as the shaman. "What is it?"

After a moment, Sky Dog pointed one finger in an eastward direction. "One man...on foot."

Bear's hand clasped the stock of his lever-action Winchester, snugged in a beaded and fringed scabbard. He inquired hopefully, "A white man?"

Lowering the binoculars, Sky Dog shook his head. "No."

Bear in the Woods turned his animal eastward. "Let's find out who it is and why they're out here so early."

Bidding the Kit Foxes to wait, Sky Dog and Bear galloped through the winter-browned grasses. The shaman was more than perplexed; he was fearful, suspecting he knew the identity of the lone man and not wanting to acknowledge it.

After a minute of hard riding, a figure could be discerned, walking in a very curious fashion. He stumbled and staggered and he appeared to be holding his arms behind him. Then he fell and vanished from sight among the grasses.

The two Lakota kicked their ponies into a faster pace. They almost rode past the nearly naked figure lying on the ground. Bear and Sky Dog reined in their mounts and leaped from their backs.

The man lay on his face, his wrists bound tightly at his back with leather thongs. His left ankle was swollen and discolored, his feet caked with mud and blood. His limbs bore a crisscross network of scratches and blood-oozing cuts. Sky Dog eased him over onto his back and Bear exclaimed in horror, "Fleet Deer!"

Sky Dog eyed his nephew's youthful face and the layer of dried blood crusted over his naked torso. Fleet Deer was semiconscious, gasping for air, his lips blue. Bear touched the rawhide thong half buried in the young man's throat. Three small but very hard knots pressed cruelly into his windpipe.

Carefully, the Kit Fox chief drew his knife and used the point to slash through the thong but so deep was it sunk into Fleet Deer's neck that the blade opened a shallow cut. Sky Dog recognized the purpose of the rawhide about his nephew's throat. It was an old but effective means of torture and eventual execution, not practiced by his people in many centuries.

While Sky Dog lifted Fleet Deer into a sitting position, Bear cut the leather cords binding the young man's wrists. When Sky Dog touched Fleet Deer's swollen ankle, the young Lakota cried out and the shaman subsided. The young man's eyes were open but judging by their glassy sheen, his life force was ebbing fast. He was in the last stages of hypothermia, exacerbated by exhaustion and shock.

"Did white men do this to you?" demanded Bear in the Woods.

Fleet Deer shook his head and said in hoarse whisper, "Catamount."

Sky Dog's lips peeled back from his teeth in a silent snarl. "And Chikala?"

"He is dead…." Fleet Deer touched the coat of dried blood adhering to his chest. "Killed by the demon cat, Deathmaul. Catamount took coup upon his body. This is his blood."

Bear growled deep in his throat. "Where is that witch? I will take coup on her and all who follow her!"

Fleet Deer coughed rackingly. "You must not…she is in league with the evil white men. They have many blasters."

"These white men," Sky Dog ventured. "Was a man with hair and face like snow among them?"

Fleet Deer nodded. "He gave the orders. He killed Long Nose personally." He reached up and touched Bear's shoulder. "And your grandson, Buffalo's Ghost. All of the Lakota who went to their camp on Medicine Mountain…dead. Butchered."

"Aiee!" The cry of pain bursting from Bear's throat was fierce and sharp, rising toward the sky.

Fleet Deer groped for Sky Dog, catching his sleeves,

pulling him close. "The murderers will come to you and tell you what our people must do to safeguard the *tai-me*. If you do not obey then the *baykok* will rouse...the Owl Prophet will live again...."

A rattling exhalation passed the young man's lips and his eyes went vacant, fixed on some faraway point. He shuddered and then slumped lifeless in Sky Dog's arms, dying very quietly and with such brave dignity it nearly clove the shaman's heart in two.

Sky Dog laid the body of his nephew down and stood up. He hadn't understood everything the young man had said. He knew of the *baykok,* the night spirit, the revenant who preyed only on warriors. He also knew how the *tai-me* figured into the legends. He clenched his fists and gazed up at the fleecy clouds, struggling to control the misery roiling in the pit of his belly. He tried to think of something he could possibly say to his sister-in-law that would justify the death of her son, but no thoughts came.

Bear in the Woods bowed his head and brushed tears away from his cheeks. When he rose, his expression was composed once more. "We will avenge him."

Sky Dog shook his head. "You heard his words. We must not. The *tai-me* is at stake."

Bear didn't bother to repress a growl of rage. Sky Dog knew that religious artifacts and ancient legends about the walking dead wouldn't stand in the way of the Kit Fox society as their warriors tracked down and exacted vengeance on the murderers of striplings.

The other warriors joined them and Sky Dog repeated Fleet Deer's final words. Blue Cloud, who was not much older than either him or Chikala, gripped the feathered shaft of his lance so tightly the wood creaked and his knuckles stood out in stark relief on his hands. "We cannot allow this to stand," he hissed.

"We will not," Bear promised, casting Sky Dog a challenging stare.

Sky Dog met that stare with an unblinking one of his own. "We know where the black-shelled whites rendezvous with the curs of the snow-head, do we not?"

Reluctantly, Bear nodded. "On the Chaka dee Wakpa…Powder River."

"That is where we will go," Sky Dog announced. "We will not climb the face of Medicine Mountain and let our enemies know we are coming. We will come in between their feet."

The Kit Foxes swiftly constructed a travois from lance shafts, blankets and leather lashings. Leaden clouds covered the face of the sun, casting an appropriately gray pall over the procedure.

Within twenty minutes, the blanket-covered body of Fleet Deer reclined on the travois behind Sky Dog's pony and the group of Sioux marched toward a pass in the foothills.

Sky Dog and Bear in the Woods didn't speak, riding silently side-by-side, buffeted at intervals by a cold wind. The shaman focused his thoughts on the *tai-me* rather than on the corpse of the boy whom he had essentially sent to his death. He knew only the legends but that was almost all any native peoples had left of their culture—legends, folklore, myths, handed down from generation to generation.

The *tai-me* was an idol carved from a stone that had allegedly fallen from the sky many, many centuries ago, lovingly adorned with ermine skin and tufts of eagle down. During the sun dance ceremonies, the *tai-me* was attached to the end of an oak staff and the Grandfather of All Spirits would imbue it with his essence. Then and only then would the Native peoples embark on their hunts and raiding forays. If they were not so blessed, their year would be a poor one, marred by misfortune and scarce game.

But the legends regarding its powers were too vague and indefinite, too wrapped in myth and folklore. Almost all plains tribes paid homage to the sun, although Sky Dog felt that they really worshipped a supernatural being, the Grandfather who lived beyond the sun, rather than that star itself.

Earth, too, was highly regarded by the Sioux. Since Earth was the mother of all Indians, everything provided by this universal mother was received with prayer and thanksgiving. The first whiff of tobacco smoke, the first morsel of food, after being held aloft to the sun, was given to Mother Earth.

The *tai-me* was instrumental to the sun dance, and without it to attract spirits of good fortune, the Grandfather would pay their offerings and prayers no heed. That was why it had become the centerpiece of a century's worth of bloodshed and intertribal war.

Over three hundred years before, the Kiowa had been in possession of the *tai-me*. The holy artifact was entrusted to Chief Islandman, a great leader and holy man. When his warriors unwittingly encroached upon the hunting grounds of the Osage Sioux, a medicine man who wielded more power than the chief called for war against the Kiowa.

The medicine man's name was Towasi but he was known as the Owl Prophet. He too was a Kiowa, but he had been banished from the tribe for practicing the blackest of sorcery, which included human sacrifice. He had secretly coveted the *tai-me* for many years and used the retaliation against the Kiowa's trespass to claim it.

Towasi ordered all of Islandman's people killed and decapitated, their heads put in buckets and set adrift in canoes down the Carrizo Creek as a warning to other Kiowa not to try to recover the *tai-me*.

The warning wasn't heeded. For the next four years, the Kiowa waged war against the Osage, the white man, Mexicans, against anyone who was not of their tribe who foolishly strayed within their field of vision. The Kiowa saw to it that the Santa Fe Trail ran crimson. Their longtime allies, the Comanche, joined their unilateral war with a fierce joy. They had become bored with burning the Catholic missions, for the fat friars were not fit opponents. Captured Sioux were tortured and humiliated, flayed and dismembered and returned piece by piece to their people.

Finally beset from all sides and weary of bloodshed, the Sioux sent to the white chief of the bluecoats at Fort Gibson to intercede. The chief, a Colonel Henry Dodge, secured the Kiowa's promise to cease warring along the Santa Fe in return for the *tai-me*—and Towasi.

But the Owl Prophet didn't wish either himself or the Grandfather's idol to be put in the hands of the Kiowa. The best he could hope for was a long, agonizing death by torture and he escaped, but he left the *tai-me* behind, swearing to return for it.

As a simple matter of ritual restitution, the Sioux had to include a pony with the exchange to compensate for the missing Towasi, but the horse was not much of a loss. The animal they traded was in the first stages of grass tetany. Although the Comanche rejected the proposal to leave the Santa Fe Trail alone, they promised not to attack white men unless attacked first. But Mexicans were a different matter. Colonel Dodge was satisfied with this compromise and the war ended.

But that was not the end of the Owl Prophet or his involvement with the *tai-me*. A sudden gust of chill wind stung Sky Dog's eyes and brought his thoughts back to present realities, not legends derived from events from long ago. The wind carried a faint but familiar noise—the rising and falling growl of several engines.

The Kit Foxes reined their mounts to a halt, gazing

across the plain as they tried to pinpoint the source of the sound. Sky Dog placed the binoculars to his eyes and swept them back and forth. Then, out of a declivity in the terrain, nearly a mile distant appeared four black figures astride motorized steeds.

"Black-shelled ones," he stated for the benefit of his companions, although he knew very well they were called Magistrates. "There are only a few."

Bear in the Woods replied grimly, "Then we should have no trouble tracking them down and slaying them."

From his parfleche he removed pouches containing his face paint and he began applying the colors vigorously to his cheeks. The other Kit Foxes followed suit, chanting *"Oo-oohey!* It is time! *Oo-oohey!"*

Sky Dog lowered the binoculars and regarded Bear grimly. In a low voice, he said, "Do not force me to order you to obey me, my friend. The time to disagree with my tactics is at a council fire, not here."

Bear's lips compressed, his eyes narrowed to slits but he said, "You are right. I apologize."

Suddenly, with a surprised snort from the pony and a short fierce cry, Blue Cloud kicked his mount into a gallop. Hooves thundering and throwing up clots of frozen earth, the animal carried his young master in the direction of the Magistrates.

Sky Dog started to shout a command for the young man to return, but he was drowned out by encouraging yells and howls from the other Kit Foxes. They didn't follow Blue Cloud, but they certainly approved of his initiative.

Unsuccessfully trying to suppress a grin, Bear said, "He will be punished."

Sky Dog bumped his pony's flanks with his heels, saying gravely, "Let us hope he lives long enough for that."

Chapter 9

The lead of a second .44-caliber bullet flattened against the rock, fragments of mica and metal whining in all directions, pelting his boot. Kane kicked himself away from the motorcycle, knowing that by the time he managed to restart it, the Indian's third attempt to shoot him dead would be the charm.

Hitting the hard ground on his left shoulder, he cursed in pain as his back muscles twinged. He heard Brigid blurt in wordless alarm. He tucked, rolled and came up on his right knee, unslinging the Copperhead in the process. He fired it upward one-handed, not really aiming.

At the same instant Grant opened up with his own subgun, twisting awkwardly on the motorcycle seat. The two weapons hammered out twin rattling drumbeats, and gouts of dirt exploded from the rim of the overhang. Grit and gravel burst up in fountains. The ponies of the Indians shied and reared, neighing in panic. They backed away from the edge in eye-rolling terror.

The Sioux with the Winchester resolutely struggled to stay astride his horse and return the fire. Dropping the rope reins, he worked the rifle's lever and trigger in a swift but unsteady rhythm. His wild shots didn't come close to the Cerberus warriors, but the whine of ricochets added to the cacophony of gunshots and the squeals of terrified ponies.

Leaping from her motorcycle, Brigid raised both arms over her head and shouted at the top of her lungs, *"Heyah! Colapi! Colapi!"*

The Sioux swiveled the rifle barrel toward her and she pointed to Kane, crying out, "Unktomi Shunkaha! *Unktomi Shunkaha!"*

At those words the Lakota peered over his rifle rather than sighting down its length. He stopped shooting and so did Kane and Grant. They saw his lips move as he repeated Kane's Sioux name. It meant "Trickster Wolf." It had been bestowed upon him by a warrior named Standing Bear, who had also given him the thin scar traversing his left cheek.

Turning his head, the Lakota shouted to his companions, *"Colapi!* Unktomi Shunkaha!"

The feather-bedecked man thrust up the Winchester high over his head with both hands, a peace sign. Kane slowly climbed to his feet. He didn't aim his Copperhead at the Indians on the overhang but he didn't lower it, either. He sidemouthed, "Thanks, Baptiste."

"Saying to them 'No, we're friends,' didn't work," she replied lowly. "But telling them they were shooting at the lovely and talented Trickster Wolf stopped the hostilities."

Grant, his eyes snapping black sparks of anger, glared up at the Sioux warriors. "Good thing you're so popular, Kane. Is this a bunch of Sky Dog's boys or are you a household name in every Indian village now?"

Kane started to make a disparaging, dismissive remark then realized he had no answer to his friend's question. With the way the Sioux had distorted their features with war paint, it was hard to recognize any familiar faces among them.

"Unktomi Shunkaha!" The sharp voice spoke loudly from behind.

Kane whirled, leading with the Copperhead. Sky Dog and four Lakota moved into the open, sidling around a scattering of boulders where they had apparently been hidden. Releasing his pent-up breath in a relieved, profanity-seasoned exhalation, Kane lowered the subgun. "Sky Dog, you have *no* idea how glad I am to see it's your gang shooting at us."

The shaman's rigid features didn't twitch in even an imitation of a smile. Although he had no a weapon, his right hand didn't stray far from the butt of the autopistol thrust through his beaded belt. The other warriors wielded a variety of firearms, all provided ironically enough by the Cerberus armory. They regarded the outlanders with glittering eyes, bright and wary. They cradled their guns so the barrels pointed Kane's way.

"In truth I don't know how I feel about seeing you three out here, Kane," Sky Dog intoned flatly.

His delivery held an undercurrent of menace and

Kane felt his nape hairs tingle and lift. Gesturing to the corpses of Indian and horse, Brigid said, "Surely you don't think we had anything to do with this."

Sky Dog stepped closer to the bodies, his face as immobile as if it were carved from brick. "Did you?"

"You know better than that," Grant snapped, anger edging his voice with steel. "Or you damn well ought to after all this time."

Sky Dog swept his dark, penetrating gaze over the three people. "Perhaps I do, but my people want to know what you're doing here in the lands of the Lakota and the Cheyenne. They are very keen to find out."

"Is that so?" Kane inquired carefully, cradling his own weapon in such away the bore fixed on the tallest of the warriors.

"Blue Cloud pursued four Magistrates on motorcycles." Sky Dog nodded toward the three machines. "I count three of them there."

"Three is not the same as four," Kane stated acidly. "At the least it wasn't the last time I checked."

"And the last time *I* checked," Brigid interjected, "the three of us still weren't Magistrates."

Sky Dog frowned at the sarcasm. His tone became a bit less formal. "Then what the hell are you doing out here? You're a long way from home."

"We're chasing four Magistrates on motorcycles," Grant answered gruffly. "And you're as long a way from home as we are."

Nodding in acknowledgment of the observation, the

shaman stated, "Perhaps we should parley, compare notes on why we're all so far from home. It might be our reasons are related."

Kane imitated the nod. "Good idea. This inscrutable noble-savage act of yours is starting to get on my nerves."

Sky Dog's lips twitched, then stretched in a grin. "I thought you knew, Kane. It's meant to."

SKY DOG'S VILLAGE LAY in the tableland in the foothills of the Bitterroot Range and as such, the mixed band of Sioux and Cheyenne were Cerberus redoubt's nearest neighbors.

Well over two years before, direct contact been established between the redoubt's personnel and the tribespeople. Kane had managed to turn a potentially tragic misunderstanding into an alliance with Sky Dog. Not so much a chief as a shaman, a warrior priest, Sky Dog was Cobaltville-bred like they were. Unlike them, he had been exiled from the ville while still a youth due to his Lakota ancestry. He joined the band of Amerindians living around the Bitterroots and eventually earned a position of high authority and respect among them. Part of that position was to serve as the keeper of his people's great secret—the war wag.

According to tribal lore, more than a century before, a group of *wasicun* adventurers had ridden inside the iron belly of a predark mobile command post up the single treacherous road wending its way around deep ravines to the mountain plateau. When the vehicle made its return journey, it ran out of fuel, and the Amerindians had set upon the people inside it. After presumably killing them all, they had hidden the huge machine and removed all of its weapons except the fixed emplacements.

When a set of circumstances brought Grant, Brigid and Kane first into conflict, then alliance with the Indians, Sky Dog proposed the residents of Cerberus make the MCP operational again. They had agreed, since a fully restored and armed war wag would make a solid first line of defense against a possible incursion from Cobaltville. The task to bring back to life a machine that had lain dormant for at least a hundred years entailed far more effort and time than any of them, particularly Kane, who had acted as the Cerberus diplomatic envoy, had foreseen.

First the engine had to be taken apart piece by piece, and then put back together again. All of the instrument panels needed to be rewired. Upon its initial manufacture in the twentieth century, the control systems were designed to be operated and linked by computers, but its postskydark owner had rerouted all the automatic circuitry to manual-override boards.

Periodically over a stretch of months, Grant and Kane visited the Indian settlement to complete the refitting of the MCP. The front-mounted 20 mm cannons had been repaired, the side and rear rocket pods made fully functional and a drum-fed RPK light machine gun reinstalled in the roof turret. Once the huge vehicle was completely operational with all of its weaponry in perfect working order, it became a true dreadnought, a mobile skirmish line, far superior to the ville Sandcats.

Those efforts that earned Kane his high standing among the tribespeople. The name Trickster Wolf was at first conceived as an insult, then it became synonymous with cunning and courage after he orchestrated the Lakota victory over the Magistrate assault force.

Two years before, a squad of hard-contact Mags dispatched from Cobaltville made an incursion into the Bitterroot Range as part of a ville-wide cooperative effort. The squad's mission was to investigate the Cerberus redoubt and ascertain if it was playing host to three wanted seditionists—namely Kane, Grant and Brigid.

The Magistrates were stopped and soundly defeated by Sky Dog's band of Amerindians in the flatlands bordering the foothills. Grant and Kane were instrumental in the victory, although they managed to keep their involvement concealed from the invading Mags.

While the body of Blue Cloud was attended to, Sky Dog drew the Cerberus warriors aside to confer. They were joined by the Winchester-toting Bear in the Woods and two other high-ranking Kit Foxes. Kane recalled meeting them during his frequent visits to the village, but they were considerably less cordial than before. Even before the incursion of Team Phoenix had resulted in so many Lakota deaths, the influence of the soldier society on the band had increased. Since then, the Kit Foxes seemed to wield more and more authority.

Kane in particular wasn't pleased by the prospect for a number of reasons. First and foremost, a political upheaval among the Sioux could have a serious impact on the security of Cerberus. He had kept his visits to the settlement at a minimum since that incident so as not to inflame anti-*wasicun* passions.

He viewed the Indian village as something of a holiday resort, a vacation getaway when he suffered from redoubt fever. No one asked what he did down there among the Amerindians but after remaining with the band for a few days, Kane would show back up at the Cerberus installation, often times dirty and disheveled but always relaxed. Grant and Brigid often wondered if Kane had a willing harem of Indian maidens who always looked forward to a visit from Unktomi Shunkaha, but they never inquired about it.

The truth was a little more metaphysical than seeking a sexual release. With the recent influx of female émigrés from the Manitius Moonbase, Kane had no lack of willing partners. He felt a strong affinity for Sky Dog's wild and free people and their unfettered way of life. Perhaps it had something to do with the vision he had glimpsed some years before during a bad gateway transit.

At the time he had dismissed it as a dream caused by an out-of-phase mat-trans lock. Lakesh had explained long ago that when the modulation frequencies of two gateway units weren't in perfect sync, jump sickness would result, a symptom of which was startlingly vivid hallucinations.

The hallucinations Kane had suffered weren't mere dreams—they were more like glimpses of past lives, vignettes from his soul's journey over the long track of time. In one of the visions, he had seen himself astride a pony, feathers in his long, streaming hair as he galloped down on the bluecoat soldiers in place called Greasy Grass. The soldier's chief had been named Pahaska.

It wasn't until much later, delving secretly into the Cerberus database, that he learned Greasy Grass was what the Lakota called the Little Bighorn and Pahaska's *wasicun* name was Custer.

Kane had wondered why such obscure historical details that weren't in his conscious storehouse of knowledge would bubble to the surface during a bout of jump sickness.

Following that incident, after gaining pieces of the Chintamani Stone, Lakesh postulated that so-called jump dreams might not be hallucinations at all, but brief, inchoate peeks into other lives and other realities.

The Cerberus and Lakota warriors sat inside a circle of stones, munching pemmican and strips of dried elk meat offered by Bear in the Woods. Grant, Kane and Brigid forced it down without registering much revulsion. A few of their MRE packs weren't superior in the area of flavor. However, they did insist on providing the water, distilled and carried in sealed bottles.

"Why are you here?" Sky Dog asked bluntly.

Brigid narrowed her eyes at his autocratic tone but she answered him, explaining in Lakota for the benefit of the others about their mission. Sky Dog already knew about the fall of the baronies and the anarchy that over-whelmed many of them. She told him about reports from a Roamer band that led Cerberus to investigate the tales of the Hell Hounds and then embark on a mission to stop their raids.

"That was accomplished early this morning," she announced. "All but four are dead."

Bear in the Woods bobbed his head enthusiastically. *"Hecheto welo!* It is good!"

Sky Dog didn't seem as pleased. In English, he asked, "Domi and Lakesh are on their way to Sweetwater Station in the convoy?"

"Yes," Brigid answered.

Sky Dog called over a warrior. The shaman spoke quickly and quietly but urgently into his ear. When he was done, the Lakota ran to his pony, leaped onto its back and galloped furiously away.

"Where is he going?" Grant asked suspiciously, star-ing after him.

"I sent Goes-Ahead to spread the word to the other bands in the region not to attack the convoy, to let it pass in peace."

"Smart move," Grant replied dryly. "Seeing as how

Domi is aboard. The Sioux would take more losses than any possible gain."

Sky Dog's eyes flashed in momentary resentment, but he didn't address the observation. "We have heard much of the Wakansica Yanka—the Hell Hounds—ourselves. When they crossed our path, Blue Cloud struck out on his own after them. The rest of us followed at a distance...then we heard gunfire. We waited, but Blue Cloud never returned. We came across his body only moments before you arrived."

"You're not out here to hunt the Hell Hounds down," Kane stated confidently.

Sky Dog shook his head. "No...they are only the curs."

Kane washed down a mouthful of sour pemmican with a swallow of water. "Let me guess...you're after the leader of the pack. A man named Benedict Snow."

Sky Dog raised his eyebrows in mild surprise. "I have met with the man you name, but no, he is not who I seek. A clever and ruthless man he is, but at this stage he is but a pawn."

Brigid cocked her in head in puzzlement. "In whose game?"

Sky Dog pursed his lips and he sighed thoughtfully. He took so long to reply, Brigid almost repeated the question, but at length he said slowly and almost reluctantly, "That is a difficult question to answer. I have cudgeled my brains deep into the night, seeking the answer. I have no choice but accept the obvious. It is a game played by a man who died at least 325 years ago...Towasi, the Owl Prophet."

Chapter 10

Sky Dog flicked his eyes back and forth across the faces of Kane, Brigid and Grant. They returned his gaze stolidly. Sounding almost disappointed, the shaman said, "You don't seem very skeptical by such a crazy statement."

Kane shrugged and exchanged wry looks with Brigid and Grant. "We've heard crazier…and seen worse."

Sky Dog's lips quirked in an appreciative smile. "I should have known."

He couldn't dispute Kane's statement as being anything less than truthful. Even a peripheral relationship with Cerberus had shown him the inhabitants of the redoubt were accustomed to lives of high strangeness.

"Even so," Grant said, "it probably wouldn't hurt to explain what you mean."

Sky Dog sighed, shifting position on the rock upon which he sat. "It has to do with a holy object of my people. It is called the *tai-me*. It is heaven-sent stone. I don't expect it to mean anything to you, but—"

He broke off when he saw Kane angling ironic eyebrows in Brigid's direction. "What?"

Kane nodded to Brigid. "If you would be so kind—"

Sounding almost embarrassed, Brigid Baptiste said, "The *tai-me* has been compared by Indian historians to the Ark of the Covenant…it was a symbol of religious veneration not entirely dissimilar to the sacred statues, paintings and other relics so highly regarded by the religions of other races throughout the world."

Sky Dog couldn't help but smile. "And do you know why?"

"According to myth," Brigid answered, "it contained the essence of the Grandfather, basically spirit of God. There were ten lesser idols, the *a'dalbeahya,* which translates as 'Grandmother' gods. They were preserved in pouches made of human scalps. They were held in respect only slightly less than that accorded the *tai-me.*"

Sky Dog gazed at her in frank admiration. "How do you know all of this?"

"I studied," she replied simply. "And remembered."

"It helps to have a photographic memory and access to probably the most comprehensive database on the planet," Grant interposed.

"You seem to know more than most of my own people," Sky Dog commented bleakly.

Brigid shrugged. "That's really not unusual. Most of these stories were all oral history even three hundred years ago. Even though native religions were studied and reported upon by a number of ethnologists throughout the nineteenth and twentieth centuries, it's doubtful if all the permutations were made understandable, even to the Indians themselves."

"What do you mean?" asked Kane.

"The cosmogony of deities and rituals were too vague and indefinite," Brigid declared, "too wrapped up in contradictory legend and folklore, particularly the sun dance ceremonies."

Sky Dog nodded. "My village practices them, but much of the meaning behind the rituals has been lost, particularly since we perform them without the unifying symbol of the *tai-me*. I fear it is empty posturing, only going through the motions."

Brigid smiled at him sadly, sympathetically. "I know. But according to the information I studied, the sun dances were more than simple religious ceremonies. They were festivals, a combined church social and picnic, even a family reunion. Old friends and relatives met for the first time in perhaps a year, warrior societies held meetings, elections and initiations, young men met their future wives, newborn infants were medicated and charmed against disease and epidemic by the shamans.

"The whole religious atmosphere of the tribe was toned up and given a rebirth, the achievements of warriors of the past year were given proper publicity and growing boys launched in their careers as full-fledged members of the tribe. The institution tended to maintain tribal and racial solidarity, and through its influence the traditions of the people were preserved."

"Why is it called a sun dance?" Grant wanted to know.

A somewhat sly smile touched Sky Dog's lips. Using his hands to suggest shapes, he said, "A large east-facing lodge is built for the ceremony and forked pole is erected in the center. In the fork we place sacred objects...long ago, it was the *tai-me*. The young warriors dance around the pole, always facing the sacred objects. They dance until exhaustion, going without food or water until they collapse.

"Then a shaman cuts two small holes through the skin and muscle on both sides of their chests and sticks wooden skewers through the holes and tie them to two ropes. The ends are fastened to the forked ends of pole. The warriors dance again, straining against the ropes. Once they received their visions from the Grandfather, the ropes will break and free them."

Kane winced. "Sounds like it hurts like hell."

Sky Dog's smile broadened. He opened his tunic, revealed two vertical raised weals on his pectorals. "Every single time."

Grant's eyebrows knitted at the bridge of his nose. "Then why do it?"

"When the ceremony is over," explained Sky Dog, "the tribe can count on enjoying health, fertility and food. The world is renewed, its harmonies restored, ready once more to work for the welfare of the people...or it used to be so when the *tai-me* was involved."

"All of that invested in a rock?" inquired Kane.

Sky Dog frowned. "I don't expect you to understand."

"It's a little far-fetched, you have to admit."

Brigid cast Kane an irritated glance. "It's not like we haven't had dealings with stones with unusual properties before."

Rather than respond to Baptiste's oblique reference to the Chintamani Stone, Kane said, "We might understand more than you give us credit for. If the *tai-me* was so important, hasn't any Indian looked for it after all these centuries?"

Sky Dog shook his head. "No."

"Why not?" inquired Grant.

"Because we've known where it was since the 1870s." The shaman hitched around on the rock and waved toward the broken line of mountains jutting up from the horizon. "There, atop Medicine Mountain, buried beneath the Tohan Pejuta in the Wanagi Awape Yata."

Brigid squinted toward him. "Beneath the what in the where now?"

Sky Dog chuckled. "So there are some gaps in your knowledge… I'm glad to hear that. It's beneath the Medicine Wheel, in the Place where Souls Wait."

"What the hell is that?" Grant asked impatiently.

"A cavern, or so I'm told. A network of caverns."

"Why the hell is it there?" Kane demanded.

All humor vanished from Sky Dog's demeanor. "To contain an great evil. And now, that evil may be released and spread a far more monstrous form of tyranny on the world than the barons ever schemed. It shames me to admit that some of our own are involved in the dark design."

BRIGID, GRANT AND KANE weren't amused by Sky Dog's melodramatic turn of phrase. The shaman had long ago explained to them the basic mind-set of his people. He had told them of the way his and other groups of Indians had reacted to the nukecaust. The Indians had interpreted it as the time prophesied for so long by their seers and wise men, the end of a time cycle when the *wasicun* and their ways were swept away.

Judgment Day arrived late in the first month of the year 2001. A long-prophesied apocalypse had scorched clean the world with waves of atomic fire. For nearly thirty more years the judgment had continued—earthquakes, massive coastal flooding, killer chem storms and years of darkness resulting from the nuclear winter. At the end of it, nearly ninety percent of the planet's population had perished.

The few Indians who survived skydark rejoiced in the coming of a new age. They left the reservations and journeyed to the plains and they grew in number and strengthened in spirit. The old ways returned. The tribes re-formed and bred mighty warriors in the second age of their history.

Remembering how their people had been deceived and robbed by the *wasicun* centuries before, they protected their ancestral lands ruthlessly, particulary the Cheyenne and Lakota. These two tribes of over one thousand souls were divided into various orders and warrior societies. They obeyed rules like the samurai of feudal Japan. No member of a warrior society like the Kit Foxes could return from war except with added honors; he had to either win coups, or not come back at all.

But time moved in cycles and the second age drew to a close. The tribes, still in the minority, were safer now from *wasicun* depredations than they had been in five hundred years. A few of the more enlightened Indians of influence realized that even the whites had been victimized and deceived by the power mongers, by the barons. With the collapse of the ville governments, attitudes were changing, and the Indian hand— which had once held a war club—was now open, extended in a cautious form of friendship.

At least, that was the hope.

Sky Dog said dolefully, "We know that after the skies grew dark, terrible days overtook everyone, no matter their race or skin color. But there are some among the Lakota who believe that Wakan Tanka, the Grandfather, meant to destroy everyone who is not Indian."

"Hard-liners," Grant grunted, folding his arms over his chest.

Sky Dog nodded. "There are a few soldier societies who still maintain that the *wasicun* are our mortal enemies whom we must outwit and kill before they destroy us again. It is the fear of the predark days returning that makes them want to kill all who are not like them."

Brigid glanced over at Bear in the Woods, who sat cross-legged atop a rock, obviously not understanding the conversation but assuming Sky Dog would provide him with the gist of it later. "You're not talking about the Kit Foxes, are you?"

"No, but there are a few warriors among them who feel that way. I speak now of the Lynx Soldiers."

Kane frowned. "I don't believe I've heard of them."

"I would be surprised if you had," Sky Dog replied. "Even my own village no longer speaks of them—or of their chief. They were banished from the tribe because they sought their own path with no regard for the consequences of their actions that befell their brethren."

"Who is their chief?" Brigid asked.

Sky Dog sighed deeply, as if he regretted answering the question. "Her name is Catamount."

"*Her* name?" Brigid echoed in surprise. "A woman is the chieftain of a warrior society?"

"All of the Lynx Soldiers are women," Sky Dog stated. "Many things have changed since the sky fell."

"Traditions fell, too," Kane commented dryly.

"There were women warrior societies among the Blackfeet," said Brigid. "I never heard of any among the various bands of Sioux."

"Catamount is not a full-blooded Lakota," Sky Dog

responded. "Her father was Spotted Hawk, my mentor. When he died, I inherited his title of shaman." He touched the white feather dangling behind his ear and a chunk of polished turquoise inserted into a loop on his belt.

"Who was her mother?" Grant asked.

Sky Dog shrugged. "No one knows. Spotted Hawk refused to say. It's thought she was a witch from the Absaroke, the Crows. The women of the Crow tribe are the most winsome of all native peoples and often suspected of having magical powers. Other say Catamount's mother was an *acheri,* a female demon who seduces men in their dreams."

"Which corresponds to the legend of the succubi," Brigid interposed. "When Spotted Hawk died, did Catamount resent you for assuming his position in the village?"

Sky Dog's bright black eyes dimmed with sorrow. "Yes. Her heart was filled with much bitterness. As a girl, though devoted to her people, she could be cruel and ungovernable. That was why she was not trained in the arts as I was. But it wasn't jealousy that turned her heart so black—when her father was killed in a Roamer raid, Catamount lost all sense of restraint."

He paused, taking a deep breath. Then in a hoarse half whisper, he intoned, "She was captured and raped repeatedly. After many days, she managed to kill several of the Roamers and return to the village. When she heard the wailing of the women mourning the dead,

Catamount decided to become a warrior herself. She undertook a vision quest in the wilderness and claimed the spirit of the mountain lion, the panther, entered her."

"Interesting," Brigid commented noncommittally.

"You might say that," Sky Dog retorted bleakly. "Particularly since she returned with a huge cougar as her companion. She named him Iwohtaka Winconte."

Brigid nibbled at her underlip. "Roughly translated, that means 'Deathmaul.'"

"Exactly. She somehow tamed it. Some said the devil-cat had found a more savage heart in her breast and yielded to it. After that she formed her own warrior society, the Lynx Soldiers."

"To protect the Lakota?" Kane inquired, noting how the shadows were lengthening across the ground.

The shaman shook his head. "No...for hate. For revenge. For power. There was a streak of arrogance, of cruelty in Catamount long before the Roamers captured her."

"What brought about her banishment from the tribe?" Grant asked, checking the impulse to consult his wrist chron.

"No single incident was the cause...it was cumulative. While we council of chiefs negotiated with the Crow, she'd raid their hunting parties. When white traders from the villes crossed the farthermost lands of our territory, instead of leaving them alone, she would draw their attention by staging attacks. She harried Roamer bands most of all, traveling hundreds of miles to seek them out."

"She sounds rather obsessive," observed Brigid. "But courageous."

"Brave but reckless," the shaman countered darkly. "Not a good combination."

"I thought being 'the bravest of the brave' was the whole point of a warrior society," Grant ventured. "Promotion to the next higher orders is through merit alone, right?"

"True, but Catamount and her Lynxes didn't plan their sorties well. Although I have no solid proof of it, I have long suspected it was due to her attacks on the Roamers that drew Le Loup Garou to our village." Sky Dog's lips compressed as if he tasted something unpleasant. "I'm sure you remember that."

Kane only nodded, not needing the reminder of the time Le Loup Garou's Roamer attacked Sky Dog's settlement and carried off captives. Only by his, Brigid's and Grant's timely intervention had the prisoners been freed—and only by the intervention of Sky Dog had Kane avoided being buried alive by Le Loup Garou.

"The Lynx Soldiers were away from the village that day," the shaman continued. "On a foolish mission which garnered them nothing—no plunder, no ponies, no coups. When they returned, the council of chiefs ordered Catamount to disband the Lynxes. She refused, choosing exile instead. Most of the women followed her."

Sky Dog's ruddy face creased in an indefinable expression, a mingling of grief and anger. "Catamount accused us of repeating the suicidal shortsightedness of our ancestors. She claimed we would bring down the same doom as befell our forefathers at the hands of the *wasicun*. She swore she would do anything to keep that from happening, use any weapon no matter how foul, commit any sacrilege."

Brigid's eyes widened in sudden comprehension. "The *tai-me*…she's manipulating the Millennial Consortium into recovering the *tai-me* for her. Is that the sacrilege you mean?"

Sky Dog stirred uneasily on the rock, saying slowly and deliberately, "There is more to it than that. If the Medicine Wheel's holy alignment of stones is dislodged, if the *tai-me* is removed from the Place of Souls, then the *baykok* will awaken."

Brigid blinked. "*Baykok*? I'm not familiar with that word."

Trying to keep the impatience he felt from being heard in his voice, Grant asked, "Is that an animal or a man or what?"

Sky Dog's eyes grew misty as clouds of dread seemed to drift across his face. "*Was* a man. Long, long ago my people feared the *baykok*. The drums and storytellers spoke of them. It was once a death sentence to even speak of a *baykok* to a *wasicun*. The *baykok* is one of the Grandfather's forbidden secrets. A mistake in his divine plan."

Kane and Grant eyed Sky Dog with growing exasperation, but they waited for the shaman to elaborate.

Voice pitched to barely above a whisper, Sky Dog said as if by rote, "A *baykok* is no longer human. It knows no love, no family, no tribe. It has joined with the creatures of the Black World, those that exist in the gulf between nightmares and waking.

"It can be slain by steel, but unless it is slain it will never die. It can only be contained. It lives forever, dwelling in eternal darkness. The passage of years means nothing to a *baykok*…an hour or a century, all is one. It can control humans if their hearts are hard and it can command the lifeless body of an evil person until the last drop of their blood has fallen. As long as blood flows, the corpse is its servant. Its only pleasure is inviting the darkness within the human soul and feasting upon it as a starving man will gorge himself on food. To seek the *tai-me* is to seek the *baykok*."

Sky Dog fell silent and for a long, awkward moment, no one spoke. Then Kane cleared his throat. "So according to your legends, a *baykok* guards the *tai-me*, like the old stories of dragons guarding treasures."

The shaman regarded him resentfully. "It is no legend…and I mean the exact opposite. I thought you understood."

Nettled, Kane shot back, "Maybe I would if you talked facts instead of folklore."

Sky Dog fixed his unblinking eyes on his face. "Very well. Fact one—if Catamount gains the *tai-me*, she will free the *baykok*—who is Towasi, the Owl Prophet, the sorcerer whom the Lakota and the Kiowa sacrificed the *tai-me* to imprison within Medicine Mountain...nearly four hundred years ago."

He paused and added grimly, "*Now* do you understand?"

Chapter 11

They climbed a hill, descended, climbed another and halfway down the next slope saw the surface of the Powder River winking in the late-afternoon sunlight.

Kane, Sky Dog, Brigid and Grant all peered through ruby-coated lenses of identical binoculars. On the banks of the river sprouted dry, leafless willow trees and snarled thickets of briar. Set back in a grove of winter-dead cottonwoods was a flat-roofed blockhouse.

Rust-pitted corrugated metal covered the walls. The visible windows were crisscrossed with iron slats. They were meant to serve more as gun ports than a means of letting light and air into the building. Four motorcycles stood outside the building on the hard-packed earth.

"Looks like an old toll takers station," Grant murmured.

Years before, self-styled toll takers staked out and barricaded sections of road or river crossings and charged exorbitant and sometimes bloody fees to travelers.

"This used to be a trading post," Sky Dog said. "Long ago."

Kane nodded absently, still scanning the immediate area around the structure, looking for camouflaged machine-gun nests. He saw none, but he knew from experience most of the Outland trading stations were heavily guarded and fortified. Very close to the riverbank, he spotted an oblong wooden structure resembling a slightly oversized, upright coffin and guessed it was an outhouse.

The few people who lived in the territory brought their trade items to the station on designated days, things they'd made, trapped or grown or salvaged, and they bartered with traveling traders for other goods. Judging by the condition of the place, business had fallen off dramatically over the past decade. If not for the parked motorcycles, he would have assumed the place had been abandoned long ago.

"Look off to your right," Brigid said quietly.

Sky Dog, Grant and Kane did so and saw a dock made of splintery planks extending from the bank near the rear of the building. The rushing water foamed white at the support posts, the current running swiftly southward. He figured the water was deep and, due to the mountain meltwater, exceptionally cold.

A bulky barge, nearly thirty feet long and almost twenty feet wide, was tied up at the end of the dock. The barge looked as if it had been put together with everything from old automobile parts to driftwood. A small box-shaped wooden superstructure formed a pilothouse. Rubber tires roped to the hull acted as cushions of sorts as the current bumped it incessantly against the pilings of the dock. A paddle-wheel contrivance with wide wooden blades enclosed within a wire cage protruded from the stern, nearly spanning the breadth of the barge. It in turn was connected by a long black rubber belt to the flywheel of a big diesel engine mounted at the back of the craft. Canvas shrouded a tall, upright object bolted to the deck amidships.

The words *Crazy Woman* were painted on the bow in bright red letters. They contrasted so starkly with the drab colors of the rest of the barge that at first glance they looked almost fluorescent.

Lowering the binoculars, Kane commented, "Now we know how the Hell Hounds transported their goods and labor to the consortium's operation."

"Yeah," Grant rumbled. "And now that we know, what are we going to do about it?"

"Kill them," Sky Dog retorted bluntly. "What else?"

Kane's lips quirked in a rueful half smile. "That's tempting, but let's try to get some information first before we go to throat-slitting."

"I don't think they're going to be in a talkative or sharing mood," Brigid opined.

Sky Dog fingered the long handle of the steel-bladed tomahawk hanging from his belt. "My people can be very persuasive."

Kane nodded absently, studying the area around the outpost. "I'm aware of that, but revenge for your nephew should come after we get what we need."

Grant tilted his head back, eyeing the position of the sun through the tree branches. "Whatever we're going to do, it ought to be soon while we can still see what we're doing. It gets big-time dark out here."

A little over an hour before, they had resumed their journey, leaving the motorcycles behind. They continued tracking the Hell Hounds on horseback, carrying most of their equipment with them. Sky Dog had arranged for three of the Kit Foxes to volunteer to lend their ponies to Unktomi Shunkaha and his two companions. The trio of Lakota didn't seem happy about the prospect of waiting mountless in such a gloomy place, despite the fact that the three people were Ocastonka, famous all over the plains.

To ease their dissatisfaction, the Cerberus warriors gave them several MRE packages, although Kane silently wondered how long their good moods would last once they dug into them. As tiresome a diet as pemmican and jerked venison could be, he figured they would taste like gourmet treats after the Indians ate a couple of the ration packs. Although the MREs contained all the minerals, vitamins and proteins a human needed to keep healthy, they all seemed to share one of two flavors—bland or repulsive. No middle ground seemed to exist, and even the most undiscriminating of palates eventually ended up in a form of shock.

As it was, neither Brigid nor Grant particularly enjoyed being on horseback again. With only blankets serving as saddles, riding the Indian ponies wasn't much different from trying to keep their balance while straddling a split-rail fence for a couple of hours. The toes of Grant's boots nearly dragged in the dirt.

Kane, however, didn't mind. He loved horses even though his experience with them was limited. At one time he had considered trading with the Lakota for a remuda of ponies so the Cerberus exiles would have alternate means of transportation to and from the plateau. He had discarded the idea when Brigid and Lakesh reasonably pointed out that the animals would require a great deal of time and care—and they weren't about to muck out whatever lodgings Kane found for them.

Fortunately for Grant and Brigid, the party of Sioux and outlanders didn't travel very far. They followed the tire tracks until they reached a narrow, rocky pass. Navigating it would be slow and arduous on motorcycles and not much easier on horseback. Sky Dog, Kane, Brigid and Grant dismounted, leaving the seven Kit Fox soldiers to wait for them.

During the short journey on horseback, Sky Dog had related how over a period of a year reports of the Millennial Consortium's activities around ancient native holy sites had circulated through the Outlands. He had personally gone to investigate the organization's presence at Carver's Cave. There he met Benedict Snow who claimed to be an archaeologist seeking only to preserve the lost knowledge of America's native people.

Sky Dog instantly suspected he was a liar. He realized it when Snow asked him questions about the location of the fabled *tai-me*. Only a handful of Kiowa and Sioux shamans knew where the relic was hidden so Sky Dog, although angry about the defilement of Waken Tipi, didn't take action against the millennialists.

The consortium was too well-armed for a direct attack to result in anything but a massacre. Sky Dog felt that with the lack of solid information from which Benedict Snow could work, his search for the *tai-me* would remain desultory and ultimately end in failure or death, particularly if he and his crew wandered into Apache country, in the deep Southwest.

Then, only a few weeks before, word reached him that Catamount had been seen among the millennialists as they traveled across the Bighorn Basin. With a sense of horror, Sky Dog realized Catamount's father, Spotted Hawk, had possibly told her of the *tai-me*'s location. After all, the old man had imparted the tales as part of his shaman training.

Four volunteers, young Kit Foxes in training, embarked upon a spying mission to Medicine Mountain. Only one returned and Fleet Deer lived just long enough to confirm Sky Dog's worst fears.

Brigid said softly, "If the Hell Hounds looted the Cobaltville armory, they could have everything from mortars to flamethrowers in there."

"I'll go back and fetch my men," Sky Dog stated.

Kane shook his head. "By the time you get back, it'll be full dark. I'd rather do this while we still have a little light."

Grant scowled. "Do what?"

Unholstering a pistol, he thumbed off the safety and jacked a round into the chamber. "Our tried and true strategy of brazening it out."

Both Grant and Brigid groaned simultaneously.

KANE SAUNTERED from the tree line, affecting a casual, relaxed gait as if he had been out picking wildflowers and become bored. In reality, his stomach muscles were knotted in the same way they had when he was a Magistrate, preparing to kick open a door to a pesthole down in the Tartarus Pits. But he knew once the bullets began to fly he would be loose and fast, anything but relaxed.

As he approached the trading post, he pretended a desultory interest in the four motorcycles resting on their kickstands. He paused to examine them, carefully withdrawing a blunt cigar from a jacket pocket. Placing the end of it in his mouth, he set it afire with a simple flint-and-steel lighter. He began smoking with what appeared to be a preoccupied intensity.

He peered through the wreath of gray smoke, eyes searching for blastermen atop the roof or hidden at the edge of the riverbank. He saw no one and nothing. Surreptitiously and alert for anything that looked like a gun barrel, he glanced toward the barred window, catching shifting shadows from within.

Kane figured the Hell Hounds inside would choose one of two strategies—shoot him down before he reached the door, or admit him and then shoot him down once he was trapped inside.

He puffed on his cigar and, when no object that resembled a gun poked out from between the bars, he guessed the ex-Mags had talked it over and decided to adopt the latter strategy.

Taking a few slow steps closer to the door, he blew a cloud of smoke, removed the cigar from his mouth and called, "Hel-*lo*, the shit hole."

For several moments he heard no sound whatsoever from within. Then his ears caught a faint shuffling as of feet on a dirt, and a youthful voice demanded, "What the fuck do you want?"

"For right now, I want to talk."

Another voice, one as euphonious as a metal rasp being dragged over wet flint, snapped, "Got nothin' to talk about, you bastard."

"That's where you're so very wrong. Is Carthew in there?"

He heard a brief, mumbled conversation, a scuff and scutter of movement, then Carthew's voice called, "I'm here, Kane."

The man's tone was tight, brittle, as if he was struggling to control either his emotions or intense pain.

"You don't sound so good," Kane stated cheerfully. "My, whatever could be wrong?"

Hoarsely, Carthew half shouted, "I'm dying, that's what's wrong! I'm all busted up inside, thanks to Grant and his goddamn rocket launcher."

Kane let a lazy smile spread across his face. "Funny you should mention that." He hooked a thumb over his right shoulder. "Guess who is aiming what at your exclusive men's lodge right now?"

"Figures." Carthew didn't sound surprised or even apprehensive. "How the hell did you find us?"

Meaningfully, Kane nudged the rear wheel of a motorcycle with the toe of a boot.

"Oh," said Carthew in glum understanding. "Did you come across any Indians while you trailed us?"

"Just the kid and his pony you shot and killed. Not very sporting."

"Hell, it's not like the little son of a bitch gave us any choice." Carthew sounded genuinely angry, even a little regretful. "We tried to scare him off, but the kid wouldn't scare."

Kane exhaled a stream of smoke through his nostrils. "How about you? Do you scare?"

"What do you mean?"

"I mean I want some information. You can either give it to me without me having to persuade you, or Grant can just blow the shit out of this place with you slagjackers still inside."

After several seconds of silence, Carthew said in a dead, defeated tone, "All right. Come on in."

Kane raised an eyebrow. "Just like that? You don't want me to toss my gun in the river or anything like that?"

"Would you do it if I told you to?"

"Most likely not."

"Then I won't waste my time. Besides, you're the one with the ace on the line, not us."

"Very astute." Kane's sixth sense, what he called his point man's sense, howled an alarm. The skin between his shoulder blades seemed to tighten, and the short hairs at the back of his neck tingled. His point man's sense was really a combined manifestation of the five he had trained to the epitome of keenness. Something—some small, almost unidentifiable stimulus—had triggered the mental alarm.

Under the guise of taking a final drag on his cigar before dropping it and crushing it underfoot, Kane murmured, "I'm going in."

Over the Commtact, Grant said, "Nice bluff about the rocket launcher."

"Yes," Brigid put in dryly. "Let's hope they don't call it."

"They're definitely up to something," Kane said softly.

"No shit," Grant commented sourly.

As Kane took his first steps toward the station, he heard a metallic clank and clatter and the door swung open. A big man in overalls and a red T-shirt and sporting a wild beard stepped up and blocked the doorway into the building. He carried a .30-30 lever-action rifle, keeping his body turned so he could bring it up at a moment's notice. The fast fading light glinted dully from the Millennial Consortium button pinned to the frayed, stretched-out collar of his shirt.

"I'm Broderick," he announced arrogantly in the harsh, flinty voice Kane had heard earlier. "I own this place. How many are out there in the bush?"

Kane shrugged. "Does it make any difference? It's the issue of your being outgunned, not outnumbered."

Broderick glowered, considered the implications of the comment and moved aside. Kane stepped over the threshold, squinting until his eyes adjusted to the gloom. The interior of the station glowed from animal-fat lanterns hanging from ceiling hooks. He saw three of the Hell Hounds still in their body armor, shifting in the chairs where they sat at a big wooden table. Earthenware mugs, poker chips and cards were scattered across it.

Carthew stood in a corner near the window, peering out intently for any sign of Kane's companions. At first Kane thought the one-eyed man had his arms folded over his chest, but then realized he was cradling his torso.

"Take a seat," Carthew wheezed between clenched teeth.

Kane scanned the room. It was barren of any creature comforts, possessing only a long wooden slab serving as a bar and the half-dozen chairs scattered around the table. Behind the bar, a long board rested on spikes driven into the planks at forty-five-degree angles. Bottles and jugs were lined up on the makeshift shelf.

Yellowed animal skulls were nailed to the walls between old regional maps of the western states. The floor was hard-packed dirt, bisected in several places by deep cracks. The cloying stench of human sweat and home-brewed liquor clung to the air.

Broderick began pushing the door closed.

"Leave it open," Kane told him. "This place really needs to air out."

The bearded man snorted and shut the door firmly. Kane didn't react until he heard the locking bar dropping into place. Then, uncoiling almost too fast for the eye to follow, he pivoted at the waist, drawing his pistol in the same motion. He hit the man across the forehead with the barrel, the blade sight tearing a bloody gash in his flesh.

The man crashed backward, bounced off the door and staggered forward, right into Kane's left fist. It pounded deep into the pit of his belly. All the air left Broderick's lungs with an agonized grunt. He dropped his rifle and fell, landing at the feet of the Hell Hounds at the card table.

Cursing, they went for their weapons.

Chapter 12

The Hell Hounds still wore their Mag-issue Sin Eaters, snugged in power holsters strapped to their right forearms. Tiny electric motors whined as they flexed their wrist tendons. Sensitive actuators activated flexible cables in the forearm holsters and snapped the Sin Eaters smoothly into their gloved hands.

As fast as they were, Kane was faster. The Bren Ten spit three subsonic rounds through the tabletop. Chips and cards jumped into the air and a mug shattered amid a spray of acidic liquor.

"What's going on?" Brigid's agitated voice blared into his head.

"Under control," he answered in a calm, cold voice. "Just making a point."

One of the Hell Hounds, a black-haired man in his midthirties, wiped at the stinging liquid on his face, muttering sourly, "We got it."

"Hands on the table," Kane said curtly, kicking Broderick's rifle out of reach. "And you, Carthew, put yours where I can see them."

Carthew flashed him a grin with red-filmed teeth.

"I'd like to accommodate you, Kane, I really would. But my hands are all that's keeping my guts off the floor."

Kane flicked his gaze toward him. The one-eyed man's face was drawn, his chin speckled with blood. He breathed shallowly, laboriously, with a faint liquid gurgle underscoring his respiration. Kane figured he suffered from punctured, perhaps even collapsed lungs. Several ribs were probably broken, too.

"And your side arm?" he asked the former Magistrate.

"Out of ammo."

"Take it off anyway."

Carthew grimaced. "I'll try."

"Just do it." Kane returned his attention to the three men still seated at the table. "You, too. Move slow."

As they complied with Kane's order, undoing the straps and Velcro tabs of their holsters, Broderick stirred on the floor. One hand clapped over the bleeding laceration on his forehead, he crawled away from the table and pulled himself up, sitting down in one of the chairs. He steadfastly avoided looking in Kane's direction.

Kane backstepped to the door and lifted the locking bar, pulling the door open, glad for the whiff of fresh air.

"We're in position now. Ready for your signal," Grant said.

"Stand by," Kane whispered.

After the three Hell Hounds had stripped off their Sin Eaters and tossed them to the floor near the bar, Kane glanced back over at Carthew. The man leaned against the wall, struggling to undo a buckle.

"You need any help?" Kane challenged. "Want me to shoot it off?"

"Leave him alone," snapped a black-armored man with curly blond hair. He looked and sounded very young, still in his teens.

Kane gauged him at no more than eighteen years old. "What's your name, boy?"

With a defiant sneer on his lips, the young man announced, "Vance."

Gesturing negligently with the barrel of his Bren Ten toward the red embossed disk on Vance's left pectoral, he asked, "How long were you badged before you went rogue?"

"Two months," Vance shot back. "How about you?"

Kane narrowed his eyes, presenting the image of a man pondering the question. "I was closing in on seventeen years, I guess. That's why I knew how to keep my fucking mouth shut when facing a man with a gun."

He paused and showed the edges of his teeth in a wolfish grin. "But if you were a Mag for only two months, I suppose you never had the chance to grasp that. So look at this as a learning experience—if I let you live through it."

Vance swallowed hard and lowered his gaze. Kane's hard, humorless grin widened. Women sometimes confused him, circumstances disturbed him, but he knew how to deal with Magistrates, even former ones. If they saw even a glimmer of fear in his eyes, so much as a twitch of apprehension on his face, the four men would react like predators scenting fresh-spilled blood.

At the sound of an object thudding heavily to the dirt floor, Kane cast his gaze toward Carthew. The man's Sin Eater and holster lay at his feet. Hugging himself, the one-eyed man husked out, "Done."

"Thanks," replied Kane. "Now it's time for a Q and A."

"A what?" Carthew squinted toward him, not understanding the old slang Kane had picked up from Lakesh.

"Question and answer. For example, I know who's paying the bills on this marauder operation of yours, but I want to know where and why."

"You know how it works, Kane." Carthew's voice was strained, barely above a whisper. "What do I get out of it?"

"Your life, for starters."

The man's lips twisted, either in a smirk or a rictus. "I don't think I have much more of it. You'll have to offer me a trade…like give me something for the pain. A good Mag like you wouldn't be out here in the ass-hole of the world without a medical kit."

Kane snorted contemptuously. "I think you'll be more talkative without being doped up." He gestured with the barrel of his autopistol. "Move over into the light. Sit down with the rest of your crew."

Biting back a groan, Carthew took a shuffling side-step toward the table, then sagged, nearly doubling over. "Can't make it—"

He coughed up pink foam, squeezing his eyes shut. Kane moved toward him, repressing a curse. Eyelids fluttering, Carthew said in a faint, aspirated voice, "Losing it…"

As if his legs had turned to molten wax, he sank toward the floor, half-falling forward into Kane's arms. As soon as he caught him, Kane knew he had fallen for a ploy so old, he nearly gagged on the humiliating realization.

Carthew's arms whipped from around his midsection and clasped Kane tightly at the elbows, pressing them close against his sides. The cracked section of the dirt floor rose, a man and a gun rising with it.

IN A FRACTION of a second, Kane understood the mechanics of the trap—Carthew had lured him into a position to be backshot by the long-haired man who had lain doggo in the shallow trench. He swore at himself for not heeding the alert sent up by his point man's sense.

Because of the fading light, Kane couldn't make out the man's features, but he definitely recognized the outline of a big revolver. Holding it with both hands, the long-haired man hauled back on the hammer with his thumb.

At the same time the section of disguised floor rose like a trapdoor, the three Hell Hounds leaped from their chairs, reaching for their weapons. Broderick made a wild scramble for his rifle, which was lying almost in the doorway.

Before the pistol spit fire and lead, Kane took the first course of action that occurred to him. Pivoting at the waist, he swung Carthew around so he was in the line of fire. Snarling out a stream of profanity, the ex-Magistrate grappled with Kane, trying to wrestle him back in front of the revolver's muzzle.

Setting his feet firmly, Kane said loudly, "A little help here."

"Won't get it from me, bastard!" growled Carthew, more pink froth flecking his lips.

Kane resisted the urge to inform the man he wasn't addressing him. Although Carthew wasn't as seriously wounded as he had made out to be, he was still injured. However, he retained enough strength to immobilize Kane's arms and stab him repeatedly with the knife blade he had concealed in his gauntlet.

Kane felt the knife thrusts as a repeated poking pressure—uncomfortable and even a little irritating but not painful. The blade couldn't penetrate the dense molecular structure of the shadow-suit fabric. The manufacturing technique known in predark days as electrospin lacing had electrically charged polymer particles to form a single crystal metallic microfiber with a molecular structure that wasn't easily penetrated. The outer Monocrys sheathing went opaque when exposed to radiation, and the Kevlar and Spectra layers provided protection against blunt trauma.

Kane believed the shadow suits were superior to the polycarbonate Magistrate armor if for nothing else than for their internal subsystems. They were almost impossible to tear or pierce with a knife, but a heavy-caliber bullet could penetrate them. Unlike the Mag body armor, they wouldn't redistribute the kinetic shock.

Twisting, Kane stopped trying to fight his way out of Carthew's hug. He lifted his right arm, bending it at the elbow, and squeezed the trigger of the Bren Ten. The automatic banged like a door slamming. He heard Vance yelp in pain and surprise and glimpsed him and the other Hell Hounds turn over the table. They scuttled behind it as if it were a shield.

"Kane!" Brigid's agitated tones came over the Commtact. She sounded breathless so he knew she was running toward the building. "What's going on?"

Rather than diverting his concentration from staying alive so he could formulate a sarcastic rejoinder, Kane drove the top of his head into Carthew's face, right at the bridge of his nose. The ex-Mag's head snapped back, blood springing from his nostrils.

As he stumbled backward, his grip loosened and Kane wrenched himself from between the prison of the man's polycarbonate-shod arms. Even as he did so, the man standing knee-deep in the ditch bellowed, "Look this way, you interferin' son of a bitch!"

Kane whirled toward him, noting how the slagger's face was contorted in fury, his eyes shining in homicidal rage. The man squeezed the trigger of the big-bored hand cannon, the booming report painfully loud.

The heavy-caliber round struck the barrel of the Bren

Ten with a spurt of sparks and a sound like a sledge pounding against an anvil. White-hot agony exploded up and down Kane's arm, a nova of pain flaring in his wrist and metacarpals. The pistol was torn from his grasp and clattered end over end across the interior of the trading post.

The man brayed a laugh of malicious triumph. "I meant to do that."

He stepped up out of the trench, aligning Kane's head in front of his pistol's sight. Through his pain-blurred vision, Kane recognized the revolver as a .357 Colt King Cobra, known in the predark days as a "man-breaker."

Kane waited to be broken—but instead of another explosive report, he heard a meaty thud and the man's face acquired an expression of vacant foolishness. His lips worked as if he were trying to think of something to say. Then he fell forward. From the rear of his skull protruded the blade of a tomahawk, the long handle extending down between his shoulder blades. Kane glimpsed Sky Dog on the other side of the barred window.

After a second of shocked stillness, Kane threw himself forward over the back of a chair, somersaulted and came up running, holding the chair ahead of him by the legs, using it as a shield and a battering ram.

One of the Hell Hounds raised himself from behind the table and snapped a shot at him. Kane shielded himself with the chair. One bullet bit a wedge out of the corner of the thick wooden seat, while another bullet chunked solidly into the seat but didn't penetrate.

Kane threw the chair at the armored man and as he ducked, he left the floor in a long dive, hurling himself behind the bar, ducking instinctively as another bullet plowed through the flimsy wood and lodged in the wall behind him.

Broderick and the three Hell Hounds fired a ragged, poorly aimed fusillade, the impacts of the rounds dislodging the shelf above him. He covered up, trying to protect himself from the shower of falling jugs and glasses. They shattered all around him. He crawled swiftly through the broken shards and pools of foul-smelling liquor, his right wrist in agony. Bullets smacked the woodwork with loud thumps.

A notion occurred to Kane and he peered up at the underside of the bar, groping with his left hand until his fingers touched the walnut stock of a sawed-off shotgun, attached to the slab of pine by a hook and a length of wire. He yanked it down, cocked both hammers and scrambled toward the end of the bar. Peering cautiously around it, he could see the doorway with Broderick standing beside it.

Not fifteen feet away lay the overturned table behind which three of the Hell Hounds knelt. He spotted Carthew crouched in the corner, but trying to nail him was risky. With presumably only two shells in the double-barreled gun, he couldn't risk firing one at random, hoping to score a hit by good luck alone.

At that second, Grant and Brigid Baptiste burst into the trading post, through the front and back doors. Brigid kicked in the rear door and Grant lunged through the open front door, leading with his Copperhead, the butt jammed against his shoulder, the laser autotargeter casting a bright red killdot on the bib of Broderick's overalls.

"Drop it!" he roared, using the Mag voice, a well-practiced tone of intimidation and power, meant to break violent momentum.

Broderick didn't drop it, but he froze for a split second, finger around the trigger of the rifle. Kane saw Vance's blond curls rising smoothly into sight from behind the table, his Sin Eater coming up to center on Grant. He swung the shotgun at him and squeezed the first trigger. The noise inside the close confines of the trading post was deafening, stunning. Kane received a chaotic impression of Vance flying backward in a red-tinted haze. He flailed across the room, tripped on the body of the man lying half in and half out of the trench and toppled against Carthew.

The other two Hell Hounds turned their attention to Kane, Sin Eaters hammering. Brigid squeezed off a long burst from her Copperhead. Three bullets caught a man on the right side of his head. Hanks of hair, a flap of scalp and piece of ear exploded outward in a clot of blood.

Several more rounds pounded into the other ex-Mag's armored torso, sending him stumbling, arms windmilling, his boot soles grating on the floor, seeking purchase.

Broderick's bewhiskered lips writhed back over his discolored teeth, and he jerked the barrel of his rifle in a short arc toward Grant, hand working the trigger and the lever, a little spear point of flame dancing from the bore. The first two shots went wild. Grant fired his subgun immediately. A triplet of dark holes appeared in the bib of the man's overalls, stitching him from navel to sternum.

The bearded man staggered, still firing the rifle. Grant shot him again, through the throat. Gobbets of muscle and tissue tore away. A few globs of blood spewed from his lips, but he didn't fall. With a liquid, gasping snarl of rage, he recovered his balance, put the rifle to his shoulder and aimed at Grant.

The room suddenly shivered with a thunderclap. The left side of Broderick's face erupted in a scarlet spray, his eye and nose vanishing in a bloody smear. Driven by the devastating impact of the double-aught pellets fired from the sawed-off, he performed a graceless half cartwheel and hit the floor heavily. For a couple of seconds, his feet twitched like landed fish.

The surviving Hell Hound pushed himself from the fallen, cursing Carthew, holding up both hands, bawling loudly, "Don't kill me, I'm done, I give up!"

Kane scrambled erect, the acrid fumes of cordite burning his nostrils and eyes. He exchanged swift glances with Brigid and then Grant. They surveyed the

smoky, blood-splattered, corpse-littered interior of the
trading post with silent, almost shocked eyes.

Sky Dog cautiously peered around the door frame,
surveyed the shambles and commented dryly, "So this
is what you mean by brazening it out."

Kane automatically he checked his wrist chron. He
estimated that less than thirty seconds had elapsed since
he first began grappling with Carthew. The time com-
pression of combat was something he had never grown
accustomed to.

Exhaling a long breath, Brigid aimed her Copperhead
at the two armored men in the corner. The crimson
thread of the laser autotargeter cut through the haze and
glowed brightly in the exact center of Carthew's eye
patch.

Tersely, she bit out, "Between the two of you, I hope
you can come up with one good reason to convince us
to spare your lives."

To the disappointment of Grant and Kane, they managed to come up with several.

Chapter 13

Under the watchful eyes and gun barrels of Brigid and Grant, the uninjured Hell Hound, a middle-aged man named Glupp, dragged the bodies out of the building. Kane and Sky Dog stared somberly at Carthew during the procedure, who stared back just as somberly.

The two men had been stripped of their Magistrate body armor and wore only their black undersheathings of Kevlar weave. Although the fabric was tough, it wouldn't turn a bullet or even a bladed weapon wielded with sufficient force.

Perched on a chair, arms wrapped around his torso, the former leader of the Hell Hounds coughed occasionally, bringing up red-hued phlegm. Carthew discreetly spit on the floor, a small indication that he was willing to bargain for his life. Otherwise he would have spit at his captors.

Outside twilight had swiftly deepened into a full, impenetrable night. Before moonrise, visibility was limited to only a few feet. Sky Dog lit the animal-fat lanterns, which shed a sickly, yellowish glow and exuded a foul stench, a combination of old grease and rotting meat.

Gingerly massaging his throbbing right hand, Kane remarked conversationally, "Looks like we're back to where we started."

"More or less," Carthew admitted, his voice nasal and snuffling due to his broken nose. "Like you already know, we have an arrangement with the Millennial Consortium. They give us what we need to operate and we give them what they need."

"Which is slave labor?" Kane asked.

Carthew nodded. "That and anything else useful we found in the convoys. Tools, food, clothing."

Standing at the open doorway, Grant declared flatly, "They sure as hell didn't give you those motorcycles."

"We found the bikes in the Cobaltville armory," the one-eyed man said. "They were stored in pieces. When me and my crew lit out, we took everything that we could cram into a Sandcat or tie onto the outside."

"Why'd you cut and run?" Kane asked. "With your ambition, seems like you would've proclaimed yourself the grand ville vizier."

Carthew chuckled, which turned into a cough. "Don't think I didn't try. But I wasn't the only one with that idea. There were too many factions shooting at each other. Allies one day, enemies the next, everybody switching sides, cutting dirty deals with competitors. You know what it's like there." He flashed a feeble grin. "Fun and games, man. Fun and games."

"Yeah," Kane said in a studiedly neutral tone. "So we heard."

Carthew eyed him quizzically. "Heard how?"

Kane shrugged. "We have our ways."

He referred to the eavesdropping system Cerberus had established through the communications linkup with the Comsat satellite. It was the same system and same satellite used to track the subcutaneous biolink transponder signals implanted within the Cerberus personnel.

Everyone in the redoubt had been injected with a transponder that transmitted not just their general locations but heart rate, respiration, blood count and brainwave patterns. Based on organic nanotechnology, the transponder was a nonharmful radioactive chemical that bound itself to an individual's glucose and the middle layers of the epidermis. The signal was relayed to the redoubt by the Comsat, one of the two satellites to which the installation was uplinked.

Bry, the resident tech-head of Cerberus, had worked on the eavesdropping system for a long time and had managed to develop an undetectable method of patching into the wireless communications channels of all the baronies in one form or another. The success rate wasn't one hundred percent, but Cerberus had been able to eavesdrop on a number of the villes and learn about baron-sanctioned operations in the Outlands. The different frequencies were monitored on a daily basis, and over the past six months they had heard little from the villes aside from sporadic reports of pure chaos.

The barony of Cobaltville, with eight others, had

been consolidated by the Program of Unification into a network of city-states, walled fortresses that were almost sovereign nations. They were named after the barons who ruled them, and they all conformed to standardized specs and layouts—fifty-foot-high walls with Vulcan-Phalanx gun towers mounted on each intersecting corner. There was a single legal way into and out of the villes, and that path was deadly to anyone who didn't have business walking it.

Inside the walls, the ville elite lived in the residential Enclaves, four multileveled towers joined by pedestrian walkways. A certain amount of predark technology was available to the elite, the so-called "high towers." Only four thousand people were allowed to live in the Enclaves. Another thousand lived below, in the Tartarus Pits. Since ville society was strictly class and caste based, the higher a citizen's standing, the higher he or she might live in one of the residential towers.

At the bottom level of the villes was the servant class, who lived in abject squalor in the Pits. The population was ruthlessly controlled so as not to exceed a thousand. The Pits were consciously designed as ghettos.

The residential towers were connected by major promenades to the Administrative Monolith, a massive cylinder of white stone jutting three hundred feet into the air, the tallest building in the villes.

Every level of the Administrative Monolith fulfilled a specific ville function. The base level, Epsilon, was

NO POSTAGE
NECESSARY
IF MAILED
IN THE
UNITED STATES

BUSINESS REPLY MAIL
FIRST-CLASS MAIL   PERMIT NO. 717-003   BUFFALO, NY

POSTAGE WILL BE PAID BY ADDRESSEE

GOLD EAGLE READER SERVICE
3010 WALDEN AVE
PO BOX 1867
BUFFALO NY 14240-9952

If offer card is missing write to: Gold Eagle Reader Service, 3010 Walden Ave., P.O. Box 1867, Buffalo NY 14240-1867

Get FREE BOOKS and a FREE GIFT when you play the...

LAS VEGAS GAME

Just scratch off the gold box with a coin. Then check below to see the gifts you get!

YES! I have scratched off the gold box. Please send me my **2 FREE BOOKS** and **gift for which I qualify.** I understand that I am under no obligation to purchase any books as explained on the back of this card.

▼ DETACH AND MAIL CARD TODAY! ▼

366 ADL D749

166 ADL D747
(MB-05R)

FIRST NAME

LAST NAME

ADDRESS

APT.#

CITY

STATE/PROV.

ZIP/POSTAL CODE

7	7	7	Worth TWO FREE BOOKS plus a BONUS Mystery Gift!
🍒	🍒	🍒	Worth TWO FREE BOOKS!
🔔	🔔	🍀	TRY AGAIN!

a se..ufacturing facility. At the bottom of E Level was pending t section where convicted felons were held

Although i.on. often deliberately ws were complex, convoluted and tenced to a term of im rary, violators were never senment in the cell blocks. Locking away a criminal ei.. r for rehabilitation or punishment was not part of the p. ..ram. Perpetrators of small crimes, those involved in petty thefts or low-level black marketeering in the Tartarus Pits, were sentenced to permanent exile in the Outlands. The only penalty for any crime adjudged to be against the welfare of the barony was death.

Brigid herded Glupp back into the outpost at gunpoint. She directed the man to sit down beside Carthew and announced, "The bodies are laid out by the riverbank. There wasn't enough time or stones to build decent cairns. I imagine the wolves and coyotes will finish the job we started."

A hint of bleakness edged her words. Essentially a gentle soul, she had never developed Grant's or Kane's pragmatism in regards to taking human or animal life, even when situations warranted no other options.

Standing over Carthew, Sky Dog demanded bluntly, "How do you exchange goods with the millennialists?"

For an instant, the old Magistrate arrogance glinted in Carthew's single eye. He didn't like being questioned by a man he considered one of the lesser breeds, but his ego didn't get the better of his sense of self-preservation. "The *Crazy Woman*." He jerked his ~~~~ the general direction of the river. "That bar~ our trades." sail down to a rendezvous point an~the ditch cut into

While he spoke, Brigid peere~ ~~ hands resting on her the dirt floor, leaning over wi~~~ knees. "What do you ge~ ~ of it?"

Carthew hesitate~ ~or a few second, and she announced, "Never ~und. I think I see it."

Grant gla~ed toward her. "See what?"

Climbing down into the trench, Brigid stretched her left arm into a space, groped for a few moments, then straightened. A small rectangular object in her hand reflected the lamplight. "This is what's known as an 'aha' moment."

Kane stepped closer to her. "What've you got there, Baptiste?"

"See for yourself," she replied, holding it out to him. "There's a least a hundred more in this homemade vault."

A brightly polished gold ingot gleamed in her hand. Even in the dim light, Kane made out the words U.S. Mint embossed on its surface. In a tone suggesting a vexing mystery had at long last been resolved, he said, "*Now* we get it."

Sky Dog glowered down at Carthew, his expression one of disgust. "You traded human lives for *gold?*"

Carthew met his scowl. "That's the way of the world, Chief. With enough gold I can buy myself a position of authority somewhere, either in a barony or a settlement."

Grant snorted derisively. "And be a baron yourself—
is that the plan?"

Carthew shrugged, then winced. "Being a Hell
Hound was a strictly temporary proposition. It's not
like it had a lot of job security. Only a means to an end."

Sky Dog demanded, "You expect us to believe that
the Millennial Consortium is running a gold mine in the
Bighorns?"

"No," Brigid interposed, climbing out the hole. She
tossed the gold bar to Sky Dog for inspection. "This is
predark, the ore smelted and refined."

Kane fixed his pale eyes on Glupp. "You've been
pretty quiet. Why don't you contribute something to the
discussion?"

Glupp shifted in his chair uncomfortably, casting a
questioning glance at Carthew.

Grant snapped, "Why are you looking at him? We're
the ones you need to please."

The middle-aged man cleared his throat self-
consciously. "We don't exactly know what they're
doing up there. They never let us travel much past the
rendezvous point. Benedict Snow calls the shots, not
us."

"Shut up, Glupp," Carthew growled.

"No, talk it up, Glupp," Kane said encouragingly.
"I'm starting to feel pleased. And that's a good thing for
you."

Taking a deep breath as if to fortify himself, Glupp
said in a rush, "The millennialists never told us what

they're doing. I talked to a couple of Snow's grunts one time and they said they found a wheel or something inside the damn mountain."

Sky Dog's eyes narrowed. "A wheel *inside?* A medicine wheel?"

Glupp shook his head, his brow furrowed. "No, not that kind of wheel. A wheel that works with a machine."

The Lakota shaman frowned in annoyed confusion. Kane and Grant exchanged puzzled glances. Then Brigid spoke up, "A *cog* wheel?"

Glupp's eyes brightened and he threw her a fleeting, appreciative glance. "Yeah, that's it! A cog wheel!"

Sky Dog's scowl deepened. "What the hell is he talking about?"

Brigid smiled wryly, lifting three fingers one at a time as she enunciated the letters. "Cee-Oh-Gee. Continuity of Government. The Millennial Consortium has found a COG facility inside Medicine Mountain."

"Discovering a COG base would explain the gold bar," Kane said thoughtfully, "since we know the places were used for storage. But that doesn't tie in with the consortium's activities in Carver's Cave. Unless there was a COG facility there."

Brigid shook her head. "Not likely, since Redoubt Tango is only a few miles away."

The redoubt to which she referred was located about thirty-five miles to the southwest of Ragnarville. Before the nukecaust, the Tango installation had served as the Totality Concept's research center into new forms and applications of cryonic science.

Crossing his arms over his chest and staring steadily at Glupp, Grant intoned, "You know something you're not telling us."

Glupp nodded nervously. "Yeah, but it's just stuff I heard the grunts talking about...crazy crap about magic and changing the world with it."

"Did they mention the *tai-me?*" Sky Dog asked.

Glupp shook his head, perplexed. "Not that I recollect."

"Towasi?"

Glupp shook his head again.

"Baykok?"

"No."

"Catamount?"

The faces of both ex-Mags registered fear at the name. "You know that sick bitch?" Carthew asked angrily.

"We're asking the questions," Kane reminded him. "You know her?"

Glupp ran a hand over his forehead. "Yeah, kind of. Her and her Lynx Soldiers. Catamount and them kill-crazy sluts were at the first rendezvous we had with Snow. I don't like talking about what happened."

"Why not?" Brigid asked in an amused tone. "Did a Hell Hound get overly familiar with her and she humiliated one of you big bad ex-Mags?"

Carthew slitted his good eye as he stared hard at Brigid. "Merrick, one of my men, put his hands on her. I mean, why not? She was walking around damn near naked, acting like she was too high and mighty for us. In about five seconds, the slut had him down on the ground. She took a knife…."

He paused, swallowing hard. "It happened so goddamn fast. One second she was knocking Merrick down. The next second, his balls was in her hand. Then while he was screaming, she cut out his tongue. Then she scalped him and crammed his own hair, tongue and balls in his mouth to shut him up."

Brigid didn't react, but Kane, Grant and Sky Dog made reflexive protective movements toward their groins.

"Merrick went into shock," Carthew continued. "Bled to death."

Glupp did a poor job of repressing a shudder. "I stayed aboard the boat at all the other rendezvous after that…didn't want to risk running into her."

"Can't say as I blame you," Grant muttered. "I'd want to stay out of her way, too."

Grimly, Carthew said, "Staying out of her way might not be as easy as it used to be. She and her Lynx Soldiers act as the consortium's sec squad. They've been extending the range of their patrols the last few days, coming into the flatlands."

"Why?" Sky Dog asked.

Carthew regarded him expressionlessly. "Probably looking for you."

Before Sky Dog could respond to the statement, Brigid interjected, "How do you arrange a rendezvous with the consortium?"

When Carthew seemed reluctant to answer, Glupp blurted, "We load up the barge and take 'er downriver about ten miles to a little sand spit, near a waterfall. We signal with flares. After a couple of hours, the millennialists meet us."

"Sounds simple enough," Kane commented.

"Yeah," Carthew agreed, eyeing Glupp venomously. "So simple you probably expect us to guide you there."

"Very perceptive," Grant rumbled. "You're not as stupid as I thought you were. I'll bet you're astute enough to guess when all of us will be leaving, too."

Again Carthew didn't seem eager to talk so Glupp ventured, "First thing in the morning?"

Kane glanced out the window and saw that a three-quarters Moon shone brightly above the treetops, casting a silvery illumination over the terrain. "It looks like there's enough light for you to get back to the Kit Foxes and fetch them here, Sky Dog…and all of our equipment. I have a feeling we'll need it."

The shaman nodded, stepping toward the door. "I'll get right on it."

"How about letting me go a little ways with you?" Carthew said.

Grant gazed at him in disbelief. "Yeah, that'll happen."

Carthew smiled in response to the sarcasm. "Suit yourself. But there's no facilities in the place, if you get my drift. I'm guessing you plan on staying the night inside here just to keep from freezing to death. But, hey, if you don't mind the stink, neither do I."

Kane sighed in weary exasperation. "All right." He unholstered his second pistol, holding it in his left hand. "But you're walking on your own and if I get even a half-assed idea that you're up to something other than—"

Carthew shook his head, rising from the chair slowly. "I've had enough violence for the time being, Kane. My day turned to shit early, and it's going to end the same way."

The one-eyed man preceded Sky Dog and Kane outside. The air was sharp and cold, very refreshing after the stink of the trading station. The Moon shone bright in the sky and Kane's sight adjusted to take in every detail of the silver-splashed clearing around the building. Carthew walked slowly, still bent over. Kane prodded him with the barrel of the Bren Ten, guiding him toward the outhouse. From the corner of his eye, he caught a brief, almost subliminal flicker of movement in the brush bordering the perimeter.

Grabbing Carthew and pulling him to a halt, he said quietly, "Hold it."

Sky Dog did so. Kane visually probed the shadows beneath and between the trees. His ears strained to sort out the noises of rushing river, the breeze rattling branches and anything else.

Carthew straightened, saying impatiently, "Look, I really have to go—"

There was a thud and Carthew staggered, a long feathered shaft sprouting from his left eye socket and about an inch of wet, red razor-sharp metal jutting out from the back of his head.

He whispered hoarsely, "Ow."

He dropped first to his knees then onto his side. Sky Dog and Kane crouched beside him, eyes and gun barrel questing for a target. They heard the faint drumming of horse hooves, then a woman came riding out of the tree line astride a great black mare. She wore the pelt of a cougar like a hooded cape. Her bare breasts bounced in cadence with the rhythm of the horse's gallop.

A cry of astonishment, even of fear, was torn from Sky Dog's lips. *"Catamount!"*

Kane stared at her, rooted to the spot in astonishment. Sky Dog's description of the woman had not even hinted at her savage beauty, or the way a tigerish flame of force seemed to burn within her.

He saw that her eyes were big and brown under level brows, with a bold nose and finely sculptured curve of cheek and chin. She was taller than he expected, longer and leaner of limb than was usual for Amerindian women. Firm of bosom, there was no trace of softness underlying her feminine curves. She moved with the smooth grace of her namesake.

Wielding a crossbow, Catamount was a fierce Amazon warrior, a Valkyrie, a chooser of the slain. Behind her rode a half-dozen other women, all young and lean muscled, copper skinned, their black hair plaited into long braids hanging down their shoulders. Like

Catamount, they were bare breasted, fur kirtled and wearing boot moccasins. They carried long slender spears and small round rawhide shields.

A huge panther loped alongside Catamount's horse, its eyes shining with an eerie green-yellow luminosity.

Sky Dog broke Kane's paralysis by bellowing, "Shoot her! Kill her now, Unktomi Shunkaha!"

Catamount repeated his name and stared at him, stark surprise in her dark eyes. Then she heeled her mount around and the woman and the Lynx Soldiers thundered into the trees and out of sight. The panther paused long enough to voice a marrow-freezing yowl, then it too vanished into the darkness.

Sky Dog stood up, fists clenched, his fierce obsidian eyes glinting with anger. "You should have killed her when you had the chance, Unktomi Shunkaha. Now that she has put a face to your name, she will add your scalp to her coups. It will be a great honor for her."

Kane glanced down at the motionless form of Carthew and swallowed down bile. "She'll have to work hard for it."

Sky Dog nodded gravely. "She would have it no other way. Make no mistake."

Chapter 14

The first rays of the morning sun slanted over the *Crazy Woman*'s gunwales. Kane drew a deep breath of the frigid air into his lungs. There was something exhilarating about the postdaybreak chill, about watching dawn arrive and drive away the streamers of damp mist hanging among the trees.

Kane had only half slept the night before, tossing about on the hard floor, clutching at a blanket, his nerves jangling. His dreams were full of fragmented images of naked women turning into ferocious, spitting cats.

He awoke at three-thirty, shivering, despite the thermal controls of his shadow suit. The chill of the earth and the nearby river worked through him, settling into every one of his old wounds. His right wrist ached abominably, as if the panther he had glimpsed the night before had sunk its fangs into the marrow. The bones had been fractured a few years before by exposure to an infrasound wand, and the bullet fired by the Colt Cobra, even deflected by his Bren Ten, had aggravated the injury. He had gotten off lucky, although the auto-pistol was damaged beyond repair.

Still, Kane always enjoyed getting away from the vanadium-sheathed confines of the Cerberus redoubt. He took keen pleasure in exploring new lands, which made him an exception among the redoubt's residents.

Most of the people who lived in Cerberus acted in the capacity of support personnel. They worked rotating shifts, eight hours a day, seven days a week. For the most part, their work was the routine maintenance and monitoring of the installation's environmental systems, the satellite data feed and the security network.

Everyone was given at least a superficial understanding of all the redoubt's systems so they could pinch-hit in times of emergency. Kane and Grant were exempt from this cross training inasmuch as they served as the enforcement arm of Cerberus and undertook far and away the lion's share of the risks. On their downtime between missions they made sure all the ordnance in the armory was in good condition and occasionally tuned up the vehicles in the depot.

Time within the huge trilevel installation was measured by the controlled dimming and brightening of lights to simulate sunrise and sunset. Since most of the people there were either ville bred or had lived in artificial environments for many years, they didn't mind the electronic changeover from dawn to dusk. Rarely had any of them strayed more than a few miles from the redoubt's mountain plateau, even the émigrés from the Manitius Moon colony.

With the fall of the baronies and the rising threat of

the overlords, most of the émigrés had shown a disin-
clination to wander too far from the Cerberus redoubt.
But more the crowded it became, the less satisfied Kane
felt to stay there for any length of time. The pull of ad-
venture, of exploring the remote places, grew stronger
with every passing day. Despite the sense of danger, he
also experienced a profound sense of peace while in the
wild regions.

Only the steady chugging racket of the *Crazy
Woman*'s diesel engine spoiled the panorama of the
wide river cutting through the rocky country on both
sides of them. He gazed at a line of cliffs about three
miles ahead. The early-morning mist half hid them,
wreathing the summits in wispy white.

At the sound of metal clinking against metal, he
glanced over at Grant, testing the gimbel of the GEC
minigun on its upright swivel mount. The multiple-
bored barrel of the weapon protruded between slabs of
abbreviated but thick steel shielding. According to
Glupp, the heavy machine gun had been appropriated
from a Cobaltville blockhouse as he and his companions fled the barony. It was one of the rifle-caliber ver-
sions that had been used in the ville's checkpoints.

Standing in the stern, Glupp manned the big tiller as
he expertly piloted the barge down the center of the
river. It was about a thousand feet from bank to bank at
that point, the fast current foaming white all around the
hull. The Kit Foxes sitting on crates around the deck
didn't look comfortable. Canoeing across placid lakes

or hugging the shorelines of streams was one thing, but they were plainsmen and didn't trust large bodies of water, particularly one as wide and wild as the Powder River.

Glupp seemed cheerful, despite losing all of his comrades and commander the day before. Kane figured he had never been happy as either a Mag or a Hell Hound and exulted in a newfound sense of freedom. The man turned more forthcoming after the death of Carthew, explaining that the Millennial Consortium had built its own defense perimeter around the rendezvous point.

Glupp didn't know the extent of the defenses, either in matériel or men, but he felt sure they had a large boat of their own. The consortium grunts he had seen were well armed, too—not with home-forged muzzle loaders but up-to-date and meticulously maintained automatic weapons. He added that they should assume Catamount had raised a general alarm by now. He could only guess at the reasons why she had killed Carthew—mainly to keep him from betraying the millennialists to enemies.

When Kane asked Sky Dog how the chieftain of the Lynx Soldiers knew him, the shaman shrugged, claiming the exploits of Trickster Wolf had spread very far. Kane couldn't deny that, but he doubted Sky Dog's facile answer. He suspected Catamount's recognition of him—or his name—was more than just him being famous.

Brigid Baptiste stood portside amid ships, scanning

the distant bank with her binoculars. Sky Dog stood next to her, doing the same thing, pointing out objects of interest. The shaman made a comment that Kane didn't catch and she laughed. He felt a quick, irrational flash of jealousy. He chided himself for his childishness and returned his attention to the river ahead.

When he and Brigid were first thrown together, their relationship had been volatile, marked by frequent quarrels, jealousies and resentments. The world in which she came of age was primarily quiet, focused on scholarly pursuits. Kane's was a world wherein he became accustomed to daily violence and supported by a belief system that demanded a ruthless single-mindedness to enforce baronial authority. Despite their differences, or perhaps because of them, the two people managed to forge the chains of partnership that linked them together through mutual respect and trust.

Brigid was structured and ordered, with a brilliant analytical mind. However, her clinical nature, the cool scientific detachment upon which she prided herself, sometimes blocked an understanding of the obvious human factor in any given situation. Regardless of their contrasting personalities, Kane and Brigid worked very well as a team, playing on each other's strengths rather than contributing to their individual weaknesses.

His partnership with Grant displayed a similar balance of strengths. As Magistrates, he and Grant had served together for a dozen years and as Cerberus warriors they had fought shoulder to shoulder in battles around half the planet, and even off the planet. Through it all Grant had been covering Kane's back, patching up his wounds and, on more than one occasion, literally carrying him out of hellzones.

At one time, both men enjoyed the lure of danger, courting death to deal death. But now it was no longer enough for them to wish for a glorious death as a pay-off for all their struggles. They had finally accepted a fact they had known for years but never admitted to themselves—when death came, it was usually unexpected and almost never glorious.

Grant finished his examination of the GEC and called over to Glupp, "How much farther?"

"Not very," Glupp replied, shouting to be heard over the rush of the water and the drone of the engine. "Another three or four miles. We're making damn good time."

Grant glanced over at Kane, who had turned toward him to listen to the exchange. The big man said bleakly, "I wish I knew if that was good or bad."

Brigid lowered her binoculars. "I suppose that depends on what we're sailing into."

Glupp announced loudly, "We got some rough water coming up...stay away from the sides 'less you feel like taking a cold bath!"

Taking out his own binoculars, Kane gazed at the river and country stretching ahead of the bow. The Powder River began narrowing steadily and as it did so, the swiftness of the current increased. The barge bounced on the increasingly rough water as it entered a bottleneck, and icy spray spumed over the sides. Whitecapped rapids splashed violently around rocks thrusting up from the river bottom.

The concourse cut through gigantic tumbles of granite and basalt, huge boulders that had fallen from the cliffs due to the monster quakes of the nukecaust. The rock formations were split by small inlets and channels drawing away from the main waterway. Many of them were clotted by thickets of brown, thorny brush.

In the distance, a dark looming shape resolved into sharper detail, a broad waterfall spreading like a translucent veil over the face of a cliff. Kane's point man's sense flared at the first glimpse of it, but he was too preoccupied with not pitching overboard to give it much thought.

For the next minute or so, the barge bobbed and swung sideways in the current, the rubber tires roped to the hull cushioning it from the glancing collisions with rocks. Then the river channel widened and the current gradually slowed.

"Pretty calm sailing from here on," Glupp called. "You can relax."

Soaking wet, Grant muttered contemptuously, "Yeah, that's what we'll do, all right." He rested his hand on the butt of the Colt Cobra he had appropriated from the dead man at the trading station. The heavy revolver was secured in a gun belt and holster. "We all feel like kicking back and relaxing."

Kane scarcely heard him. His attention was completely absorbed in watching the river ahead of the *Crazy Woman*. The water frothed under the keel as she breasted the quick-flowing channel. It turned and twisted amid sand spits and patches of thicket so that he could not see clear water ahead for more than a hundred yards.

The *Crazy Woman* continued to slosh along, her wake washing up against the muddy banks on either hand. At another bend Kane saw how the river was shadowed by overarching trees. In the tangled, leafless boughs nothing stirred but a flock of birds taking frantic flight, but he didn't spy anything that could have set them to wing.

Then, without an instant's warning, the thicket on the portside spit a tongue of flame and thunder. Kane caught a fragmented glimpse of a quick darting streak, then the *Crazy Woman* shuddered under a blow that shook her frame and popped caulk up from between the deck planks. The river erupted astern and one of the Kit Foxes fell overboard, tumbling headfirst into the water. He surfaced once, already pushed yards away from the barge by the current, turning and flailing in a mad thrash of arms and legs. Then he was swept around a half-submerged boulders and was gone.

Automatic fire stuttered in a cacophony from the rocks and the shrubbery. Bullets punched little dimples in the water and hammered dents in the metal-sheathed hull of the barge and the cabin housing, thumping into the tires. Up ahead Kane saw a wall of shrubbery far too green for the winter-browned thickets and he realized the barge was fast approaching a foliage-masked weapons battery.

"What'd I tell you?" Glupp howled, wrestling with the tiller as the craft fishtailed back and forth between the banks. "They were waiting for us!"

"Shut up!" Grant bellowed, ducking into the wheelhouse and dragging out the plastic case that held the LAW. "You didn't say anything about this kind of reception!"

Kane crouched on the heaving deck, pistol in hand. "Sky Dog! Get your men to returning the fire! Baptiste—"

"I know what to do," she snapped irritably as she ran across the deck, taking up a position at the GEC, crouching behind the shielding.

Kane heard the tearing rush of a second rocket, and another eruption of water burst from the river's surface in front of the barge, drenching him. The craft shuddered from the impact. As the echoes of the explosion bounced back from bank to bank, the deep voice of Grant bellowed, "Fire in the hole!"

Kane glanced over his shoulder as flame and smoke gouted from the hollow bore of the missile launcher. Propelled by a wavering ribbon of vapor and sparks, the HEAT round leaped from the tube, accompanied by a ripping roar.

The warhead impacted in a thicket, the brush vanishing in a roiling ball of billowing orange-yellow flame and an eardrum-knocking concussion.

The crash of the exploded shell resounded as Kane yelled, "Slow astern!"

Twin spears of flame lanced from the masked battery. Two geysers of water erupted portside and Kane heard and felt the splintering smash of a hit somewhere below the waterline.

"The bastards have *two* rocket launchers!" roared an infuriated Grant.

The *Crazy Woman* heeled over as a crackle of automatic gunfire came from the opposite bank—hidden riflemen. A bullet hit the pilothouse and whined away just an inch shy of Kane's left shoulder. He turned aft, seeing two of the Lakota down and bleeding on the deck, then aimed his Bren Ten at the sniper's position.

Taking a double-handed grip on the weapon, he fired the autopistol in a steady roll at the shapes hunkered down atop the rocks, the bullets chiseling dust-spurting notches in the stone. A man wearing a tan uniform slithered over the edge of the boulder and fell into the water, a Bushmaster M-17 assault rifle dropping with him.

Four men wearing identical dun-colored shirts and pants rose to their knees, rifles at their shoulders. Kane put the Bren Ten's sights over one of the men and squeezed the trigger. The bullet slammed through his head, jerking him sideways and throwing him against the man beside him. Both of them toppled from their perch and splashed into the river below.

The other pair of men directed a steady barrage of fire toward the *Crazy Woman*. Kane squeezed off another round, then the slide of the Bren Ten blew back into the locked and empty position. He flung himself backward, behind the shield of the corner of the pilothouse. Bullets crashed into it, tearing away long splinters.

Brigid swiveled the GEC toward them, raking the boulders with a jackhammering ferocity, geysers of dust and stone shards flying in all directions. A barrage of return fire was directed toward her, and the clang of bullets on the protective cowling sounding like a gang of riveters hard at work. The steel sheathing acquired a constellation of shiny stars.

Rounds from the heavy machine gun clawed open the torso of one of the men from sternum to groin. As he fell, doubled up, into the river, his companion slid down the opposite side of the boulder and out of sight.

Ejecting the Bren Ten's empty clip and replacing it with a fresh magazine, Kane yelled to Glupp, "Where the hell is this rendezvous point of yours?"

Glupp, still struggling with the tiller, didn't answer. He took his right hand away from the wooden handle long enough to point urgently ahead.

Kane turned just as the *Crazy Woman* swept around a bend. A wide sand spit projected out into the water, cutting the river's width at that point to less than fifty feet. Stretching out from the tip of the spit, Kane saw that the channel was blocked by a double row of dead trees and timber. He yelled, "Full astern!"

Grant fired the LAW again. The rocket streaked across the surface of the water, pushing ripples ahead of it. As the warhead struck the bank, the blast swept away the thicket as if by a giant scythe. Four dun-colored figures then plunged through the smoke and flame like disjointed marionettes. There was no answering fire.

"I think we managed to fight them off!" Kane announced.

The *Crazy Woman* backtracked clumsily away from the barrier, the GEC still blazing, the rounds from the spinning barrels digging out mud and rocks in a wild spray. The rifle fire from the banks had tapered off since the detonation of the LAW's warhead.

Rising to his feet, Kane ran across the slippery deck to the stern, helping Glupp wrestle the tiller around. Through the smoke drifting over the surface of the water, Kane saw a dark shape shove out into the river from one of the side channels, right across the barge's course and nearly a thousand yards away. He caught only a fragmented glimpse of a mass of foliage triced up all around the gunwales and the bow, as well as a long, fluted metal cylinder. He had time to murmur in gloomy acceptance, "Well, shit."

With a pop and a whoosh, the shell left the long barrel. Trailing a plume of smoke, the warhead vectored in its target. Kane grabbed Glupp and dragged him away from the tiller.

The next instant Kane was flung to the deck by an impact that knocked the breath from his body. His eyes were dazzled by a brilliant flash of fire as the shell exploded directly against the *Crazy Woman*'s stern. Fragments of the paddle box and metal clattered down all around him. The rubber belt attached to the diesel engine's flywheel separated with a loud pop. The faint sound of men screaming filtered through the roar in his head.

Glupp writhed on the deck beside him, folded around a three-foot-long splinter ripped from the tiller. His intestines oozed out along the point of the bloody wood. His waxy face showed no real pain, only surprise, then his expression became vacant, mouth hanging open slackly. Kane wasn't sure if he had passed out due to shock or died, but he had no time to make sure.

Staggering to his feet, clinging to the rail, Kane blinked his eyes against the stinging smoke, trying to focus them on the gunboat that had lunged so suddenly from the side channel to cut off the *Crazy Woman*'s withdrawal. The craft was small and black, lying low in the water to accommodate the 150-pound weight of the tripod-mounted H&K grenade machine gun. It fired 40 mm high-explosive rounds, with a maximum reach of a mile.

Leaning around the edge of the GEC's shielding, Brigid shouted, "Kane, are you all right?"

"Hell no, I'm not all right!" he bellowed angrily. "We're about to be sank!"

"Sunk!" she corrected him, ducking back behind the cowling.

Fire stabbed from the muzzle of the H&K again and the grenade burst in a hellfire blossom close alongside the *Crazy Woman*, just behind of the wreckage of the paddle box. As smoke streamed over the water, he saw the maddened Lakota leaping and bounding to return the fire with their rifles, their painted faces making them look like denizens of Hell. Sky Dog shouted an order in his own language and the rifles of the Kit Foxes crashed in unified volley. Water spumed in little geysers all around the camouflaged gunboat but because of its screen of foliage, they couldn't see if their shots found human targets.

Brigid hunkered down behind the GEC and depressed the trigger. She swung it on its gimbels in short, left-to-right arcs, tongues of fire lipping from the spinning bores. Spent cartridge cases tinkled down on the deck at her feet.

Grant hastily reloaded the LAW, a race between the H&K 40 mm grenade machine gun bolted to the black craft's bow and the swiftness with which he could achieve target acquisition. As he shoved the rocket into place, smoke and flame spit from the hollow bore of the H&K.

"Brace yourselves—" Kane shouted.

The deck smacked upward beneath his feet as though a fist had punched up through the *Crazy Woman*'s keel. Kane felt the jar of the detonation just below the waterline, the river leaping skyward in a fountaining column over the gunwales.

Chapter 15

Grant fell over backward, dropping the LAW. The rocket within the launcher leaped from the bore, streaked into the wheelhouse and detonated with the fiery roar of an exploding volcano. The opposite side of the structure burst open in a sleet storm of flinders and kindling. The open doorway vomited a cascade of flame, briefly touching him.

Grant rolled frantically, his jacket smoldering. The deck was already awash with the Powder River, so his roll across it doused the flames. Although his shadow suit protected him from serious burns, he felt the sting of fire on his face. Scorched, dazed, choking, he staggered erect at the rail. The *Crazy Woman* tilted astern. Hungry tongues of flame licked up through every crack in the planking, but the river streaming over the deck extinguished them, with loud sizzles and puffs of steam combining with the smoke to form an almost impenetrable haze.

As his stunned ears recovered from the explosion, he heard Sky Dog exclaiming in Lakota, then Brigid cried, "Grant!"

Fanning the acrid vapors away from his face, he called back, "I'm all right."

Brigid moved into sight, one hand on the side, the other pressing against her right hip. She grimaced as she walked, favoring her right leg. Grant reached out for her, but she waved him away. "I took a spill. Nothing broken—I hope."

A moment later, Kane, Sky Dog and three of the Kit Foxes joined them. All were soaking wet and bedraggled, their face paint runny, their feathers drooping. Without preamble, Kane said, "We're all that's left."

"I'd say we've just been officially outsmarted and outgunned," Grant observed grimly.

"You helped a little bit in that area," Kane bit out snidely. "That last rocket of yours pretty much took the bottom out of the *Crazy Woman*."

Glaring at him, Grant opened his mouth to voice a profane rejoinder, but Brigid interjected, "We've got to get to shore fast."

Sky Dog squinted through the smoke toward the spit of land. "I don't see anybody, but they could be lying in wait for us."

"It's not like we have any choice," Brigid said tersely, swinging a leg over the side. "Let's do it, not discuss it."

The others followed her lead, but Grant hesitated. He wasn't much of a swimmer, a deficiency he had managed to conceal from Kane for the past fifteen years. But, over the side into the river was their one chance while they were still screened by the smoke. Otherwise, they would be either shot to pieces, burned to a crisp or blasted apart when the flames reached the crate of grenades in the shattered wheelhouse.

Kane called up in a hoarse, impatient whisper, "What the hell are you waiting for?"

Grant slid over the gunwale, hitting the water with an awkward splash. He went deep, arms and legs threshing as he fought to get back to the surface. The water was bone-numbingly cold, but it felt good against the burned flesh on his face. His head rose up in the smoke-filtered sunlight. The heavy Colt Cobra dragged at his waist. He loosened the buckle of the gun belt and let it go, but he kept his Copperhead.

Just ahead of him he saw Brigid and Kane swimming easily, steadily for the sand spit. Farther ahead, he saw the Sky Dog and the three surviving Kit Fox soldiers, stroking in a neat crawl. He did his best to emulate their movements, fighting the current that tugged at him, pushing him toward the deadfall of fallen trees.

The muffled roar of an explosion rolled across the river. A few seconds later, debris came splashing down around the swimmers. The flames had found the case of grenades before the barge sank.

In a few more strokes, Grant's kicking feet hit the bottom and he stood up. Brigid and Kane waded ashore just ahead of him. Kane swung anxious eyes toward the *Crazy Woman*. The vast cloud of dark gray smoke spread out from the burning, sagging hulk. The smaller black craft, outfitted with the grenade machine gun, was not in sight.

The seven people slogged onto the sand spit and stood for a moment, coughing, panting, shivering and in Sky Dog's case, cursing, "Goddamn the luck! Son of a bitch it to hell and back on a round trip!"

Kane and Brigid were startled into laughing. Wringing water out of her heavy mounds of hair, Brigid said wryly, "I think we need to get out of sight before our luck improves any further."

"I don't see how it could," Grant rasped bitterly, breaking into a jog.

They sprinted across the open ground of the spit onto a narrow animal path running between heavy tangles of vegetation. Wet boots and moccasins made loud squishing sounds. Once away from the river among a copse of pines and ferns, the six people stopped again to take inventory of their injuries and their possessions. Although none of them were hurt, all of them were stripped down to their bare essentials.

Kane and Brigid had managed to retain their side arms and Copperheads, but they were down to one full clip of ammunition for each weapon. Grant had only his subgun and his fourteen-inch combat knife. The blades were part of his and Kane's standard field ordnance, so both men had them sheathed securely at their hips.

Sky Dog and his Sioux saved only their edged weapons, knives and tomahawks, although the shaman's parfleche was still attached to his belt. Everything else, from their survival packs to the medical kit had gone down with the *Crazy Woman*.

Kane shrugged, as if the losses were negligible. "We've been in worse situations with less than this."

"When?" Brigid and Grant challenged simultaneously.

Before he could reply, the slow chugging pulse of a diesel engine reached their ears. Crouching among the tree trunks, they peered through the ferns at the point of the sandspit. The black, flat-keeled boat pushed through the scraps of smoke. The camouflage of intertwined brush had been discarded and they saw three men aboard.

All of them were attired identically in dun-colored khaki uniforms, gun belts and long-visored caps. Two of them stood on either side of the H&K grenade launcher mounted in the bow. The third man sat behind it, hand on the charger handle. The man on the left scanned the bank of the sand spit through binoculars.

He inched them across the ground, paused, moved on, then came back. He spoke to the gunner and handed the glasses to him. The man peered through the eyepieces, nodded, then handed them back. He shifted position behind the H&K, squinting into the scope and making adjustments on the calibration knob.

"They've spotted our tracks," Sky Dog whispered angrily. "We should've been more careful—"

"Since they didn't see our bodies floating in the river," Kane interrupted, "then they'd assume this was the most likely place for us to have swum ashore. Erasing our footprints wouldn't have made any difference."

He didn't need to add that the Millennial Consortium operatives were far more than the grunts Glupp made them out to be—they were slick professionals and knew their jobs.

They watched in breathless silence, and the man peered through the scope, estimating elevation and angle and pulled back on the H&K's charger handle. Smoke, flame and an ear-knocking crack spit from the long barrel. Everyone dropped flat as the grenade streaked overhead and struck the trunk of a tree several yards to their rear. Bark exploded in a shower. Pine needles rained down as the pine, broken in the middle, toppled forward. Branches snapped with a sound like multiple gunshots.

"They can have only the most general ideas of where we are," Brigid husked out, green eyes bright with apprehension.

"Yeah," agreed Grant lowly. "But they can just shell the whole area until they drive us out."

Sky Dog began a backward crawl on elbows and knees. "Then let's get the hell out of range before they get too close."

As they followed Sky Dog's actions, suspicion and fear welled up within Kane in equal measure. Thus far, the consortium agents had shown themselves to be canny tacticians, allowing them to sail into a cul-de-sac before springing the trap and cutting off their retreat.

The millennialists didn't seem to be the type to fire random shots at the trees in the hopes of flushing out their quarry like a flock of common quail. Kane's point man's sense sent out a constant alert, telling him that the men on the gunboat were hoping they would react exactly in the way they were.

Three more grenades were fired from the H&K, but the Lakota and Cerberus warriors went deeper into the forest, wincing as the explosive rounds sheared through the tops of trees and showered them with twigs.

Within a few minutes, they were clambering through ravines and climbing along ridges. Much to Sky Dog's irritation, Kane took the point but not because he was more attuned to the wilderness. Walking point was a habit he had acquired during his years as a Magistrate, and he saw no reason to abandon it. Both Brigid and Grant had the utmost faith in Kane's instincts.

During his Mag days, because of his uncanny ability to sniff out danger in the offing, he was always chosen to act as the advance scout. When he walked point, Kane felt electrically alive, sharply tuned to every nuance of his surroundings and what he was doing.

Over the next two hours, the sun rose higher in the sky, warming their chilled bodies and drying their clothes. They reached a treeless escarpment shortly before noon and stopped to rest and take their bearings. The blue-hazed height of Medicine Mountain loomed up from the horizon, surrounded by slate outcroppings, plateaus and massive crags. The waterfall was much closer, less than two miles away as the crow flew. To reach it, the small party would have to descend into a shallow valley filled with rocks, scrub brush and bordered by shrub-ensnarled pine trees.

Grant surveyed their surroundings and, unconsciously lowering his voice, said, "Now I know what the word *desolate* means."

Kane sourly reflected that Grant's admission was made for melodramatic effect inasmuch as the man had once traipsed across the white pumice deserts of the Moon and even the Cydonia plains of Mars.

Brigid, sitting down on a rock, shivered slightly and massaged her right hip. "No sound. Not an animal or even a bird."

"This is sacred land," Sky Dog said dolefully.

Grant ran a hand over his jaw. "Yeah…it sort of feels that way."

Rather than join in the conversation, Kane sat down and dismantled his Bren Ten, laying out the pieces on his jacket. He used a strip of cloth torn from his jacket lining to dry each part and each cartridge. Swiftly, he reassembled it and dry fired it on the empty chamber. The firing pin clicked solidly, so he reloaded the automatic and returned it to his shoulder holster. Fortunately, the holster was made of vacuum-formed plastic, not leather.

Brigid checked over her TP-9 and Grant quickly examined his Copperhead and found their weapons in working condition. "Now what?" Brigid wanted to know.

Kane saluted the lofty peaks of Medicine Mountain sharply. "Now we go there."

Although the four Kit Foxes didn't understand English, they easily the gleaned the meaning of his gesture and murmured to one another, then to Sky Dog. The shaman didn't need to translate their trepidation but he did say, "The Kit Fox Society does not fear man nor animal, but this is the land of the Grandfather. They fear to trespass."

"And are we not their grandchildren?" Brigid asked. She spread her arms to include Grant and Kane. "We have come to drive any trespassers, and so we must walk on the sacred ground ourselves. Our cause is just and the Grandfather will recognize that. He will reward, not punish us."

Sky Dog's mouth quirked in an appreciative smile. "You've picked up Sioux warrior psychology pretty quickly. They're very angry and upset about losing our friends and need some sort of motivator to go against conditioning and seek revenge."

"I figured as much," she replied. "Repeat what I said to them and see if it works."

Sky Dog did so and the Lakota nodded in approval, saying, *"Wayo, wayo!* True! True!"

They smiled in relieved gratitude at Brigid as if she had solved a knotty problem for them. Kane wished he could be so easily reassured. The feeling that they had willingly strolled into a trap increased with every passing second.

"Where's the Medicine Wheel on the mountain?" Grant asked.

Shading her eyes, Brigid gazed at the distant, snow-covered parapets. "On a shoulder of one of the peaks," she said uncertainly. "I think."

She glanced up at Sky Dog and asked, "Do you know?"

He shook his head. "I've never seen it."

"So you don't know what it's supposed to be, either?" Grant challenged.

"I really don't think it matters," the shaman replied unperturbed. "Stones, stars, the directions, time—these can speak to us out of the silent past. Sometimes their language is intuitive, spiritual and the meanings will be felt by the sensitive, but can't really be communicated by your dead predark science."

"Sometimes that's true," said Brigid, "and some-times scientists, rather than shamans, can hear the cosmos speak, and they can hear it through various scientific disciplines. What shamans think may have been lost in the mists of time can be found again through science."

"Speaking of dead predark science," Kane ventured with a wry smile, "if there is a COG facility inside the mountain, do you think it'll have a gateway?"

Brigid pondered the question for a moment, then shook her head. "I really couldn't say. Not even Lakesh knows how many of the modular mat-trans units were built or where they were shipped to."

Kane wasn't surprised by her answer. Two hundred years ago, after Lakesh had debugged the gateway system, the Cerberus redoubt became, from the end of one millennium to the beginning of another, a manufacturing facility. The quantum interphase mat-trans inducers, known colloquially as "gateways," were built in modular form and shipped to other redoubts and installations.

In the five years preceding the nukecaust, the gateway system, the Cerberus network had been set up all over the globe. By then, even the Totality Concept itself had begun to schism along faction lines. Certain project personnel decided to hedge their bets, putting gateways in places other groups didn't know about to further their own partisan agendas.

Kane led the six people down the opposite side of the escarpment and into the rugged terrain of the valley. As they walked across it, he tried to listen for sounds, but he heard very little. Visually he searched the boulders they would have to pass, moving his gaze slowly around and between them. He saw nothing unusual, but he drew his Bren Ten anyway.

There was a sudden, subtle shift in the atmosphere. He couldn't explain it, yet his point man's sense reacted to it. If he had been a true wolf, his hackles would have bristled and he would have tucked his tail under his belly. The sun was unchanged, its brightness undiminished. A haze lay across the outcroppings butting up against the foot of Medicine Mountain, but he sensed a difference in the brush-snarled area they approached.

Brigid moved up close beside him. "What's wrong, Kane?"

He shrugged. "I wish I knew. I only know that something's damn out of tune."

Brigid knew better than to attribute his feeling of disquiet to overstressed nerves or his imagination, so she drew her own autopistol as they drew closer to the edge of the valley.

Kane suddenly rocked to a halt, gesturing for his companions to do the same. "What is it?" Sky Dog asked quietly.

"I don't know."

"Something scares the Trickster Wolf?" the shaman asked with a touch of sarcasm in his tone.

He glanced over at Sky Dog, not bothering to conceal the irritation on his face or in his voice. "Yes, something scares the Trickster Wolf. A man of your age ought to know that sometimes you have to be smart to be scared."

Sky Dog glowered at him. "What scares you here?"

Kane shook his head. "Everything. Nothing."

"There's not even a lizard," Sky Dog pointed out.

"That's another thing that bothers me. Let's find another way out of here."

Peevishly, Grant rumbled, "We're almost out now."

Kane didn't mention he was experiencing the unshakable feeling of being watched. "Just humor me."

"Like that's a new thing," Grant muttered half under his breath but loud enough for Kane to hear.

They began backtracking, the Kit Foxes grumbling under their breath in Lakota. Suddenly, a panther screamed. It was answered by others on the other side of the brush, like a hunting pride whose leader had found the scent of prey.

Sky Dog blurted in a hoarse whisper, "The Lynx Soldiers!"

Kane resisted the urge to ask him who was scared now. Instead, keeping his eyes and gun on the border of trees and undergrowth, he said, "Run. I'll cover you."

From behind the brush line came a sequence of little puffballs of white smoke and thudding reports. A multitude of small canisters burst open against the ground.

Chapter 16

Kane didn't need to shout to his companions to drop. They did so automatically as clouds of vapor spread across the area. A tart chemical sting burned his nostrils, and he immediately held his breath and slitted his eyes.

Through a part in the undergrowth poured a column of dun-attired men, all of them armed with spidery, long-barreled rifles. Their faces were turned into something inhuman and insectoid by gas masks. The canopy of drifting gas obscured their numbers, but Kane guessed there were at least a dozen. The pall of vapor made it impossible for him or his two partners to fire their weapons with any degree of accuracy.

Rather than expend their limited ammunition, they adopted the first course of action that occurred to them—they rose and began running. Only the realization that the uniformed men apparently preferred to take the six people alive kept Kane from going to ground and shooting it out. Still, he lingered for a few moments, firing three random shots at the uniformed men to buy his companions a little time.

Brigid, Grant, Sky Dog and the Kit Foxes scattered, sprinting in different directions to confuse and confound the millennialists. To his surprise, Kane didn't hear gunshots but faint sounds like high-pitched whistles combined with the sneezes of infants. Displaced air thumped near his left ear, but he didn't look behind him.

Exhaling, Kane got to his feet and started running through the planes of vapor. The chemical fog seared his eyes, lungs and nostrils. After he inhaled a whiff of it, the world darkened and teetered around him. He fought against the blackness, conscious of a lancing pain in his skull that bored through both temples. Absently, Kane realized the gas, delivered by scatter-pack launchers, was not of the CS variety nor an opiate but some kind of nerve agent. He had no idea of its full effects, nor did he care to find out.

Fixing his gaze on a tall blue spruce on the opposite side of the valley, Kane ran headlong as fast as he could. He inhaled lungful after lungful of fresh air, and the pain in his head abated a bit and the darkness creeping in on the edge of his vision receded. Still, the skin between his shoulder blades itched in anticipation of a bullet drilling into his flesh.

The toe of his right boot struck an object at ground level and he fell heavily, barely able to catch himself him on his hands. He managed to keep his grip on the Bren Ten. Hitching around, he saw one of the Lakota lying sprawled facedown, arms flung out, legs twisted.

Clutching him by the shoulder of his buckskin tunic, Kane carefully turned him over. Despite the dirt and smeared war paint on his face, the features of Bear in the Woods were easily recognizable. The warrior's eyes were half-open, but they were dull and lusterless. Spittle drooled from the corners of his mouth. He breathed rapidly, his chest rising and falling spasmodically, but Kane didn't think he was suffering from the effects of the neurogen.

Then he saw the small, metal-walled dart protruding from the side of Bear's neck. At the same instant, he heard the snapping of a twig behind him and a spitting whistle. Kane hurled himself to one side, rolling up onto his right knee as a twin of the hypodermic dart that had felled Bear buried itself in the ground an inch from his foot.

A gas-masked millennialist, scarcely discernable in the wafting vapors, stood behind a four-foot-high boulder, less than fifty feet away, a spindly rifle at his shoulder. Without hesitation, Kane squeezed off a single round from his Bren Ten, knocking the man over. He didn't wait to see him fall. Rising to his feet, he began running again. What sounded like two bugs whipped by over his head, missing him inches.

He zigzagged, running broken-field style, although he doubted one of the darts could penetrate his shadow suit. He heard the screech of a puma again and the thud of hooves, but he couldn't see either a cat or a horse. Even as he sprinted, he wondered why the millennialists apparently wanted them incapacitated not dead. The attackers on the river had displayed no such merciful tendencies. He guessed the situation had changed but he couldn't imagine why or how.

Kane's lungs burned with the sustained effort of trying to run as fast as he could while breathing in short, swift gasps. He made it to the spruce tree—and a consortium operative stepped out from behind it, holding one of the long-barreled tranquilizer rifles.

He dug in his heels and dodged to the right, raising his pistol at the same time. He heard a wheezing whistle and an exquisitely sharp, wicked pain stabbed through the left side of his neck, just beneath the hinge of his jaw where it wasn't protected by the high collar of his shadow suit.

Kane's finger jerked in reflexive reaction on the trigger. The Bren Ten boomed and the millennialist clapped a hand over his right thigh and staggered back, a muffled squawk of pain bursting from beneath the gas mask.

As he pivoted on his toes, Kane's autopistol quested for another target. At least, that was what his instincts told his body to do. Instead, he achieved a kind of stumble-footed quarter turn, and he leaned against the tree. His arms and legs suddenly felt as if they were hollow straws being pumped full of half-frozen mud. The fingers of his left hand explored the side of his neck, found the metal hypodermic dart there and pinched it away.

He aimed the Bren Ten at the man writhing on the ground, clutching at the blood-pulsing wound in his right thigh. His finger tightened on the trigger—or he thought it did. His finger remained stiff and straight. His mind sent frantic messages to his hands: Squeeze, pull, squeeze...

He stared incredulously at his pistol. His limbs could move, sluggishly and laboriously, but not his extremities. His fingers and toes were numb, as if they had been amputated. When the millennialist saw Kane couldn't squeeze the trigger of his automatic, he didn't crawl away. Elbowing himself up to a half-sitting position, he fumbled with his rifle, breaking it open and using a thumb to insert a needle-tipped dart into the chamber. Kane was afraid to try to take cover behind the tree. If he fell down in the process and couldn't get up, the man could literally pincushion him with the trank darts while he lay there helpless.

Shoving himself away from the tree trunk, Kane took two shambling steps forward and let himself drop atop the consortium agent, swinging his automatic over his head and down like a club. Powered by 185 pounds of virtually deadweight, the long barrel crashed across the gas mask, shattering the plastic lenses in the eyelets. The man stopped moving, his limbs going slack.

Cursing breathlessly, Kane struggled atop the man's body, managing to get to his hands and knees. He heard the thump of running feet and, alerted by movement in his peripheral vision, he pushed himself, swaying, to his knees. He waved his pistol menacingly, but he realized he probably looked like a belligerent but ultimately incompetent drunk to the four millennialists converging around him.

Despite the gas masks on their faces, the profanity they spit when they spied their companion lying unconscious and bleeding on the ground was clearly audible. A heavy-soled combat boot pounded into Kane's right rib cage and he sprawled onto his side, the Bren Ten leaving his nerveless hands, vanishing from sight in a clump of high grass.

Breath knocked out of him from the impact, Kane tried to force himself to his knees again. Through the amoeba-shaped floaters swimming across his vision, he glimpsed the hollow bore of a trank gun aimed at his face. Then Grant smashed full-tilt into the men, shoulder-slamming them aside, wresting the rifles out of their hands.

His teeth bared in fury, Grant's left leg arced up, his foot burying itself in a millennialist's crotch. As the man went down, Grant whirled on another just he launched a roundhouse kick at him.

As the millennialist's boot snapped toward his belly, Grant's hands came together, catching the ankle and twisting savagely. The consortium agent spun in the direction of the twist, and when Grant released him he hit the ground full length with such force dust puffed up around his body.

The other two men recovered their trank guns and fired darts at Grant, but they stuck in his jacket, failing to penetrate the shadow suit beneath. In response, he unslung his Copperhead and squeezed the trigger, holding it down. The subgun stuttered, and bright streamers of blood splashed from the series of holes punched through a man's chest. Loose limbed, he toppled to the ground.

At the same time, the surviving millennialist dropped his trank rifle and drew a spike-nosed autopistol from a holster at the small of his back. He took swift aim on Grant—just as a .45-caliber round crashed into the occipital region of the man's head. The impact of the slug drove him forward, the broad cranial bone at his hairline breaking open and popping the lenses out of the gas mask. Only then did they hear the eardrum-knocking report of the gun.

Holding her TP-9 in a double-fisted grip, Brigid strode into view. Although Kane felt a surge of both relief and gratitude at the sight of her, he also experienced a queasy sensation of dread at her pronounced pallor and the perspiration pebbling her forehead.

Even Grant looked distinctly unwell, his lips grayish, his face gleaming with a film of clammy sweat. Reaching down, Grant secured a grip on Kane's right arm and tried to lift him to his feet, but it wasn't easy— the numbness had spread further through Kane's legs, making his knees feel as if they had been replaced by jelly.

Brigid stepped up and helped Grant haul Kane to his feet. In a strained, aspirated voice, she said, "It's that damn gas. It doesn't work as fast as the darts, but even brief exposure works on you eventually. It's probably a diluted derivative of VX. The symptoms seem similar. Our shadow suits provided us protection from the full effects."

Kane grimaced as he tried to stand on ankles that felt rubbery. "I guess the idea is that the gas slows you up enough to get tranked."

Grant grunted, wiping sweat from his face with his free hand. "Seems that way. Let's get out of sight."

Slinging his arms over their shoulders, Brigid and Grant half dragged Kane through a hedgerow of undergrowth and into a boulder-strewn, sparsely treed field that led toward a line of cliffs about a mile ahead. For half the distance, the ground was level and covered with waist-high grass and weeds. A narrow trail little wider than a deer path threaded among the grasses and intersected with a house-sized rock formation a hundred feet ahead.

"That place looks defensible," Brigid said. "Nobody can sneak up on us. We'll hole up there and get this gas and juice out of our systems. Then we can plan our next moves."

"Anybody see Sky Dog?" Grant rasped, his respiration labored.

Kane shook his head. "No…came across Bear in the Woods…he'd been tranked. But if the Lynx Soldiers are around and they spot Sky Dog—"

Brigid interjected, "There's not much we can do to help him in the shape we're in—"

Suddenly, she broke off and Kane saw the quick flash of alarm in her eyes. Sweeping around both sides of the rock formation came a troop of thundering horses. Kane caught only glimpses of the near naked female figures astride them, all voicing shrieks reminiscent of the hunting cries of mountain lions. Kane recognized Catamount in the lead, leaning over her black mare's neck, teeth bared in either a grimace of determination or a grin of delight, her cape of panther pelt streaming behind her.

Galloping hooves kicked dirt clots high in the air as the Lynx Soldiers bore down on them. Grant tried to bring up his Copperhead, but he was hampered by Kane's weight. The flank of a horse clipped him and both men went down heavily, Grant sprawling atop Kane.

Brigid raised her TP-9, trying to achieve target acquisition on the nearest of the women, but as a horse swept by, the haft of a long feathered lance struck the nerve ganglia atop her right shoulder and she fell, banging her knees on rocks. She tried to keep her jaws clamped shut on the cry of pain that tried to force its way out of her mouth. Her arm went numb.

She heard another cry behind her, a piercing, warbling howl. Twisting, she looked behind her. Catamount charged forward, a long plaited whip inscribing a humming, hazy circle in the air over her head. Her horse galloped at a frightful, reckless speed, hooves tearing up bucketfuls of turf. Brigid transferred her pistol from her right to her left hand and raised it, finger curling around the trigger.

The snapping of the lash was lost in the drumming hoofbeats. The whip snaked around Brigid's left forearm, a streak of fire across her wrist. She dropped her pistol as she clawed at the whip, staggering as Catamount galloped past, the length of oiled, braided rawhide stretching taut. Rather than risk a dislocated elbow joint, Brigid didn't resist the pull. She went with it, kicking herself forward, but she lost her balance, tripped and fell. Dragged along on her belly, she disappeared among the high grasses.

The mounted Lynx Soldiers rushed by in a bustle of shouts and drumming hooves. They pounded on past Grant and Kane, who were struggling to their feet, then turned their mounts expertly. They charged back and dismounted in graceful vaulting leaps, piling atop the two men, bringing them down again.

Kane slammed a fist into a flat belly, brought up a knee and heard a woman yelp, then he planted an elbow under himself and almost gained his hands and knees with at least three Lynx Soldiers clinging to him. Bare breasts pressed against him, strong thighs gripped him, but his physical reaction was anything but arousal. Then a very hard object cracked against the back of his skull. Pinwheels of light spun behind his eyes, but he didn't lose consciousness.

Reeling, Kane tore one arm free and tried to swing a blow from the shoulder, but he couldn't force his mind

and body to work in tandem. A deerskin-shod foot
slammed up between his legs. The shadow suit had a
reinforced cup made of quadruple layers of Monocrys
and Spectra in the crotch, but the impact was still transmitted into his groin. Without it, his testicles would've
caught in his throat.

Kane stumbled, sick and dizzy and he heard Grant
blurt his name. He caught a blurry impression of the
man going down under the butts of lances. Then he collapsed facefirst into the dust and lay there, unable to
move for what seemed like a very long time. At the
thunder of hoofbeats, he lifted his head. It took an eternity.

He glimpsed Catamount on her mare, and once more
she reminded him irresistibly of a Valkyrie but this time
because she carried on the saddle blanket before her, not
the soul of a slain warrior, but Brigid Baptiste. Her
wrists were bound behind her by stout thongs, and her
face hidden under the veil of her red-gold hair.

Catamount cried out in strident triumph then rode
away, voicing a strange undulating chant. The other
Lynx Soldiers followed her on their own horses, joining in with wild vocalizations. The tawny shape of
Deathmaul loped alongside the black mare, his muzzle
darkened and glistening with fresh blood.

Sweating and swearing, Kane fought to push himself upward, his mind racing, although his body seemed
somewhere else. He strained to regain control of his
body, arms and legs flopping like fish stranded on dry

land, but the effort exhausted him. He was immobi-
lized. He tried to call out to Grant, but he couldn't force
a sound past his lips. His throat felt swollen, closed. He
tried to brace himself with his hands, but he couldn't
feel them and he was sure he hadn't the coordination to
spit, but much less stand up.

Then the world darkened around him, shutting out
everything but anger and humiliation, and they spun like
enraged hornets within the walls of his mind.

Chapter 17

Waves of pain jostled Brigid Baptiste like a ceaseless surf. Grinding her teeth, she tried to see through her screen of hair and the tears of pain occluding her vision. Cramping needles of agony stabbed into her stomach. Judging by the constant rocking and jumbled images of ground, brush and hoof, Brigid realized she was folded over the back of a horse, belly down, legs on one side, her arms tied behind her. Draped over the blanket saddle like a sack of potatoes, she saw the world upside down.

She retained only vague, chaotic memories of how she came to be jackknifed over the horse. She recalled the excruciating pain in her left elbow and shoulder as she was catapulted off her feet and dragged through the grass behind the black mare, experiencing a crazed eternity when the ground and the sky skidded around her, changing places with one another. Dirt filled her mouth and eyes, and dust clogged her nostrils.

When the mad plunge ended, she was too dazed, too blinded and in too much pain to do anything but lie motionless and gasp for a long moment. In that moment, her arms were forced behind her, her wrists bound and she was heaved up and over the back of a horse like a deer bagged by a jubilant hunter.

A persistent pressure compressed her wrists, squeezed them tightly. By a tentative exploration with her fingertips, she felt strands of rawhide wrapped tightly around her wrists. She was helpless, blind and sick. Nausea was a clawed animal trying to tear its way out of her stomach. It was all she could do to swallow the column of burning bile working its way up her throat.

With great, tendon-straining effort, Brigid raised her head and saw, through strands of her hair, blurred trees whipping past. Mallets of pain hammered at her, striking in time with the clopping sound of the horse's hoofbeats as it galloped along an overgrown path. She wanted to shout, but lacked the necessary strength to open her mouth and form the words. It was all she could do to breathe, and even that was labored and painful through a compressed diaphragm and an aching rib cage.

The horse cantered swiftly, and with each movement a new flare of pain burst at the end of every nerve ending in Brigid's bruised and battered body. She attempted to move, shifting her lower body where it folded across the beast's backbone, but the end effect was to make her fear that her stomach lining would fall out of her mouth. She was grateful she hadn't eaten anything solid since before dawn.

A twist of cruel laughter touched her ears, and she felt a sharp, stinging blow on her buttocks. A sharp female voice said in English, "If you want to get down, white woman, I will help you—headfirst."

Brigid clenched her teeth but said nothing. After what felt an interlocked chain of eternities, the horse's rocking, swaying gait slowed to a walk. She heard it snorting noisily as if tired. She tried to lift her head, but the pressure of a hand on the back of her neck held her down.

"Be patient, white woman," she heard the woman say. "We're almost to my camp...but you have only completed the first leg of your journey."

Brigid began to hear an incessant hissing, which swiftly built to a dull roar. The temperature grew warmer, the air feeling moist. The horse came to a halt, and Catamount spoke a few words in Lakota but the roar in Brigid's ears impaired her hearing. Strong hands clasped her and hauled her off the horse's back. She expected to be dumped unceremoniously and roughly on the ground, but instead she was placed down gently and eased into a sitting position.

Brigid sat motionless for a long moment, hanging her head, waiting for the vertigo to subside and the nausea to ebb in her belly. The roaring continued, and she realized it wasn't coming from inside her head. After a few seconds, she felt strong enough to move, although still sick and weak. She tossed her head, flinging her hair out of her eyes. Above her reared high plateaus, crags jutting against the sky, massive ranges lost among a monstrous mountain, trackless, uncharted and forgotten.

To her left rose the huge bastion of a perpendicular cliff. Over its gray face gushed a wide torrent of water, roaring and foaming as it fell, the mist from it wavering over the rocks. Brigid felt a fine spray touch her face, settling on her dry lips, and she licked them gratefully.

The only vegetation in the area were beds of ferns, most of them surrounding little pools of water above which wreathes of vapor floated. She guessed the pools were natural hot springs.

Indian girls dressed in bleached doeskin smocks emerged from teepees and took the horses from the Lynx Soldiers, leading them to a split-rail corral, where they rubbed them down with the saddle blankets. Brigid stared, noting that the girls ranged in age from eight or nine years old to teenagers. She noticed one of the Lynx Soldiers brandishing a pair of Copperheads. She assumed one of them was hers, the other Grant's.

Suddenly the huge cougar padded across Brigid's range of vision, cold green eyes fixed on her, blood-wet muzzle glistening. She instinctively recoiled and the giant cat hissed, revealing yellow, saliva-slick fangs. Brigid knew the animal smelled her fear.

Catamount's voice called out sharply, and the mountain lion turned, trotting toward her like an obedient dog. Reaching down, the woman caught the animal's jowls between her hands and whispered. The panther appeared to listen intently, then when Catamount released it stalked away, its posture suggesting sullenness. Brigid received the distinct impression the woman had chastised the animal.

Catamount turned toward her. "Deathmaul will not harm you unless you give him a reason to...or I give him a specific order to do so."

Although Brigid's throat felt as if it was coated with dust, she retorted stiffly, "That makes me feel much better about all of this. Thank you."

Catamount favored her with a piercing glare, then removed the panther pelt and hood, passing them and the coiled whip to a girl. Brigid experienced a distant quiver of surprise by how young she looked. Her skin was a dark, copper-tinted amber. Her eyes were a deep brown under long black lashes. Although her face wasn't classically beautiful, it held a wild, pagan beauty that showed no true age.

But it was Catamount's grace that caught the attention and evoked even a little envy in Brigid. Her every movement was a flowing symmetry from ankle to throat that bespoke a life very close to the roots of nature, of creation itself.

"Sky Dog told you who I am?" Catamount asked bluntly.

Brigid nodded. "Do you know who I am?"

Catamount returned the nod. "You are Magasinyanla Wayana Wicincala—Red-Haired Scholar Girl. At least

that is the name you are known by. You are the woman
of Unktomi Shunkaha."

Brigid opened her mouth to refute the casual comment, then realized it might be to her advantage to be
so classified. Rather than respond directly to it, she demanded, "Why did you capture me? To lure Kane—
Trickster Wolf?"

"I captured you because you can be of some use to
me," Catamount answered flatly, striding over to her.
"And my allies bade me to keep you alive. I care nothing for Unktomi Shunkaha except that you accompanied him here."

Inserting a hand beneath Brigid's right armpit, she
lifted her to her feet as if she weighed no more than the
shadow suit itself. A knife blade flashed in the woman's
hand. "Turn around."

Brigid hesitated, but decided if Catamount meant to
kill her, she would have done so earlier without her co-
operation. She did as the tall woman bade and felt the
sharp knife slash through the rawhide thongs binding
her wrists.

Brigid pulled away the strands of leather, feeling in-
timidated by the near naked Catamount and not liking
the feeling one bit. Catamount was a couple of inches
taller than her, leaner and longer of leg. Rubbing cir-
culation back into her hands, Brigid turned away and
the world spun dizzily for an instant. She tottered, stumbled and would have fallen if Catamount hadn't stead-
ied her.

"Are you ill?" the woman asked, although not at all solicitously.

Brigid shook her head. "It's a combination of the gas your consortium pals used and the very uncomfortable pony ride you gave me. It'll take me a while to get over the effects."

Catamount nodded. "We were warned to stay well away from the gas. Come with me."

She strode purposefully through the camp, not looking back to see if Brigid followed her or not. After a second or two of hesitation, Brigid fell into step behind her, trying to make her steps surefooted and project an attitude of fearlessness. It wasn't easy, since every glance directed at her by the other Lynx Soldiers and the doe-skin-clad girls was either hostile or mocking. But if she had learned one thing from Kane, and from her association with Grant and Domi, it had been to accept risk as a part of her way of life, taking chances so that others might find the ground beneath their feet a little more secure.

She had never considered her attitude idealism, but simple pragmatism. She had come to understand that death was a part of the challenge of existence, a fact that every man and woman had to face eventually.

She could accept it without humiliating herself if it came as a result of her efforts to remove the yokes of the overlords from the collective neck of humanity. Although she never spoke of it, certainly not to the cynical Kane, she had privately vowed to make the future a better, cleaner place than either the past or the present. She suspected he knew anyway.

Brigid followed Catamount on her path through the teepees, noting the crude, colorful glyphs painted on them in bright primary pigments. If the illustrations told stories, they were beyond her current abilities to comprehend or care.

As the chieftain of the Lynx Soldiers marched swiftly ahead, tall, lithe and vibrant, Brigid smiled in rueful envy. Watching the sensuous play of muscles beneath the smooth skin of her bare back and the slight swagger of her flaring hips, Catamount reminded her of Ambika, the genetically engineered Lioness of the Western Isles. However, Catamount didn't exude the calculatedly seductive sexuality affected by the self-proclaimed pirate queen.

Catamount stopped before a teepee and thrust aside a door flap. Steam filtered out. "Go in there," she instructed. "Bathe. You will sweat out the poisons."

Brigid eyed the interior, then Catamount, but she didn't move. "What did you do to my friends? Kane and Grant and Sky Dog?"

Catamount's expression didn't change. She gestured sharply to the triangular entrance to the teepee. "Go in there. Bathe. I will return shortly and we will talk."

Brigid stared unblinkingly into Catamount's dark eyes. Catamount stared back, just as unblinkingly. With a sigh, Brigid turned and entered the lodge. Catamount dropped the flap behind her. Warm vapor arose from a hot-springs pool. Brigid fanned it away from her face, considering her options. Escape didn't seem to be one of them. Not only did she not know in which direction to go, but also she didn't feel up to running. She estimated the Lynx Soldiers had traveled a minimum of five miles from where she was captured.

The heat from the pool played invitingly over her face, and she made up her mind. Brigid shucked out of her jacket and pants, then sat down and tugged off her boots. She stripped out of the shadow suit by opening a magnetic seal on the right side. The garment had no zippers or buttons and she peeled it off in one continuous piece from the hard-soled boots to the gloves.

She slid into the pool, noting that the water temperature was just a few degrees shy of being uncomfortable. She completely submerged to wash the dirt and twigs out of her hair. She sat on the smooth bottom, leaning her head against the soft ferns overhanging the edge, trying to relax in the soothing heat of the water, letting the warmth push away the ache in her arms and legs.

The memory of her last sight of Kane and Grant surrounded by the Lynx Soldiers flashed through her mind, and she struggled with the sudden stab of panic and fear. With effort she reminded herself of all times she and the two men had cheated death and turned the tables on those who sought to kill them.

Lakesh had once suggested that the trinity they formed when they worked in tandem seemed to exert an almost supernatural influence on the scales of chance, usually tipping them in their favor. The notion had amused Brigid. She was too pragmatic to truly believe in such an esoteric concept, but not even she could deny that she and her two friends seemed to lead exceptionally charmed lives, particularly Kane.

The head ruled the heart, thinking came before emotions, but Brigid always shied away from examining the bond she shared with Kane. On the surface there was no bond, but they seemed linked to each other and the same destiny.

She recalled another name she had for Kane: *anam-chara.* In the ancient Gaelic tongue it meant "soul friend." Dreams they had experienced during a bad mat-trans jump years before suggested that not only had they lived past lives, but also in all those lives their souls were continually intertwined with each other in some manner. The idea that she and Kane had existed at other times in other lives had seemed preposterous at first. Perhaps it still would have if she hadn't experienced those jump dreams herself, which symbolized the chain of fate connecting her soul to Kane's and Kane's to hers.

Only once had the links of that chain been stretched to a breaking point: Over two years before, Kane had shot and killed a woman, a distant relative of Brigid's, whom he perceived as a threat to her life. It took her some time to realize that under the confusing circumstances, Kane had no choice but to make a snap judg-

ment call. Making split-second, life-and-death deci-
sions was part of his conditioning, his training in the
Magistrate Division, as deeply ingrained as breathing.

What conflicted her during that time was not the
slow process of forgiving him, but coming to terms
with what he really was and accepting the reality rather
than an illusion. He was a soldier, not an explorer, not
an academic, not an intellectual. When she finally understood that about him, the two people achieved a syn-
thesis of attitudes and styles where they functioned as
colleagues and members of a team, extending to the
other professional courtesies and respect.

Brigid drowsily considered climbing out of the pool
but grudgingly realized that she had begun to feel better, stronger and less sick to her stomach. She felt as if
she were floating in the air, not in the water. She didn't
realize she had drifted off into a light doze until she felt
motion in the water around her.

Snapping her eyes open, she saw a naked Catamount
sliding into the pool opposite her. Brigid made a motion to climb out, but the chieftain of the Lynx Soldiers
lifted an imperious hand. "Stay."

Brigid felt her spine stiffen at the autocratic tone of
command, but she did as the woman said, sinking back
into the water. Catamount's hair was braided and fastened atop her head. The water lapped at her bare shoulders and full breasts. Her lips curved in a smile of subtle
cruelty.

"You do not like to be ordered about," she said. "That is good."

"Why?" Brigid asked.

"Because I can understand that. One must understand an enemy, particularly if it is possible they can be turned into an ally. I hated being ordered about so much I became a warrior and formed my own soldier society."

Brigid tried to match her cruel smile, but knew she failed. "Apparently you hated being ordered around so much, it got you banished from your tribe."

"I have no tribe," Catamount countered matter-of-factly.

"Not anymore, no…since you didn't concern yourself with the welfare of the people you were sworn to protect."

She paused and added, "Or so Sky Dog said."

Catamount's dark eyes flashed with anger, but it was quickly veiled. She leaned her head back against the edge of the pool. "Is that what he told you?"

"More or less," Brigid replied.

Catamount chuckled bitterly. "Sky Dog has said many, many things about me and to me. That I was wicked, ungovernable, that I was reckless and selfish. And that he loved me more than life itself."

Chapter 18

Kane tried to lift his head, listening not just with his ears but every square inch of his being, waiting for a recurrence of the sound. He thought he had heard a faint, husky whisper that to his ears sounded like "Unktomi Shunkaha."

But there was only silence—utter, complete silence. No sighing in the boughs of the spruces clustered around the edge of the meadow, no scuttling of furtive life in the underbrush, so he attributed it to an aural hallucination brought on by stress and the drugs poisoning his system. Strangely, his eyes so far seemed unaffected. Through the spires of the trees, the stars had already started to glint above the fused red-and-gold colors of sunset.

Kane shifted his gaze sideways, toward the slumped and motionless figure of Grant. He had lain without moving or even appearing to breathe for the better part of the past hour. Kane's nerve centers frantically commanded his arms and legs to do what they were designed to do, but they didn't respond.

Furious, frustrated, he silently raged against the cold

creep of the tranquilizing drug through his bloodstream. Forehead beading with sweat, he let his head drop back to the ground. Although he could feel the lump on the rear of his skull, there was no pain, since the neurogen gas had evidently scrambled his nervous system. His vision remained clear, and he could manage to crane his neck and look up but that was the limit of his mobility.

Limbs filled with molten lead, reflexes slumbering, Kane feared to call out to Grant or any of the Lakota who might be still in the vicinity. As far as he knew, millennialists were searching for them despite the approach of dusk. The high grasses in which he and Grant lay concealed them from a cursory glance.

All he could do was to lie paralyzed, consumed with worry about Brigid and Grant. The Commtact transmitted not even a whisper of static, so he assumed Brigid was far outside of its range. He didn't allow himself to dwell on any other possibility. He drifted in and out of consciousness, a symptom he attributed to the effects of either the gas or the tranquilizing drug or a combination.

IT WAS DEEP DUSK, almost full dark when Kane forced his eyes open again. Turning his head, he saw that Grant had still not stirred, lying where he had fallen under the hammering war clubs of the Lynx Soldiers. He moved his eyes, searching. Nothing appeared to have altered in his immediate surroundings. Although his range of sight was limited, his vision remained thankfully clear.

The temperature had fallen to near freezing, and flakes of light snow, barely a flurry, sifted down on his upturned face. Although the shadow suits would protect him and Grant from hypothermia, their ears and noses would still be exposed, susceptible to frostbite. Once again, on the very fringes of audibility he thought he heard the sighing whisper of "Unktomi Shunkaha," but now he was positive his senses were still scrambled by the drugs and couldn't be trusted.

He stared up at the darkening sky, straining his ears for any noise that might be produced by large animals, of the four- and two-legged variety. At first the only sounds he heard were the familiar ones of a wilderness at nightfall—the chirping of crickets, the distant but monotonous croaking of a frog and the piercing, haunting cry of a nocturnal bird of prey.

Then Kane's ears caught a new sound, the soft, stealthy rustle and swish of the high grass being parted. A vivid image of the panther's bloodstained muzzle flashed into the forefront of his mind and he held his breath, caught between the warring impulses to continue lying perfectly still or make a final attempt to fight his way to his feet.

The sound of passage through the grass ceased for a moment then began again, an almost inaudible swish-swish. Gritting his teeth, Kane knew an animal wouldn't move with such deliberate stealth unless it scented a meal nearby.

He struggled, his mind frantically ordering his

numbed muscles to move, to twitch, to display any signs of life at all. He glared, furious and panic-stricken at Grant, then at his own feet. He fought violently, but in a way he had never fought before. The struggle had nothing to do with his body; it occurred inside his mind. The thought that his entire life added up to a single night lying helpless in a Wyoming field, waiting to be eaten by an animal, terrified him.

Kane heard the rustle of the grass again, this time much closer. He concentrated on moving his feet. When his left one twitched, he almost shouted in jubilation. But he kept silent, focusing fiercely on his legs and arms.

He didn't know how long it took, but finally he was able to prop himself up on his elbows, then flop over onto his hands and knees. His face and hair were damp with sweat. Panting, hanging his head, he looked around and caught a blurred glimpse of a tawny shape gliding almost silently through the high grass only a few yards away.

Although the effort made his heart feel like it might burst, he surged to his feet—and almost immediately fell again. He didn't hit the ground. Muscular, buckskin-sleeved arms caught him, grasping him tightly.

"Easy, Unktomi Shunkaha," Sky Dog whispered. "I've been calling you."

DURING HER YEARS as an archivist in Cobaltville's Historical Division, Brigid Baptiste had perfected the art of maintaining a poker face. Because archivists were always watched, it didn't do for them to show emotional reaction to a scrap of knowledge that might have escaped the censor's notice. Now at Catamount's casually spoken claim, she felt her eyebrows rising involuntarily toward her hairline.

Catamount's superior smile widened. "Does that surprise you?"

Staring at her through the steam wavering above the surface of the hot springs, Brigid answered frankly, "Yes, it does. Sky Dog led us to believe that you and he were mortal enemies."

"We are," Catamount retorted. "Now. And in some ways, that has made us even closer."

"It is said that hate can sometimes be a stronger bond than love," Brigid replied knowingly.

The smile vanished from Catamount's face and she nodded gravely. "I am living proof of that, Red-Haired Scholar Girl."

"Call me Brigid," Brigid said curtly. "Whoever came up with that name for me wasn't even trying for anything like drama."

Catamount didn't appear to have heard her. Broodily, she said, "Sky Dog hoped his love would bind my spirit, weaken it. But I saw through his trickery, his deceit, his persuasions."

The tone and timbre of Catamount's voice didn't change, but Brigid sensed a great rage, a deep hurt simmering so close to the surface of the woman's psyche, she wouldn't have been surprised to see her fly into a screaming frenzy. Her soul was trapped in a terrible place.

Half-closing her eyes, Catamount stared at Brigid, but Brigid knew the woman was not looking at her but across miles and years of suffering as she raised memories from their shallow graves.

"My father was Spotted Hawk, a man of the Sioux," she said in a monotone. "His people and the Absaroke, the Crow, have been rivals since the birth of Grandmother Earth, but the Lakota men were ever and always drawn to Crow women. Many became highly revered seers, magicians and wise women. One who came to great prominence was named Cetan Winyan."

"Nightingale Woman," Brigid murmured.

Catamount opened her eyes a trifle wider. "You know the tongue of our peoples."

"As do you that of the *wasicun*," Brigid countered.

"Taught to me by Sky Dog." Catamount pursed her lips as if she tasted something sour. "Spotted Hawk had gone on a vision quest and while he walked the spirit path, he was told he would be a medicine man, a shaman, but he would first have to learn the Great Mysteries from a Crow conjure woman. He made the long journey through the forests and came to the Crow village. The warriors would have killed him, but Nightingale Woman stopped them. She was mighty among them, wise and just.

"She was still a girl, but the people came to her for

counsel and the settling of their disputes. She acted as midwife, prayed to the spirits to end droughts and even offered advice during times of war. The Crow believed great magic lived in Nightingale Woman."

Catamount shifted position in the water, her eyes vacant as she gazed at the tendrils of steam, as if they were veils obscuring the past. "Spotted Hawk believed so, too. She agreed to teach him the ways of the Great Mysteries, and as she tutored him, he fell in love with her. Nightingale Woman taught him everything she knew, and soon the tribe accepted him as a shaman in his own right. Spotted Hawk went among the folk as she did, healing, prophesying, teaching, counseling. After a year, he and Nightingale Woman were wed in the Crow village, and there I was born.

"As I grew, I learned the wild skills and lore of the woods and the animals. I had a special affinity for the big cats of the forests and the mountains...the lynx, the puma, the cougar. Life was good to us. My people knew of the *wasicun,* the white man, but we never made contact with them, even though our scouts brought reports of bands of them encroaching onto our lands.

"Each year there were more of them, coming deeper and deeper. They were called Roamers, we learned. Our war chiefs feared it was only a matter of time before they found us. They beseeched Nightingale Woman to find a way to turn back the *wasicun,* to far-see and learn what we might face if we made war on them."

Brigid said nothing, but she realized that Nightingale

Woman had more than likely possessed the powers of a doomseer, or a doomie, a psionic gifted—or cursed—with the psychic ability to foresee coming events. Doomseers weren't necessarily mutants, but norms with true telepathic abilities were rare. Nearly a year before, Brigid and her friends had visited a hidden city where psi-powers were bred into the populace by a method of bioengineering.

Extrasensory and precognitive perceptions were the most typical abilities possessed by mutants who appeared otherwise normal. Catamount had evidently inherited a degree of her mother's talents, judging by her empathic connection with Deathmaul.

"My mother was reluctant," Catamount continued, "because when in such a deep trance state, opening a channel to the Great Mystery, she is open to other energies. My father, Spotted Hawk had not the same level of power as she, and so convinced her she must do it. He harangued her day and night for a week."

"Why was it so important to him?" Brigid asked softly.

Catamount sighed. "All Indian peoples know that the earth must be renewed, by our prayers, our dances, our rituals and by our blood if need be. For our ways to live, we must be in a world that understands and accepts them, that knows our hearts.

"Those are some of the words my father spoke to Nightingale Woman. Eventually, she relented. She fasted for three days, then entered the sweat lodge and went into a trance that lasted four days. She did not awaken. My father violated the terms of the ritual and tried to rouse her."

Catamount stopped speaking, the sudden silence ringing like the tolling of a bell.

Brigid felt a chill creep up along her backbone, despite the warmth of the pool. "Had she died?"

Catamount did not answer for a long time. Then she said with a quiet, grave calm, "Worse. She had met a ghost in her journey on the spirit path and he had stolen her soul. When she opened her eyes again, two days later, it was not Nightingale Woman who looked at us, but Towasi, the Owl Prophet. He told us how he had ensnared my mother's soul. If we did not do as he bid, in every way, her soul would remain imprisoned."

"What did you do?" asked Brigid.

She stopped speaking again, and silence felt oppressive in the enclosed space of the tipi. Then Catamount said in a hoarse whisper, "What I had to do. I killed my mother."

Chapter 19

Between Sky Dog and the two warriors, Iron Horse and Laughing Badger, they managed to turn Grant over. The big man remained unmoving, but he still breathed. His face bore bruises and swelling from the clubbing administered by the Lynx Soldiers. Kane unsteadily knelt before him, checked the pulse at his throat and put his head on his chest to listen to his heart and respiration. Both were slow, a bit labored, but they seemed steady.

After speaking his name several times and receiving no response, Kane slapped his cheeks. Grant's head wobbled back and forth, but his eyes didn't open.

"His spirit may still be awake, but his body slumbers," Sky Dog said.

Acidly, Kane demanded, "How is that a help?"

"We will try to contact his spirit through his body." Sky Dog reached into his parfleche and removed a small clay vial. Popping open the wooden cap, he passed it back and forth under Grant's nostrils.

Kane caught a whiff of one of the most vile odors that had ever come within a mile of his nose and he recoiled. He stopped short of pinching his nostrils shut, but he did ask in tones of horror, "God Almighty, that stinks! What the hell is that shit?"

A wincing Sky Dog turned his face away from the vial as he answered, "Beaver musk, the glands from a weasel and essence of fish eggs, stewed in horse urine, allowed to ferment for the last month within the belly of a dead snake."

Kane gaped at him in shock and dismay. "Why would you cook up something like that?"

"To pour on our tracks, to cover our scents, in case we were trailed by Deathmaul. This perfume would overwhelm the sensitive nose of a big cat for several hours. It would be unable to smell anything."

Kane resisted the urge to opine that it probably wouldn't want to smell anything ever again after an exposure to the pungent and nauseating odor, but he kept his attention fixed on Grant's face. Despite the piercing stench, he had no great faith that Sky Dog's tactic would work to rouse the man. Grant's nose had been broken three times in the past, and always poorly reset. Unless an odor was extraordinarily pleasant or virulently repulsive, he was incapable of detecting subtle smells, unless they were right under his nostrils. A running joke during his Mag days had been that Grant could eat a hearty dinner with a dead skunk lying on the table next to his plate.

Suddenly Grant's eyelids fluttered, his nostrils twitched and his lips contorted in a grimace. Then his eyes popped wide. He lunged up from the waist, slap-

ping at the vial of scent in Sky Dog's hand and snarling, "God Almighty, that *stinks!*"

He started to fall backward, but Kane and Iron Horse
supported him. Grant squeezed his glassy eyes open and
shut, looking around in disorientation.

"Grant," Kane said urgently. "Can you hear me? Can
you see me?"

Grant frowned at him impatiently. "Why shouldn't
I be able to? It's my nose I'm worried about, not my ears
and eyes. What the hell is the matter with you?"

Then he winced and raised his right hand, first gingerly touching the back of his head, then the swollen
flesh on his face. "Don't tell me," he rasped in weary
disgust. "I got hit in the head again."

"Several times," Kane replied dryly. "But so did I."

Grant frowned as memory returned, peering up at
Sky Dog and the Lakota. "How long have I been out?"

"Three hours, I think." Sky Dog and Laughing
Badger pulled Grant to his feet. Breathing harshly, he
swayed from side to side.

"It's that damn gas," Kane said, still kneeling. "Not
to mention being severely drummed on by half-naked
women."

Grant scowled. "And wouldn't you know it…that's
the one thing I don't remember."

He extended a hand to Kane, who took it and allowed
himself to be heaved to his feet, even though his legs
still felt partially numb. "What happened to you guys?"
he asked Sky Dog.

The shaman gestured to the far side of the hedgerow bordering the field. "The gas got to us, too. Made us sick and weak, but we were able to hide ourselves. Bear in the Woods wasn't so lucky."

Kane nodded. "I know. I stumbled over him. He'd been tranked. Did the consortium goons find him?"

"Deathmaul found him," Sky Dog said grimly. There was no need to elaborate, since Kane retained a vivid memory of the fresh blood staining the big cat's muzzle.

Grant patted himself, feeling under his jacket and growled, "Where the hell is my Copperhead?"

"I don't have a weapon, either," Kane announced bleakly, glancing over toward the hedgerow. "But I don't feel like backtracking to hunt for it."

"It was probably taken by the Lynx Soldiers," Sky Dog said, shivering as a sudden gust of cold wind flattened the grasses of the meadow and blew a sprinkling of snow into his face. "We saw the consortium men carrying off their dead and injured and they most likely retrieved their firearms, too."

"Brigid's pistol might be around—" Grant broke off and asked, "Do you know where that Catamount bitch could've taken Brigid?"

Sky Dog shook his head. "Only that it's too far to reach on foot before the storm arrives."

"Storm?" Kane echoed, craning his neck, looking skyward. Thick dark clouds had massed in the east.

"If we do not care to freeze to death," continued Sky Dog, "we must find shelter."

"Like where?" Grant asked impatiently.

Sky Dog gestured in the direction of the lofty ramparts of Medicine Mountain. "There is a place on the lower slopes, a cave."

Kane eyed him suspiciously. "You've been there?"

"I've seen it," the shaman replied. "All holy men of the Lakota, the Cheyenne and even the Crow know of its location."

Kane glanced in the direction of Sky Dog's hand wave, started to turn away, then did a double take. He stared at the dark face of the mountain for a long moment before asking, "Sky Dog, do you still have your binoculars?"

Looking a bit mystified, the shaman handed them over, and Kane peered intently through the eyepieces. He adjusted the focus as he swept the ruby-coated lenses over the mountainside and fixed them on a tier of ledges below the domed summit.

"What's so damn interesting?" Grant asked, glancing up at the thickening cloud cover. Strong, cold gusts of wind slapped at his face.

"I'm not sure," Kane murmured distractedly. "I thought I saw something."

"Like what?"

He didn't respond in words, but his body stiffened. At first, Kane had doubted his eyes, fearing that as a lingering symptom of the neurogen and the drug, he was experiencing a hallucination. But as he stared incredulously through the binoculars, he watched a slate wall on the mountain face moving ponderously to the left like a sliding panel door.

Light spilled out, revealing a huge hollow extending deep into the mountain, illuminated by what he guessed were numerous glowing neon strips inset into the ceiling and the walls. He estimated the entrance to be at least twenty feet by twenty, wide and high enough to accommodate large mil-spec vehicles.

"I said," Grant stated in an aggrieved tone, "like what?"

Wordlessly Kane pointed in the direction he was looking. Although the light shafting through the open portal wasn't bright, Kane's companions were able to discern it with the unaided eye despite the distance.

"What the hell is that?" Grant snapped. "Is that the cave you were talking about?"

"No," Sky Dog said flatly. "I would imagine it is the COG installation Brigid surmised might be built inside the mountain."

Grant took the binoculars from Kane and raised them to his eyes. "I imagine you imagine right. She's not wrong very often."

Sky Dog uttered a spitting sound of loathing. "I wish she was wrong about this. It is one thing to commit the sacrilege of misusing the holy mountain in such a manner, but to do so in the proximity of the *tai-me* and *baykok* is utter madness."

"You still haven't explained about the *baykok*," Kane declared.

"Or this Towasi slagger," Grant interjected, lowering the binoculars.

Iron Horse spoke a stream of rapid-fire Lakota. Although neither Kane nor Grant understood his words, he sounded exceptionally peeved.

Sky Dog's thin lips stretched in a mirthless smile. "My friend has submitted the point that the longer we stand here jabbering, the greater the chance we stand of being found here at dawn with our jaws forever frozen open. He urges us to get under way."

Seeing the frowns cross the faces of Grant and Kane, he added, "I will explain all that I can once we reach the cave."

"It looks like it's at least five miles away," Kane said dubiously.

"At the very least," Sky Dog conceded. "And some of it is straight up."

Grant shook his head in exasperation. "I knew we should've come out here in one of the Mantas."

Grant referred to the transatmospheric craft found on the Manitius Moonbase and brought down to Cerberus. Powered by two different kinds of engines, a ramjet and solid-fuel pulse detonation air spikes, the Manta ships could fly in both a vacuum and an atmosphere. The transatmospheric planes weren't experimental craft, but examples of a technology that was mastered by a race when humanity still climbed trees to escape from saber-toothed tigers.

The five men began jogging toward the rocky bluffs.

The moon flew in and out of lowering, soot-colored clouds. It was difficult for Kane and Grant to move at first, since they were still woozy from the debilitating effects of the beating and exposure to chemicals. They took it easy for the first mile, stopping often to catch their breath. Afterward, they wolf trotted, alternating walking and running. The wind hadn't been dangerously cold at first, but the temperature kept dropping and their breath was a constant steam before their eyes.

Within a half hour, the wind moaning over the field turned into a shrieking wail that seemed to fill the entire world, tearing at the five people with a clawing fury. They were blinded by a white, stinging curtain of snow. Breathing in the gale was difficult, since snowflakes and sleet seared the moist, soft tissues of their mouths and sinus passages like razor-edged ice blades. The flurries danced across their eyes, clinging to their lashes.

The five men simply put their heads down and jogged onward. The cold pummeled them, slapping at their bodies. As the snowfall increased, their range of vision was reduced to only a few yards. As the hands and legs of the Lakota grew numb, Kane's and Grant's ears and teeth ached fiercely.

They had no choice but to trust Sky Dog's sense of direction. Traditionally, a Lakota's powers of recollection were phenomenal, since they had to rely solely on their memories to find water and game, without the benefits of maps or signposts. The shaman led them unerringly toward the rocky foothills.

The terrain dropped into a narrow declivity that sheltered them from the direct bite of the chill wind for a little while. Panting, putting his hands in his armpits to warm his fingers, Sky Dog said, "There is a marker near the cave, what looks like pattern of stones in the ground. If you see them, then you know we are near."

Too out of breath to answer, Kane and Grant only nodded that they understood.

After resting for few minutes, the five men moved on again. If hell were ice and snow, Kane reflected, it would be something like what they fought through. Everything was covered in ice and sleet that cut into them like animal fangs. Following Sky Dog's shouted instructions, they stumbled up the side of a bluff, clambering over boulders and squeezing between pinnacles of stone through which the wind wailed mournfully. In single file, the men eased along a ledge that inclined upward at an ever steepening angle.

On the higher parapets, the only trees that grew were twisted and dwarfed spruces that had found precarious rootholds in the crevices. The five people used them as stanchions and handholds. The darkness and the storm turned the climb into an exceedingly dangerous exercise above black ravines and drop-offs, but all of them managed to pull themselves up onto the lip of an overhanging precipice.

Kane was up first and, breasting the wind, he shambled and shuffled along the edge until he struck something hard underfoot. He stumbled and nearly fell over an irregular circle of brown, round-topped stones. They curved outward in front of a sheer cliff wall, in a U shape.

Shielding his eyes, Kane was just able to make out a dark opening through the whirling streamers of snow. He called to his companions, and they huddled on the leeward side of a massive tumble of rock that protected them from the direct onslaught of the wind. They stared into the murky depths of a yawning cavern.

"Is this the place?" Kane shouted into Sky Dog's ear.

Sky Dog gazed at the cavern for a long moment without answering. The opening was eight feet high, the width considerably less. He kicked at one of the domed stones and it ripped up from the ground like a rotten tooth. A brown human skull, missing its lower jawbone, went clattering over the rocks. Hoarsely, the shaman intoned, "This is the place. Home sweet home...at least for the night."

Chapter 20

"You killed your mother?" Try as she might, Brigid couldn't keep the horror she felt from underscoring her tone.

Closing her eyes, Catamount's expression and voice were as hard as flint. "Her body, yes."

Brigid's own mother had literally disappeared from her life some fifteen years ago. One day Brigid had returned home from her archivist's training class and her mother, Moira, was gone from the small flat they shared in Cobaltville's residential Enclaves. She found no note, no message of any sort indicating where her mother had gone or why.

She left behind a framed photograph as the only evidence she had ever lived at all. Brigid had been forced to abandon that sole memento when she escaped the barony with Kane, Grant and Domi. In the months following her mother's disappearance, she had made no inquiries into what might have happened to her. People vanished from the ville all the time, their flats never vacant for more than an hour. Asking about it only drew attention.

Years later, when the Preservationists made their first covert contact with Brigid, she had found some small comfort in the remote possibility her mother was associated with the secret society of scholars. But even that hope was dashed when she learned the group of renegades didn't exist, that they were only a straw adversary fabricated many years before by Lakesh to divert the barons from his true insurrectionist activities.

Pitching her voice to a low, unemotional monotone to hide her incredulity, Brigid asked, "How could you be so sure Towasi had stolen your mother's soul?"

Catamount opened her eyes and to Brigid's dismay they glinted with a savage, almost merciless light, not softened by the ribbons of steam. "*He* told me. Through my mother's lips and using her voice, Towasi told me. His body lay entombed in the *Wanagi Awape Yata,* the Place where Souls Wait, bound by the energies of the *tai-me.* Nightingale Woman's soul now waited there. My mother's body now played host to a *baykok.*"

Brigid shifted position slightly, intrigued in spite of herself. "I've heard that word before, but I don't know what it means."

"It means 'demon who comes in the night,'" Catamount said in a soft, almost sibilant voice. "A creature that was once human, then gave his soul over to the eternal darkness, but at a price. It must ever exist within a flesh vessel. Towasi is dead, but he is also alive and his life is the exact opposite of life as we know it. The *tai-me* kept his body trapped in the cave, and the Medicine Wheel confined his ghost."

As the woman spoke, Brigid fancied she heard the distant beating of a drum, and chanting voices, as if they echoed from the spirals of steam.

"The Owl Prophet was an evil man in life," Catamount went on. "A sorcerer who cast spells of wickedness for his own enrichment. He played his own people against each other and betrayed all who trusted him, who paid heed to his counsel."

Brigid shut her eyes and in an instant, an image flashed full-blown into her mind. She glimpsed a dancing figure, raising and lowering his fringed arms like a great bird as he stamped his feet to the drum's thumping. She tried to make out the figure's face beneath shadows of an elaborate feathered headdress fashioned to resemble the head of a great horned owl.

His features were hatchet sharp, his complexion a deep reddish brown, seamed and creased like old parchment or discolored oilcloth. His deep-set eyes glowed with a hellish yellow flame, smoldering like evil stars in an empty universe. The flame spread from the sockets and melted away the wrinkled flesh, revealing a mask of naked white bone. Then all Brigid saw was a grinning skull floating in a sepia sea, a skull of ivory in which sparks of livid red flame danced in the shadowed sockets.

Heart pounding against her rib cage like the wings of a terrified bird, Brigid snapped her eyes open and straightened, sending little waves of the warm water sloshing up over the edge. Catamount's eyes were still closed as if she were in a trance, and Brigid wondered if she might not be somehow telepathically transmitting her own subjective image of Towasi into her mind.

Or, Brigid reflected with a surge of unease, Towasi had done it himself.

"Only I knew what he had done to my mother," Catamount went on in a flat, dispassionate voice. "He had entered her body while her spirit had trod the path of the Great Mystery. He fooled my father with his imposture, he tricked the entire tribe, but he didn't trick me. I knew it was his ghost speaking when others heard only Nightingale Woman's sweet voice."

The unease Brigid felt built into fright. She speculated that Catamount's empathic talents would have enabled her to see through a psychic masquerade such as the one she described. Or she was simply mad.

"Towasi whispered to me what he wanted me to do," Catamount said, "if I wished to rescue my mother's spirit from an eternity of wandering. He wanted me to remove the *tai-me* from the Place where Souls Wait and so free his ghost. I beseeched Spotted Hawk to do as he bid, but he didn't believe me. He punished me for suggesting such a transgression. He thought I had lost my mind."

She uttered a short, mirthless laugh. "Would that I had. The fear that my mother's soul was lost consumed me. I couldn't sleep or eat. I began to waste away. I couldn't abide the thought of that thing, that *baykok,* inhabiting the body of Nightingale Woman and laughing in secret at the way it had deceived everyone. When no one was around, he would sing to me."

In a haunting, almost ethereal voice, Catamount sang, "'It is I who travel in the winds, it is I who whisper in the night, I shake the trees, I shake the earth, I trouble the waters on every land.' In my mother's voice, he would sing his song to me, like a lullaby."

Brigid's shoulders quaked in a shudder.

Catamount stared levelly at Brigid, not really seeing her. "Finally, a plan occurred to me. I pretended I had been ill with brain fever and now I was better. I began to eat again and sing and smile. After a month, my father and the rest of the tribe forgot all that I had said about the Owl Prophet and the lost souls and my mother. Then one night, while she—*it*—slept in my father's arms, I took a knife and placed it against her throat—"

As she had done earlier, she stopped speaking abruptly. After a few moments of staring unblinkingly into the mists rising from the surface of the hot spring, Catamount said matter-of-factly, "No need to tell you what happened next. The Crow elders were enraged and decided to put me to death, to burn me. I didn't care, because I had driven Towasi's ghost back into the Place where Souls Wait, trapped again by the *tai-me* and the Medicine Wheel.

"But my father wouldn't allow me to die. Knowing

it meant a death sentence even for him, he stole me away from the Crows. He brought me to his Lakota village, where he had been born but had not returned to since meeting Nightingale Woman. There we met Sky Dog."

A faint smile touched the corners of her lips, and the hard glint in her eyes softened. "He paid both my father and I a great deal of attention and deference, particularly me. It became a joke, the Dog slavering after the affections of the Cat, but I was still a maiden and was smitten by him.

"Spotted Hawk had always been well-liked among the Lakota, and so it didn't take long before he became the shaman of the village. He refused to name his wife or where she was, and so that only added to his mystique. Sky Dog became his pupil and as time passed, the wound in my heart and my father's slowly healed. Sky Dog wooed me ardently. He was in haste to marry, always eager to please me. My father wasn't opposed and wished for grandchildren, but he wanted to complete Sky Dog's training before we wed."

Brigid asked quietly, "Were you angry that Spotted Hawk groomed Sky Dog to take his place as shaman when you had inherited some of your mother's abilities?"

Catamount shook her head. "I didn't want those abilities, not after what I had gone through. Nor was I content to be a mewling maiden, waiting endlessly for a husband, but I bore no anger toward Sky Dog or my father. But I knew I would have to tell Sky Dog our story before we wed."

Brigid felt her heart jerk in sympathetic pain. "What was his reaction?"

Catamount sighed. "Before I could do so, the village was attacked by Roamers. My father and I had been in the woods, collecting herbs. When we heard the gunshots, we ran toward the village and when we saw what was happening, my father told me to run and hide. I struck off across a field and had not gone far when I heard my father cry out. I saw him go down with a bullet in his back. Four Roamers saw me and gave chase on horseback."

She smiled slightly in grim satisfaction. "They caught up to me, the filthy beasts. They thought I was a cringing helpless maid who would offer them no struggle. I killed one of them and wounded two others. But they captured me and took me miles away to their camp with their other captives, girls taken that day from the Lakota and in raids against the Crows. Their leader, who called himself Zule, at first planned to sell me to the band of Roamers led by Le Loup Garou. But he decided to keep me for himself as his own gaudy. I didn't know what that word meant at first, but he showed me. He showed me."

Brigid felt a pang of sympathy for the girl Catamount had been, dragged into a twilight world of savagery far worse than any of the wild animals she had ever encountered.

"I resisted," Catamount continued. "But I wasn't beaten by him. Zule didn't want his property scarred. That would ruin my resale value. Instead he drugged me, forcing liquor down my throat. I was raped three times a day for a week. Then on the eighth day, I managed to break the jug of the liquor he fancied and when he came to me that night, I cut his throat with a shard, then I slashed open his belly and hewed off his cock. I gouged out his eyes and stomped on them. Oh, how his blood spurted across the walls and floor of his tent."

She flashed her teeth in a feral grin. "I'll never forget how it looked, how much of it there was. I danced in it, barefooted. I painted my face, my breasts with it. I took Zule's knife and killed two guards on my way out. I freed the other captive girls and they came with me. We killed other Roamers who tried to stop us. Night fell swiftly. I didn't care about what manner of animal or demon might prowl around in the forest. They couldn't be worse than the Roamers.

"We walked all the way back to the Lakota village. It took us two days. During that time, I sensed we were being stalked by one of the great cats of the wild, but he meant us no harm. He was curious, watching me in particular. When a pursuit party of Roamers drew too close, the cat attacked them and drove them off."

"Deathmaul?" Brigid asked.

Catamount lifted her bare shoulders and a goodly portion of her breasts cleared the water in an indifferent shrug. "Who can say? Perhaps it was another animal entirely or only a figment of my imagination like my talks with Towasi through my mother." Her grin widened into an expression more deranged than feral. "Who can say?"

Brigid's belly slipped sideways at the shadow of dementia suddenly flitting over Catamount's eyes. The woman's self-control and poise were only facades protecting a soul in anguish.

"Everyone in the village had given up me and the other girls for dead," Catamount stated. "They were astonished and suspicious that we had returned. Many of the captive girls were now without husbands, fathers, brothers or even sweethearts. None of the single men wanted them, since they had been defiled by the Roamers. They were expected to become the chattel of the camp and drudge to earn their keep. I protested on their part, saying we had proved in the Roamer camp that we were warriors, not servants.

"Sky Dog wasn't happy with my attitude. He had changed toward me. He didn't say so, but he wondered how many times I had been taken by the Roamers and how much I had struggled. So he reprimanded me for not mourning my father in the way he thought I should, for protesting about all the backbreaking labor in the village being given to the girls I had set free.

"As far as I was concerned, we had killed enemies and taken coup upon them. Those accomplishments should have earned us places of respect among the Lakota, if not membership in a warrior society."

"He didn't see it that way, I guess." Brigid didn't ask a question; she made a statement.

Catamount nodded. "You must know what that is like, being the woman of a famous warrior. You are ever in his shadow."

Brigid repressed the urge to correct her, and instead opted to remain silent.

"I didn't wish to be known only as the consort of the village shaman," Catamount went on, "Not after all I had gone through and with the powers I had inherited from Nightingale Woman. I told Sky Dog this and we quarreled. For many days we argued. During one of those times of conflict, he demanded to know about my mother, claiming Spotted Hawk had mentioned something horrible had happened to her. I told him about Nightingale Woman and Towasi.

"Although he was horrified, I knew he wanted to believe me, but I no longer felt inclined to convince him of anything. I further scandalized him and the tribe by announcing my intention to go on a vision quest. They felt I wasn't worthy of the Grandfather's notice. Sky Dog desperately tried to keep me from doing so. He was very brutal. He struck me, tried to hold me against my will. But I escaped."

Brigid reflected that the Lakota believed the inspiration or messages received through visions was determined in part by the character of the person who sought aid from the spirits. Guilty of matricide, regardless of the reason, Sky Dog didn't feel she would attract sacred energy to the tribe.

Catamount's words came faster now, in short, concise bursts. "I went out in the wilderness and prayed and fasted for three days and nights. I sought the holy path like any warrior in search of a vision. Then a she-cat came to me, a female panther. Her mate was nearby, she said. She told me that the male claimed I was his true mate, and she would fight me for him.

"I was very much afraid at first and fell to my knees and begged for my life. How could I, a naked human girl fight a panther? The she-cat spit at me, called me a coward and struck me. Then a wave of anger overtook me, consumed me, possessed me utterly.

"I remembered the men I had already killed and I knew I was a predator born. My ferocity was not a transitory thing, a thing outside of the true me. It was a deep part of who I was. I knew I could kill effortlessly, as ruthlessly as any beast of prey.

"I proved it once and evermore that night. I slew the she-cat and claimed her pelt as my own and her mate claimed me. Our souls joined."

Brigid knew that in the mind of the Indian, garments made of animal skins retained the semblance of the animal, and the comfort the skin contributed to the body served to increase the warrior's confidence in the close relationship between all manifestations of nature.

"I returned to the village wearing her skin over

mine," Catamount announced proudly. "I felt a wild freedom as if I had been in prison and suddenly saw the bars broken and the table of life spread out with all the foods that had been denied me. Never again would I be the slave to any will but my own. I formed the Lynx Soldiers from the women captives of the Roamers and saw the clear path to avenging the wrong done to me, to my mother."

Brigid said softly, sympathetically, "You have been hurt, but revenge will not ease your pain, believe me. I speak from experience."

The facade of calm and restraint that had been upon Catamount suddenly dissolved. She lunged up from the pool, arched her back and, as water streamed from her nude limbs, screamed at the roof the lodge, "Towasi! I curse you! *Wasicun,* I curse you! Sky Dog, I, Catamount, Nightingale Woman's daughter, curse you! Damnation be upon you forever!"

Catamount swept her gaze over Brigid, her eyes seeming to spark. The cruelty behind them stood out for an instant, naked and raw. "And you, Red-Haired Scholar Girl—you live only to help me gain that revenge. You have the knowledge I seek, that I need. Refuse me and you die!"

Chapter 21

The storm screamed through most of the night, snow-flakes falling in a solid curtain beyond the portal of the cave. Wind-drifted snow piled up high on the far side of the opening, forming a wall they would have to struggle through when the storm ended.

The air in the cavern was stale, rank with wild-animal smell, but there didn't appear to be any sign of recent habitation. By striking flint and steel, Sky Dog managed to get a fire going. The fuel of dried spruce branches and needles was abundant, but not very satisfactory as far as producing heat. The needles crackled and flamed up wildly, lighting up the cave with dazzling yellow flares.

The branches burned out quickly, but the light they produced gave Grant and Kane enough time to give their den a quick examination. For a moment they wondered if they were the first humans to have trod the granite floors. But then they saw the petroglyphs and pictograms decorating the walls, representations of bizarre figures that were blendings of man and animal and even man and bird. A stylized horned-owl motif was repeated several times.

The firelight glinted off mineral deposits embedded in the rough walls—silvery mica, gleaming quartz and even a few twists of milky marble. Fangs of feldspar jutted down menacingly from the rough ceiling. The walls were pocked with holes and bisected by cracks. The atmosphere of the cavern, instead of feeling like a comforting shelter, made Kane's nerves tingle with an almost palpable aura of malevolence lurking in the shadows.

The two men lent their jackets to Laughing Badger and Iron Horse. Once out of the direct bite of the subfreezing wind, their shadow suits kept them comfortable. The five men were hungry, not having eaten since before daybreak as they prepared to embark on the *Crazy Woman*. Although no one complained, Grant's belly growled and gurgled in protest. They sat on rocks around the small fire, feeding it constantly with spruce branches and needles.

Kane felt wrung out and enervated. Even Grant, whose stamina was a little short of superhuman, trembled with fatigue. Despite the exhaustion settling on Kane's body like layer after layer of lead, he asked Sky Dog, "What will Catamount do to Brigid?"

The shaman sat on a small boulder between the two Kit Foxes so as to benefit from their body heat. He threw a handful of pine needles into the fire before saying dolorously, "I wish I knew, Kane. Hopefully Catamount will not harm her."

"You and Carthew both claimed she was a kill-crazy bitch," Kane pointed out.

Sky Dog shifted on the rock uncomfortably. "We may have overstated that. Catamount's temper when aroused is ferocious, but she is not irrational. Not always."

"Why the hell did she capture Brigid in the first place?" Grant demanded. The sudden flare of firelight cast eerie shadow patterns across his dark face. "Of what use is she?"

Sky Dog shook his head. "If Benedict Snow has found a predark installation inside the mountain, perhaps Catamount thinks Brigid's knowledge will be of some use."

"Interesting," Kane commented, a touch of sarcasm in his tone. "Maybe you can enlighten us as to how Catamount could possibly have any idea that Brigid had *any* knowledge about the predark, useful to Snow. Catamount recognized my name when you called it out last night."

The shaman shrugged. "Like I told you, every Indian on the plains knows who the three of you are. You are Unktomi Shunkaha." He nodded toward Grant. "You are Mata Sapa Akucita, the Black Bear Soldier. Brigid is Magasinyanla Wayana Wicincala, the Red-Haired Scholar Girl."

Despite the situation, both Kane and Grant were startled into laughing. "Just a guess, but I don't think she'd be happy with that name," Kane said.

"The point is," Sky Dog went on, "the three of you and your individual skills are well-known. Catamount assumed if Trickster Wolf was in the area, so would Black Bear Soldier and Red-Haired Scholar Girl."

"Maybe," said Kane dubiously, "but Catamount wouldn't have known we were in the area at all—except for you shouting my name loud enough for her to hear."

"I apologized for that," the shaman replied defensively. "I got excited."

"Was it excitement that had you yelling at me to kill her? Why didn't you do it? You were armed."

Sky Dog fixed his gaze on the dancing flames. He didn't seem inclined to answer, but at length he said in a voice like the chip of grated pottery, "Because I could not bring myself to cause her harm."

"Why not?" Grant demanded bluntly. "You said she was your enemy."

"She is. But before that…she was my betrothed."

Sky Dog raised his eyes and flicked them back and forth between the faces of Grant and Kane as if he expected an explosive display of astonishment. Instead, the two men exchanged dour smiles. Iron Horse and Laughing Badger leaned away from him.

"We sort of had a feeling you two had a history," Kane commented with a slight smile.

"Was I that transparent?"

"No," Grant answered. "But we've learned to read signals over the last few years. If you'd really wanted Catamount dead, you would've done it yourself, not ordered Kane to do the deed. You know him better than that."

Sky Dog squeezed his eyes shut to conceal the sudden glimmer of tears in them. In a voice raw with anguish, he whispered, "I suppose I was trying to convince myself that she deserved to die and pass the responsibility of doing it to someone else. I owe it to her. She killed my nephew. But…"

The shaman's voice trailed off and he opened his eyes again, the firelight dancing on them.

"But what?" pressed Kane.

Sky Dog drew in a shaky breath. "I can't hate her. She wasn't always a monster. She's not completely responsible for what she has become."

"Then who is?" Grant inquired.

"Towasi, the Owl Prophet."

Kane's expression became a mask of incredulity. "The dead guy who's not really dead you told us about?"

The shaman nodded. "The very same. But I didn't tell you everything about him."

"I'd say it's about time." Grant's tone didn't sound as if he intended to give Sky Dog the option of refusing.

Sky Dog threw another handful of pine needles into the fire. As flames flared up with a sizzling crackle, he intoned, "The most sinister figure who stalked through the camps of the plains Indians in the midnineteenth century was Towasi, the Owl Prophet. A self-proclaimed medicine man and sorcerer of the Kiowa, he was suspected of having inspired most of their intertribal conflicts and atrocities against white settlers over a period of twenty years."

"How do you know so much about him?" asked Kane.

Sky Dog's teeth flashed in a self-deprecating grin. "I do more than dance around and shake rattles over sick people, Kane. Like Brigid, I'm very curious. I asked questions. And of course, Spotted Hawk, Catamount's father, told me much about him.

"As best as I can determine, the first reference to Towasi dates from the winter of 1866, when a hunting party of Sioux camped here in the Powder River country were cut off from their village by a blizzard. Food ran low and the tribesmen tramped through the deep snow in a desperate attempt to find game. Many of them went snow-blind from having looked too long at the glare of sunlight. One of the blinded hunters was the son of the Sioux chief, Yellow Hand.

"They had heard of a Kiowa medicine man who lived in a cave in Medicine Mountain. He had learned healing through dreams and visions, so they sought him out and found him here."

"Here?" a startled Grant echoed. "You mean on the mountain."

Sky Dog pointed at the floor and the ceiling. "I mean *here*, literally. This was Towasi's lair."

Faintly, at the edge of audibility, came the mournful hoot of an owl. Kane repressed a shudder, his flesh crawling. His spine felt as if the individual vertebrae had been doused in icewater.

"Towasi cured the blinded men," Sky Dog stated, "by chanting and singing a song he said an owl had taught him in a dream. Shortly after that, a grateful Yellow Hand adopted him into the tribe. In a year, he was accorded the same reverence as the chief. His word was law. If he predicted good fortune for the tribe, there was rejoicing, but if the outlook was bad, few war parties went out. No raids against enemies were staged when the outlook was poor.

"Towasi became master of all medicine men of the allied tribes. The other shamans were subordinate to him—they feared him. According to legend, his prophesying went beyond determining the victor in an impending battle, but included how many warriors would be slain and who they were.

"Before a conflict, he would bring all the warriors together in a council fire, where he would chant and pray. Then out of the darkness would come the hoots and cries of an owl. Towasi would interpret their meanings. He claimed his ancestors and even nature spirits spoke to him through his oracle, the owl. From what I've been able to learn, his record for accuracy was pretty close to one hundred percent."

Both Grant and Kane knew the North American Indians believed that the Grandfather had bestowed upon all animals certain outstanding abilities or powers. They believed these abilities could be transmitted to humans who possessed a mental or spiritual rapport with the animals and birds, and those became their totems.

Skeptically, Kane asked, "What was a Kiowa medicine man doing holed up in a cave in Wyoming? Aren't the Kiowa from Texas and New Mexico?"

"Hiding, apparently," announced Sky Dog. "He had been exiled from the band of Chief Islandman, cast forth because of his delving into black magic. Towasi had been charged with stewardship of the *tai-me,* and he sought to loose its full powers, learn all of its deepest secrets. He was convinced it could restore life, so many a child and a woman died screaming on an altar under his hand. He was a fiend in human shape. When the day of reckoning came, he fled from Islandman, leaving the *tai-me* behind."

As Sky Dog spoke, both Kane and Grant experienced a tingling sensation at the back of their necks as if they were being watched. Very distantly they heard the pounding of a drum. Boom, boom, boom. When they strained their ears to try to fix its source, they heard nothing but the crackle of flames and keening of the wind.

Sky Dog said, "As Towasi's influence with the Sioux expanded, his desire to reclaim the *tai-me* grew. He convinced Yellow Hand that the holy stone belonged to all Indians, not just the greedy Kiowa. If they took it from Islandman's band, then he, the great Owl Prophet, would make sure that every red man would benefit from its sacred radiance. So, the Sioux went to war with the Kiowa over a staged incident about trespassing. At Towasi's order and against Yellow Hand's better judgment, they slaughtered many of Chief Islandman's people, butchered them and stole away with the *tai-me*.

"There was much hatred. The plains and forests ran red with the blood of incessant warfare. There were no neutrals—tribes allied with the Sioux were attacked, white settlers, anyone. Towasi's act blossomed into an orgy of atrocities, rape and murder. Yellow Hand regretted heeding the words of the Owl Prophet, but he couldn't make peace with Islandman after what Towasi had done—which was what the Owl Prophet had intended all along. Yellow Hand had been manipulated into being the instrument of Towasi's revenge."

"Why didn't Yellow Hand just give the damn rock back to the Kiowa?" Grant asked.

"He feared Towasi's mastery of the *tai-me*," explained the shaman. "Towasi had learned all the secrets pent up in the icon, the power of ancient worlds and dead chiefs. But Yellow Hand appealed to a bluecoat soldier chief, who acted as a mediator and arranged for the return of the *tai-me* to Islandman. To get the stone from the Owl Prophet, the Sioux tried to poison him. They took him out onto the plains and left him. He was sick for days and lay near death, but did not die. When he recovered, the return of the *tai-me* had been completed and Towasi found himself an exile a second time."

"Why didn't the Sioux kill the sneaky son of a bitch when they had the chance?" Grant demanded.

Sky Dog frowned. "They feared that while the *tai-me* was in his possession, he had begun to walk the Black Road and so his powers were too great. He began to wander from place to place, tribe to tribe, still lusting after the *tai-me*. As filthy as a pig and repulsive to look upon, he was involved in so many intertribal conflicts over a period of the next fifteen years, he was suspected of inspiring most of them. Towasi aided first one tribe, then the other, betraying each one as it fitted his purposes…and that was ever and always to regain possession of the *tai-me*.

"Finally, when his actions drew down the wrath of the *wasicun* military, both the Sioux and the Kiowa decided to rid themselves of the creature. They tempted him with the *tai-me*, letting it be known they would give it back to him if he could cast a spell to drive away the white man. Yellow Hand would meet him at the cave where his son first met him, many years before.

"Towasi surely must have suspected a trick, but he so coveted the stone, he disregarded his own sense of caution, of self-preservation. When he arrived back here, he was shown the *tai-me*. While his attention was enraptured, he was made a prisoner. He was tortured for many days and buried alive within a hidden chamber inside this very mountain. A holy symbol was built atop it, to contain him and the *tai-me*, which was buried with him."

"The Medicine Wheel?" Kane ventured, feeling a chill finger of dread stroke the back of his neck. He still fancied he could hear the distant beat of the drum.

Sky Dog nodded. "But Towasi didn't die as a man would die. The *tai-me,* though penting him up, had granted him a form of eternal life by turning him into a *baykok.* Now you can understand why I fear what the millennialists will release with their tampering."

"You don't really believe all of this, do you?" asked Grant, a hint of unease in his voice. "Most of it sounds like word-of-mouth legends. Ghost stories."

Sky Dog didn't reply for a long time. When he did, his voice was curiously hushed. "I may have been born in Cobaltville, but all Native Americans share a common heritage, no matter how much the different tribes war among one another. I don't blame you if you don't believe me. *I* don't want to believe in such tales. But the places and things of power must be preserved, for the sake of Grandmother Earth. The holy spots cannot be defiled. If the places and things and power are destroyed, then the *maxpe*—life circle—will be broken and all will be destroyed."

Kane studied the shaman's dark, clean-shaven face, noting absently how hardship had carved his face into inflexible lines. Sky Dog had lived in Cobaltville's Tartarus Pits until he was fifteen. After his father died, he, his sister, brother and mother were cast out. A Magistrate used a knife to dig the ID chips out of their forearms so they could never return. The ID chips were tiny slivers of silicon injected subcutaneously into all ville residents. They responded positively to scanners at checkpoints.

Sky Dog and his family had wandered for a long time. His sister was murdered by a Roamer gang, and his mother died of radiation poisoning after crossing a hellzone. When he and his brother were accepted into the mixed band of Lakota and Cheyenne living near the Bitterroot Range, Sky Dog accepted their belief system wholeheartedly.

Like most Indians, he believed the earth was not inanimate. It was a living entity, and everything in nature was alive, from birds, animals and even the great mountains. All were united in one harmonious whole. Whatever happened to one affected the others and subtly changed the interlocked relationships of the parts to the whole. The life circle that pervaded and united every creature on Earth was the manifestation of the *maxpe*.

"It has happened before," Sky Dog continued. "Before the purification, many tribes were slaughtered by the *wasicun*. Then the purification wiped out the white world. Even this can be understood. Death is part of the *maxpe*, but Towasi is outside of the circle. He cannot be allowed to wander free again."

The shaman snorted and said contemptuously, "And the scientists and soldiers of the predark—they thought they could build one of their secret bases inside a holy place? Even Indians didn't venture to the top until they had undergone purification rites. And now the millennialists think with their guns, their ambition and their greed and believe they can invade a holy place and take away a prize?"

He spit scornfully into the fire. "Blind fools rushing to their doom."

Kane didn't feel it an appropriate time to comment on Sky Dog's melodrama. He said quietly, "If that's the case, then I can't see why Catamount and her Lynx Soldiers would throw in with the consortium."

Sky Dog nodded, his expression suddenly sad. "Catamount has not thrown in with them, so much as she is using them."

"To do what?" asked Grant gruffly. "Free Towasi?"

"No," Sky Dog answered softly. "To free her mother's soul."

Chapter 22

The waterfall glistened with the silvery glaze of moonlight. Following Catamount as they approached the cascade, Brigid tilted her head back to gaze at the top of the cliff and the peaks looming above it. She saw very little detail since dark clouds passed over the face of the Moon every few moments, heralding the approach of a storm.

Catamount's moccasined feet were sure on the damp stones edging the foaming creek. The roar of the waterfall all but deafened Brigid, so she couldn't have heard anyone speak even if they shouted directly into her ear. But she didn't need to hear to know three Lynx Soldiers and Deathmaul padded closely behind her.

The mist from the downpour seemed to wrap Catamount's figure with ghostly fingers, touching the cougar pelt on her head and back with a gleaming dew. The path she followed wended around a tall outcropping, then curved into a deep hollow in the cliffside behind the curtain of crashing water.

It was raven-black between the back side of the torrent and the cave, but Brigid continued walking. She held up a hand before her eyes, but could barely discern its outline even when she faced the waterfall. Suddenly a rod of incandescence pierced the darkness, like a spear made of white light. Brigid flinched, squinting, but she glimpsed Catamount with a flashlight in her right hand.

After her eyes adjusted to the glare, Brigid saw Catamount standing beside a table-sized boulder. On the ground at its base a small, metal-walled box lay open. The chieftain of the Lynx Soldiers beckoned to her sharply with the flashlight and they continued walking. Brigid followed, occasionally confused by the writhing shadows. The path curved toward the cliff and narrowed as it did so.

Halting before the rock wall, Catamount played the beam of the flashlight over the deep fissures. A wavery funnel of red light suddenly sprayed out from a crack and washed over her face, encircling her left eye with a blood-hued halo. After a few seconds, barely audible over the thunder of the waterfall, a grinding rumble arose. A rectangular section of the cliff, no more than seven feet tall by four wide, slid aside. Catamount threw Brigid a sly, mocking smile.

Brigid's expression remained neutral. Her first surge of surprise at the sight of the concealed technology faded quickly. If Medicine Mountain contained a COG facility, then the lack of several secret exits and entrances would have been the true surprise.

Catamount strode through the opening. Brigid hesitated, but when a hand pressed against her back, she fell into step behind the chieftain. As she passed the rocks framing the entranceway, she rapped them experimentally with her knuckles. As she had suspected, they were fake, made of cunningly crafted resin.

Beyond the door stretched a concrete-stepped stairway, almost seeming to rise straight up. Every twenty feet or so, neon strips in the ceiling cast a feeble illumination. Catamount began climbing. Brigid, having no choice, did the same, not bothering to glance over her shoulder to see if the two women and puma were following. She knew they were.

Catamount hadn't offered any intelligence about the Millennial Consortium or the predark installation built inside the mountain, but Brigid hadn't really expected her to. Although half-mad, the woman was quite intelligent and didn't care to appear ignorant of anything to a stranger. Catamount wanted to keep her off balance and guessing for as long as she could.

Brigid understood that attitude. In her former life as an archivist, it was one she had assumed herself. It didn't derive so much from ego as from a sense of self-preservation, a defense and therefore survival mechanism.

The longer they climbed the stairs, the higher they went, the colder it became. Just as Brigid's knee joints began to protest the strain put upon them, the stairway led into a short tunnel and the cold air turned their breath to steam. Catamount made her way up the steep slant, leather-shod feet slipping and sliding on the snow-wet concrete.

Brigid, the two Lynx Soldiers and Deathmaul climbed through the passage and onto a rock-strewed plateau. It leveled off in a series of narrow terraces. A flag-stoned path wound among a cluster of stone cairns constructed of flat, interlocking rocks. A light snow drifted down from the cloud-clotted sky, but the Moon still provided sufficient illumination to light their way. Despite the chill wind gusting up over the peak, Catamount didn't appear to be cold although she breathed deeply, her bare bosom heaving.

"What are we doing here?" Brigid asked.

"Silence," Catamount snapped haughtily, turning away from her.

The path widened into a miniature walled plaza, lined by leaning timbers carved with pictograms. The detail work had long ago been scoured into illegibility by the harsh wind and the merciless hand of centuries.

They passed through the plaza and stopped in a clearing among the stones. No snow lay on the ground. No lichen, grass or moss grew on the earth, almost as if it had been blighted in some way. In the center of the bare patch spread a wheel-shaped pattern of stones about ninety feet in diameter. A central cairn rock served as a hub and from its base projected stone spokes. Beyond it yawned a steep precipice that dropped hundreds of feet straight down to the Bighorn River valley.

The clouds passed away from the face of the Moon and bathed the Medicine Wheel in a dim but gleaming glow. Gazing at the arrangement of stones, Brigid sensed that the air pulsed around them, like the slow beating of a heart.

"Below the wheel," said Catamount, her voice barely above a whisper, "a demon sleeps."

She strode swiftly away from the Medicine Wheel, following an almost invisible pathway that skirted it. It pitched down to a trail. Brigid and the others followed Catamount, moving carefully. There were places where they had to inch sideways, their toes protruding over the edge. The trail grew steeper and more rocky, winding in and out among crags and boulders.

Abruptly, it opened up onto a wide tierlike ledge. The stone and dirt underfoot were exceptionally smooth. The silence atop Medicine Mountain was unbroken except for the wail of the chill wind. Catamount stood facing the slate wall of the mountainside, waiting impatiently with arms crossed over her breasts and tapping her foot.

Mystified, Brigid was about to ask a question when the wall suddenly quivered and a straight vertical crack split the naked stone. Slowly, smoothly, the slate wall began slide to the left. Faintly came the sound of buried machinery, gears, chains and the prolonged hissing squeak of hydraulics.

Stepping back, Brigid managed to maintain a poker face as she stared at the twenty-foot-wide door in the mountain. It opened slowly but smoothly, revealing a hangar-sized and well-lit artificial cavern beyond. A dozen men stepped out, all wearing identical dun-

colored uniforms, zipped up tightly to their throats.
They were armed with the same kind of tranquilizer rifles she had seen earlier, but they aimed them only at
her.

A large figure appeared in the center of the doorway.
Because he was backlit, Brigid couldn't make out his
features but she heard a raspy, whispering voice say,
"Magasinyanla Wayana Wicincala. Red-Haired Scholar
Girl. Brigid Baptiste. I could scarcely believe my good
fortune when Catamount told me you were in the vicinity. I violated company policy to bring you here alive,
and I'm risking a written reprimand. I hope you can appreciate that."

Chapter 23

The rock was cold in the first few minutes after dawn, and so the five men didn't linger on it for any longer than necessary. Grant, Sky Dog, Kane, Iron Horse and Laughing Badger struggled up the rough trail that stretched to the brow of the ridge. In the dim early-morning light, it looked like only mountain goats could possibly scale it, but their fingers clutched at the ribbed surface of the cliff and found numerous footholds.

It was still an arduous climb, because the cliff bulged outward near the crest of the ridge and the strain on their muscles and tendons became almost unbearable. More than once, a hand- or toehold slipped and one of the men escaped falling only by a convulsive grab at stone.

The five people had spent a bone-chilling and virtually sleepless night in the cave, even though the storm tapered off completely by midnight. When the first roseate glow of dawn lightened the eastern sky, they roused, rubbed snow on their faces to bring them to full alertness and began climbing. Their objective was the tier where they had glimpsed the open door in the mountainside the night before.

By the time they pulled themselves over the crest of the ridge, the sun was a full handsbreadth above the horizon. Sunsets and dawn were always spectacular in the Outlands, due to the pollutants and radiation remnants still lingering in the upper atmosphere. The five men sat and tried to appreciate the beauty of the sunrise as they caught their breath, drawing painfully cold air into their aching lungs and releasing it in steamy plumes.

"How long do you figure it'll take us to get to where we're going?" Grant husked out.

Sky Dog craned his neck, studying the face of the mountain and the narrow paths cutting between crags and outcroppings. "If we're trying to sneak up on them, a couple more hours. If we assume they already know we're here, then considerably less."

"I for one am making that assumption," Kane said with a lopsided grin. "If nothing else, the millennialists handed us a major ass-kicking. So much for our reps."

Grant nodded in grudging agreement. "We underestimated them. I won't make that mistake again."

Kane shrugged fatalistically. "Maybe we've gotten overconfident and started relying on our gear and tech, instead of our own resources. The resolution of every situation doesn't always boil down to a matter of overwhelming firepower."

Grant arched a questioning eyebrow. "What resources?"

Tapping the side of his head and then his chest, Kane replied, "Wits and guts, guts and wits. That's what has kept us alive the last few years, more than anything else. I don't want to get locked into a mind-set where we rely solely on our guns and things that go boom to complete a mission."

"Good thing, too," Grant replied glumly. "Since we've lost our guns and things that go boom."

Sky Dog chuckled. "We'll make a Lakota of you yet."

Grant glanced at him, then over at Laughing Badger and Iron Horse. "You mean we're not?"

Looking up at the peaks looming above them, Kane grimaced, then smiled ruefully. If Domi was with them, she would have scampered over the summit by now. Grant compared her climbing abilities to those of a scalded monkey.

Pushing himself to his feet, Grant announced brusquely, "Let's get back to it. We're burning daylight. The sooner we get up there, the better the chance we have of finding something to eat."

"What kind of chance is that?" Sky Dog asked grimly.

Grant shrugged. "Around one percent."

Kane forced a grin. "Our favorite."

Grant returned the grin, though a little sourly. It was a private piece of philosophy between the two men, from their long careers as Magistrates. Their half-serious belief was that ninety-nine percent of things that went awry could be predicted and compensated for in advance. But there was always a one percent margin of error, and playing against that percentage could have lethal consequences.

He turned and breached the unspoken protocol observed between him and Kane by taking point. In their dozen or so years serving as Magistrates together, Kane almost always assumed the position of point man. When stealth was required, Kane could be a silent, almost graceful wraith. In a dangerous setting, his senses became uncannily acute, sharply tuned to every nuance of any environment. It was a prerequisite for survival he had learned in a hard school.

Kane didn't say anything as Grant literally began clawing his way up the mountainside. He simply fell in behind him. They struggled around and over twisted rock ridges that thrust out from splintered granite.

Kane blessed the gloves of his shadow suit many times. Without them, his and Grant's hands would have been raw and blistered. He didn't envy the three Lakota, but he did admire their unwavering stoicism in the face of such exertion.

Their progress slowed the higher they climbed, as the pitch grew steeper. As they scrambled over boulders, more than once they started miniature avalanches. Finally, after what felt like a rope of intertwined eternities, Medicine Mountain's pinnacle blotted out the sky and the bottom of the wide shelf of rock overhung their heads by a scant twenty or thirty feet. There didn't seem to be any way to reach the top of it.

The five men looked, examined, studied and concluded the only way to reach the tier other than back-tracking and scaling the mountainside from another angle was to climb up through a cleft in the granite. The cleft looked to be about six feet wide with the two faces parallel all the way up. Climbing back down would be just as hard and far more time-consuming than at least trying to keep going.

They rested for a few minutes, drew deep breaths and then wriggled one by one into the cleft. Wedging their backs against one wall, they walked up the other until their bodies were braced tight, supported by the friction of their shoulders and feet. The process was laborious and painful, pushing their bodies higher with their arms, then planting their feet firmly against the stone. Inch by inch, Grant, Kane, Sky Dog, Laughing Badger and Iron Horse wormed their way up the cleft.

The procedure of locking the knees, forcing the feet upward, scraping and pressing their backs against the rough rock became a set of automatic, machinelike motions. Grant was in the lead and Kane tried not to worry about what would happen if he lost his grip and fell. The domino effect would be devastating. Iron Horse, bringing up the rear, would be crushed beneath all of their falling bodies.

Despite the cold, sweat formed on Kane's face in a clammy film and soaked his hair. None of the men had any breath or strength to speak to one another. The only sounds were the scuffing of feet, the rustle of fabric and soft grunts of exertion.

Finally, Grant reached the top rim of the narrow channel of rock. He paused, took a deep breath, then twisted and heaved his body around. He rolled onto the solid ledge and lay there, gasping in lungful after lungful of air. Although his limbs shook with the strain put upon them, when he saw the crown of Kane's head appear, he reached down and secured a tight grip on his partner's upper arms. He fell backward and Kane came with him, flying up out of the opening like a cork popping from the neck of a bottle.

Staggering to their feet, they helped Sky Dog and the Kit Foxes one at a time out of the cleft. Panting, massaging his shoulder muscles, Sky Dog commented, "I certainly hope we can find an easier way down."

Wiping at the sweat on his face, Kane surveyed their surroundings. Even his eyes ached. They stood on a wide flat ledge that stretched between shattered rocks on their left and the mountainside on their right.

"Now what?" Grant asked.

"We try to find the door we saw last night."

"And what will we use as a key to get it open?"

Kane's lips quirked in a half smile. "Guts and brains, brains and guts."

Grant glowered at him. "Are you saying that's what we'll use, or that's all that will be left of us by the end of the day?"

There was a whispered sound, as of air gushing through a small opening. A faint, fine mist sprayed out from the cliff face over their heads. Although all five men reacted to the sound by jumping and swearing, there was nowhere to run. They stood rooted to the spot. Warm air rushed over Kane, seeming to envelop him like an invisible cloak. Sky Dog cried out garglingly, throwing his arms up before his face. He twisted, falling down.

Laughing Badger and Iron Horse stared at the shaman in horror, then they fell, too, as if struck by invisible clubs. Kane turned and then went down, arms and legs asprawl. It wasn't as though he fell. He felt more as if he were being pushed down by immensely strong hands.

He glimpsed Grant wheeling around, then striking the ground hard. He snarled, "That goddamn gas again!"

Kane knew his friend had blurted the truth. They had either triggered a hidden release or someone had opened a valve on a concealed canister. He heard the clanking sound of huge gears and the prolonged hiss of pneumatics from behind him. Slowly he turned his head just as half a dozen men rushed through an opening in the side of the mountain.

Helplessly, lying like a sick dog on the ground, Kane stared up at the men surrounding him. They wore the familiar dun-colored uniforms. Their heads and faces were enclosed in transparent plastic masks, worn over goggles and inhalers.

Grant struggled frantically, managing to lift his body to his hands and knees, but he could rise no farther. Between clenched teeth, he rasped, "We underestimated them again."

Then a foot stomped him between the shoulder blades, slamming him hard against the rock. The airs left his lungs in a hoarse, strangulated bellow. After that, he made no other movement.

Hands removed Kane's combat knife from his belt, and he glimpsed Grant being similarly disarmed. He felt himself being lifted and placed on a wheeled gurney. He kept his eyes opened a slit as he was rolled across the ledge toward the wide square opening in the mountain-side. He glimpsed Grant, Sky Dog and the two Kit Foxes being borne on wheeled litters beside his. The Lakota seemed to be unconscious.

When they had been rolled inside the square cavern, the slate walls closed, sliding back into place with a rumble and a creak of gears. Once they were inside the artificially lit cave, at a double-time pace the men pushed the gurneys to an elevator inset into the far wall. The lift was huge, Kane noted, built to accommodate cargo the size of a Sandcat.

A pair of heavy doors rumbled shut, and an overhead light came on. The lift had its own power source and Kane saw the car was almost the size of a Sandcat's interior.

Cables squeaked and ratchets clicked and the elevator plummeted downward at breathtaking speed, making Kane's stomach feel as if it was rising into his throat. The six men in coveralls removed their headpieces but didn't speak. They were all of a similar type, fair of complexion and hair, presenting very businesslike, professional demeanors.

There was no malice in their clean-shaved faces, only a calm resolve. They didn't look like they were born in the Outlands. Kane lay still and silent, not even attempting to speak or to taunt them as he had done with captors in the past.

The elevator didn't seem to slow in its descent. Instead of easing to a halt, it slammed to a teeth-rattling stop. One of the men announced crisply, "Right, let's get it done quickly now. Get them to holding so they can recover. Mr. Snow will want to talk to Grant and Kane as soon as they're able."

Kane felt a queasy, almost humiliating sense of flailing madly in very deep water, of having been outmaneuvered by the consortium yet again. He tried to find solace in the knowledge that Catamount had probably apprised Snow of their presence.

He could hear a high-pitched whine, distant and faint. Then the heavy elevator doors parted and slid back smoothly as the whine became almost deafening. It cut into Kane's eardrums like a surgeon's scalpel. The men pushed the gurneys out, trotting in their double-time gait as a white glare stabbed into his eyes from overhead.

He squeezed his eyes shut, then after a few moments, opened them by degrees. He couldn't see much, but what he did see caused his breath to seize in his throat in stunned amazement. He, Grant, Sky Dog and the Kit Foxes were being rolled through an underground city, but instead of paved streets, Kane saw the gleaming rails of tracks, lacing out in every direction.

Monorails thundered along them, coming and going through a labyrinth of elevated tracks and tunnels. Fluorescent tubes stretched across the high ceiling, blazing with a white incandescent light.

A door in a rock wall slid open. The consortium agents rolled Grant and Kane into a room, the ceiling made of vaulted brick. The men pushed the gurneys into the center of the room, then turned and went out the door, which closed silently.

Within a minute and after a few faltering attempts, Kane sat up, noting absently the millennialists had timed their exit perfectly. He saw Grant lying beside him, but no sign of the Lakota. He assumed they were probably unconscious, not protected from full exposure to the gas to the extent he and Grant had been by their shadow suits.

Kane swung his legs onto the floor and though he felt a bit weak-kneed, they held him up. He called to Grant, "It's just you and me here. Can you move yet?"

Grant shifted slowly, voicing a profanity-salted groan. "More or less. Goddamn nerve gas."

Glancing around the bare-walled room, Kane said quietly, "This place is probably under surveillance. For the time being we better act like we're still suffering from the effects."

Massaging his forehead with the heels of his hands, Grant croaked, "Who's acting?"

"Do you have a better idea?"

Grant shoved himself into a sitting position, teeth bared. He climbed off the gurney, stumbled, caught himself, then slowly straightened. "Yeah, I do. Let's make like birds and get the flock out of here."

Kane gestured toward the wall. "They brought us in through that door there. Let's see if we can open it."

As they crossed the room on unsteady legs, Grant asked, "Where's Sky Dog and the other guys?"

Kane shook his head. "I have no idea. They separated us for some reason."

They reached the wall and stared at the door. It appeared to be a single slab of metal inset into solid rock. There was no sign of a knob or a handle, or even hinges.

"There's got to be a button or switch somewhere," Grant muttered, stepping forward and running his hands along the door edges and framing.

"They opened the door from inside when they left us here. Maybe a lever or something at floor level?"

The two men gazed about on the floor. Grant shook his head. "Nothing. I guess we'll have to come up with a real escape plan."

In frustration, he struck the door with the heel of his fist. Instantly, the door glided open. Grant gaped in astonishment, eyeing his fist.

"Now that's what I call real planning," Kane commented dryly.

Grant opened his mouth to speak, then closed it again when three coverall-clad men stepped forward, the sub-guns in their hands trained on them.

Kane sighed. "Forget what I said about real."

Grant nodded grimly. "Done."

Chapter 24

The armed men prodded Kane and Grant ahead of them along the narrow walkways that paralleled the narrow-gauge monorail tracks crisscrossing the entire breadth and length of the facility.

Although it didn't seem as immense as it had when they were wheeled through it on gurneys, the installation was a bustling beehive of activity with small shifter engines of the monorail trains zipping back and forth. They raced past, the flatcars loaded with crates, disappearing into perfectly round, metal-collared tunnels perforating the walls.

The whine of many electric motors was painfully loud, as the walls, floor and ceiling all formed a gigantic hollow cube that echoed with the engine noise. The white light glinted from stacked metal crates, and elevated boom arms stretched out over the floor, cables and winches dangling from them.

They saw groups of men and women working at small platforms, unloading items from the train's flatcars, placing them on long trestle tables. Other people stood by with clipboards, consulting sheets of paper and making check marks. Although they wore the standard dun-colored garb, the workers didn't resemble the other consortium agents. Their faces were sallow and haggard, their ages and ethnicities extremely varied. Grant and Kane guessed they were refugees from the villes, taken prisoner from the convoys and forced into slave labor.

Kane walked casually on an oblique course that brought him close enough to look at the contents of the trestle tables. They held stacks of gold and silver bars, even small towers of plastic-wrapped coins and open cases of glittering gems. He experienced a surge of confusion, then realized the installation was less a Continuity of Government facility than a storage warehouse or giant vault.

One of the consortium escorts jabbed a gun barrel into the small of his back, and he obediently turned away from the tables. Kane didn't feel sufficiently recovered from the neurogen to attempt to overpower the guards. He assumed Grant didn't feel up to it, either.

The man didn't speak, but jerked his head toward an adjacent, white-tiled hallway. The incessant whine was somewhat muted in the corridor. Grant and Kane were marched down the hallway, past a number of ordinary-looking wooden doors equipped with card-swipe locks. A sign hung on the wall, written in faded red letters reading Know Your Emergency Exits!

Neither man doubted he was within a COG installation, but unlike other predark bases and redoubts they

had visited, it didn't have the sense of ever being occu-
pied. Most of the others were grimly depressing places,
haunted by the ghosts of a hopeless, despairing past age.
This one didn't possess that disquieting ambiance.

The corridor curved toward a set of double doors.
One of the men pushed the right-hand door open and
gestured for Kane and Grant to enter. The millennialists didn't follow.

The door closed behind them and they were alone in
a green-hued grotto of a room. The walls were painted
green and the fluorescent tubing cast a soft chartreuse
hue. Across the room, at the far wall, they saw a three-
foot square of glass. Without speaking they walked toward it. The glass wasn't opaque or a monitor screen.
It was more like a window looking onto the blackness
of deep space.

When Kane rapped on it with his knuckles, it gave
forth a hollow echo.

"Please don't do that, Mr. Kane. It's disrespectful to
my conversation piece."

The subdued voice spoke from behind them. The
two men whirled as a door in the opposite wall closed.
For an instant, they glimpsed a suite of incomparable
luxury, all done in restful hues of pale blue, violet and
tan. Then the door closed and they concentrated on the
figure walking toward them.

He was an unforgettable-looking man. His most
striking feature was his high, pompadoured mop of
snow-white hair, edged at the temples with jet-black. He

was also almost blind. His eyes appeared monstrous, magnified behind thick lenses in round, black-rimmed goggles. He was a big man, well over six feet, but his body was pear shaped, his legs round like gourds. He moved languidly, as if he were underwater.

Every motion appeared to exert him, and he breathed loudly with each step, gasping wetly through an open mouth. He wore military-green coveralls, zippered tightly over his swelling paunch. Fleece-lined slippers enclosed feet that looked far too small for his rotund form. His complexion was a waxy gray, a kind of dark pallor that lent him a ghostly, almost translucent appearance in the green light. Still, he held himself as erect as possible. He gave the impression of a man of consequence.

"You must be Benedict Snow," Kane said calmly.

The big man continued to walk forward, in a strange, hobbling gait. Thrusting his head forward, he peered at them through the thick lenses of his goggles. "I am he," he said, his voice a raspy whisper. "And I know who you are. Your infamy has spread far."

"We're flattered you know us," Grant said. "But to what do we owe a personal audience with you?"

The round man paused to draw in a deep breath, then he spoke slowly, gaspingly, "I want to extend a word of caution. You have been watched since you first showed up on the mountain ledge. Unless you get the kind of ideas that will prove fatal for you, you will continue to be watched and not harmed…at least for a time. So don't get any ideas that we're alone in here."

"It never occurred to us we *weren't* under observation," Kane replied. "We pretty much figured we were expected."

Snow inhaled deeply and exhaled. "But you came on anyway, letting yourselves be captured. Fools."

"And that makes you angry at us?" Grant inquired, raising an ironic eyebrow.

The stout man nodded emphatically, wheezing. "I don't like distractions."

The corner of Kane's mouth crooked in a mocking smile. "Is that what we are?"

"Not anymore," Snow replied. "I understand you are responsible for killing one of my men several months ago in Ragnarville. At the time, I was willing to write off that incident as due to an accident of unfortunate timing. I certainly didn't want our paths to intersect. I couldn't afford to have my attention and energies diverted. But now that you're here, I'm afraid that means I must turn the disposition of your cases over to the board of directors."

Snow released his breath slowly, a protracted, laborious sigh. "That's a shame, too. I had hopes you could join me and aid the Millennial Consortium's plans to build a brilliant new world."

"Oh?" Kane asked uninterestedly. "Out of the ashes of the old?"

"Something like that. More of a mixture of the best of the old and new."

"I can't say I'm very impressed with what I've seen so far," Grant commented, needling the round man.

The goggled face turned toward him. "Perhaps that is because you have seen so little. Aren't you familiar with the saying about a little knowledge being a dangerous thing, Mr. Grant?"

"I am," replied Grant. "That's why I'm always looking to have questions answered. And for starters, maybe you can tell us about Brigid Baptiste."

Snow seemed perplexed by the query. "What about her?"

Kane tried to tamp down a surge of worry-fueled anger. "Is she here?"

"Oh," Snow said in comprehension. "I just assumed you knew. Yes, of course she is. Catamount brought her to me last night. She's quite unharmed, I assure you."

Kane clenched his fists. "Where the hell is she?"

"She's busy at the moment, in one of the vaults. Her font of historical knowledge about the predark is proving invaluable in identifying artifacts and relics of which I have found no record. I could only guess at their nature and I hate to guess. It's a shocking habit—destructive to the logical faculty."

"What do you mean she's busy in one of the vaults?" Grant demanded impatiently.

A fatuous smile creased Snow's face. "Pardon me, I'm afraid I misspoke." He waved an arm in semicircular motion. "In truth, this entire facility is a vault."

"We thought it was a COG installation," Kane commented.

"It was part of the program, certainly," Snow conceded. "But not every Continuity of Government base was meant to be inhabited. Several of them, admittedly not very many, were built strictly as storage units. Huge ones, yes, but storage units nevertheless, almost like museums or even banks. They were called Cellar Complexes, a variation of the deep-storage-vault concept."

Neither Grant nor Kane was surprised by the rotund man's admission. They knew the Anthill had been designed to serve as both a stockpile and a bunker for the survivors of the nukecaust. The commander of the Anthill had been inspired by the method of keeping organic materials fresh by pumping a hermetically sealed vault full of dry nitrogen gas and lowering the temperature to below freezing. The internal temperatures inside the installation were lowered just enough to preserve the tissues, but not low enough to damage the organs.

Other scientific disciplines were blended. The interior of the entire facility was permeated with low-level electrostatic fields of the kind hospitals experimented with to maintain the sterility of operating rooms. The form of cryogenesis employed at the installation wasn't the standard freezing process relying on immersing a subject in liquid nitrogen and the removal of blood and organs.

It utilized a technology that employed a stasis screen tied in with the electrostatic sterilizing fields, which for all intents and purposes turned the Anthill complex into an encapsulated deep-storage vault. The process created a form of active suspended animation, almost as if the personnel were enclosed by an impenetrable bubble of space and time, slowing to a crawl all metabolic processes. The people achieved a form of immortality, but one completely dependent on technology.

"There were no personnel here in stasis?" Grant inquired.

Snow hesitated before answering, "No 'personnel,' so to speak." He crooked the index fingers of both hands to indicate quotation marks.

Kane narrowed his eyes. "What does that mean?"

Snow didn't respond to the question. "Cellar Complexes were built to store everything the survivors of the nukecaust would need to rebuild. The plan was that when Earth's surface was safe for habitation again, teams would be dispatched from central redoubts to open up the vaults and distribute the materials therein to rebuild society.

"Paper money of course is useless, but the Cellar Complexes hold tons of precious metals like gold, silver and platinum, gems, works of arts, and even caches of electronic equipment...all protected and shielded from electromagnetic pulses, radiation and fallout in the vaults here. When the day came, they would be unearthed and used as the foundation to rebuild."

Snow's smile became one of triumph. "Of course, that day never came. So now it's up to me and the organization I represent to carry through with the plan."

"To reconstruct the old predark system?" Grant inquired skeptically.

The big man shook his white-haired head. "Hardly. The Millennial Consortium intends to build a new kind of society."

"Based on what?" Kane's tone was cold and accusatory. "It looks to me like the same kind of master-and-slave system as practiced by the barons."

Benedict Snow waved a chubby hand languidly. "Only a temporary situation, Mr. Kane, until we reach our goals. I assure you it's only temporary."

"Right," Grant drawled sardonically.

"I hear your sarcasm, sir, but even you have to agree that some individuals are mentally inferior, born only to be servants. That will never change, regardless of the enlightened nature of any society. Even ancient Athens was served by slaves."

Kane stared at the round man, barely able to keep an expression of disgust from contorting his face. Benedict Snow was another egomaniac, another would-be tyrant who paid lip service to an idealistic cause while lusting to control and enslave his fellow human beings.

"If you're going to divide up your new society into inferiors and masters," Grant rumbled, "then it's just the same old rat race, but with different fat rats running things."

"Those 'things' will be running as they should be at long last," Snow announced dismissively. "We will be organized on business principles, on the corporate model and the doctrine of technocracy."

Kane raised his eyebrows. "The doctrine of what?"

"Technocracy, Mr. Kane. Whereas all other forms of government have their roots in political ideology, philosophy and religion, technocracy has its roots in science. It is, in fact, more of a technological than a political idea. It was first developed in the early twentieth century by scientists, engineers and other specialists seeking to understand the role of high-energy technology in our society, such as electrical generators, large earth movers, manufacturing plants and fast, motorized transportation.

"In short, the conclusion by these specialists was that an industrialized society governed by a council of scientists, of technologists as it were, would be far more productive, less prone toward crime and deviation from the standard and certainly not inclined to bomb itself out of existence."

Kane and Grant exchanged neutral glances. After a moment, Grant ventured, "So the Millennial Consortium is a group of scientists, technocrats?"

Snow nodded. "Essentially."

Kane declared, "Then the question begs to be asked—and answered—why are scientists involving themselves in Indian legends about *baykok*s and magic rocks from the stars?"

Snow pursed his lips. He looked almost embarrassed. "You know about that, do you? Well, even scientists can't deny that certain legends have a foundation in fact. Apparently, the predarkers who built this Cellar Complex discovered the same thing."

Kane cocked his head at him quizzically. "Explain."

Benedict Snow sighed heavily, thrust a slab of a hand into a pocket of his coverall and produced a small remote control box. "Very well."

He pointed it at the black pane of glass and thumbed a key on its surface. "Have yourselves a look at a certain legend with a foundation in fact, the conversation piece to which I alluded earlier. To me, it's just a means to an end."

A yellow light flashed on behind the glass, revealing a small square cubicle, the walls of rough, unfinished stone. Both Grant and Kane felt the hairs lift on their napes and their skin prickle with a sudden chill.

In the center of the cubicle rose a heavy timber, a knot-holed log stripped of its bark, with a pair of broken branches forking out from the top. Lashed to it by rawhide thongs stood a withered, wizened cadaver, the dried brown limbs crossed over the chest and trussed tightly there by the wrists.

The corpse was outfitted with a weird array of trappings—a threadbare buckskin tunic with long, beaded fringe hanging from the sleeves and rotting boot moccasins. On the skull rested a helmet fashioned out of wood and glued-on feathers, made to resemble the beaked head of a horned owl. The face below the beak was virtually a skull. The dry flesh, stretched tight over the bones, had the texture and color of dusty leather, framed by stringy strands of black hair. The lipless mouth peeled back from yellowed teeth, bared in a macabre grin. The eye sockets were empty black hollows.

Fixed to the top of the timber between the forking branches by crisscrossing straps of leather glittered a crystalline object. A yellow translucent stone roughly triangular in shape and the size of a large spearhead; it sparkled dully in the overhead light.

Lances decorated with feathers and beads leaned against the timber to which the cadaver was tied. At its feet lay a circle of stones, the base of the log forming the hub of a wheel. Behind the post, the rocky floor was bisected by a yawning crack, a minimum of four feet in width.

Kane finally got his lungs and voice working again. He dragged in a breath and asked, "Towasi?"

Benedict Snow nodded. "And the *tai-me*. Like I said, only a means to an end."

He didn't sound completely convinced.

Chapter 25

With a gasping grunt, Benedict Snow struggled into the small compartment behind the shifter engine, his broad hips and buttocks completely filling the seat. At a gesture from the guard's subgun, Grant and Kane climbed into the passenger car of the train. As they did so, the bullet-shaped engine suddenly emitted a high-pitched whine.

Hitching around in the seat in front of them, Snow said conversationally, "The monorail system is the only way to get to the many vaults here in the complex. I would imagine it's a standard feature of most COG facilities."

He eyed both men expectantly, as if hoping they would confirm his comment. The Dreamland base where Kane had been imprisoned for two weeks was equipped with a similar system of internal transportation, but he wasn't inclined to share information with the white-haired man, at least not until Snow produced Brigid, alive and unharmed.

The whine rose in pitch, and with a slight lurch the train slid almost silently along the rail. It swiftly built up speed and plunged into one of the tunnels. Overhead light fixtures flicked by so rapidly that they combined with the intervals of darkness between them to acquire a strobing pattern.

As the train sped down the shaft, Snow said, "Finding the mummy of a dead Kiowa medicine man wasn't as much of a surprise to the consortium as you might think. We already knew that the COG planners tended to hide their installations in plain sight, as it were, often in national parks. So the reference to Towasi was actually a vital clue in our search for this place."

Folding their arms over his chests, Grant and Kane regarded him stonily, refusing to be drawn into a question-and-answer session.

Snow didn't appear to notice. "My colleagues and I, the board of directors to be specific, chanced across a very old computer disk that contained a construction-status report about this particular Cellar Complex, but without actually identifying its location. You can imagine how maddeningly frustrating that was to us. The report, dated May 4, 1995, dealt in the main with a discovery made during the excavations—a body and an artifact placed in a ritual burial position, hidden in a niche within the larger cavern."

The rail curved lazily to the right, plunging almost noiselessly into a side chute. Lights shone intermittently on the smooth walls, small drops of illumination that did little to alleviate the deep shadows.

"Rather than remove the body and risk disclosure to

various Senate oversight committees," Snow went on, "the decision was made to seal off the niche for the time being. An archaeologist and ethnologist were consulted and they both shared the opinion that the remains were probably those of Towasi, the Owl Prophet. That was the only specific in the report, the only hard data the consortium had to work with regarding the possible location of this installation."

Interested in spite of himself, Kane asked, "Is that why you were excavating Carver's Cave in Minnesota? Looking for an Indian mummy and a chunk of rock?"

Snow nodded. "Exactly. If we'd found them, then we would have known we were in the right place. Of course, I wasn't the only consortium crew engaged in the search. We had crews performing excavations in a number of Native American sacred sites. Fortunately, it was my own independent investigation that brought my crew here to Medicine Mountain."

"You talked to Sky Dog," Grant grunted.

"He came to question me in Minnesota. Sky Dog denied knowing anything about an Owl Prophet or a stone from heaven. He did, however, speak briefly of Catamount and the Lynx Soldiers, warning me not to come into Powder River country for fear of her. I found his attempt at dissembling and disinformation childish, so I did the exact opposite. I came into this country and sought her out. And she led me here, to Medicine Mountain."

The white-haired man beamed, his goggled face and

upswept hair making him grotesque under the strobing
lights. "Quite the achievement on my consortium
record, if I say so myself. And I do."

"What the hell is the Millennial Consortium?" Grant
demanded loudly and exasperatedly. "Where does the
board of directors come from?"

Benedict Snow's eyes widened behind the lenses of
his goggles, giving him the aspect of a distressed frog.
"Why, I thought you knew, Mr. Grant. We come from
the same places as you two…the baronies."

The train's speed dropped and it hissed to a halt beside a broad platform. An armed man in a khaki uniform
stood sentry there. He watched impassively as the three
men climbed out, then fell into step behind them as they
entered a bare-walled corridor.

"There are seven of us who compose the board of directors," Snow stated in his wheezing voice as they
walked along the passage. He moved with a rolling,
waddling gait. "We were a distaff group of division ad-
ministrators who had spent our lives trying to keep our
respective villes running smoothly. Eventually, we all
reached the conclusion that such a goal was impossible
because the system of government was stupendously in-
efficient. All of us acted as intermediaries with the various independent traders and we saw the need for them
to be organized, like the branch offices of a predark cor-
poration.

"In order for that to be accomplished, we formed the
Millennial Consortium in secrecy five years ago. I

needn't tell you how difficult a task it was to organize the trading groups according to management theory. However, we enjoyed our greatest success with an operation run by a man named Chapman, who, although poorly educated, shared our own appreciation of the corporate model."

Kane and Grant cast surreptitious glances at each other. They had met Trader Chapman a couple of years before when he acted as an ore courier for Baron Cobalt. As far as they knew, he had died during a battle with Ambika's raiders.

Snow went on, "Acting as our agent, Chapman discovered the first Cellar Complex in Utah. It wasn't nearly as large as this one, but what it held financed the consortium's expansion. It was where we found a supply of the nerve gas and a cache of automatic weapons. Not long afterward, the seven of us saw fewer reasons to remain in our positions in the villes. Our cause-and-effect-chain charts indicated the ville system would undergo a major upheaval in the next decade, so we determined to find viable alternatives.

"Over a period of a couple of years, we left the baronies. Some of us faked our deaths—as I did—others bribed Magistrates to look the other way as they left the ville on official business and never returned. The consortium has grown and expanded ever since. And now, with the discovery of this installation, we have the power base we have sought, to build the new society we envision."

"It still sounds like the same old predark society to me," Kane remarked darkly. "Fortunes built on the backs of the unfortunate."

Snow shrugged his down-sloping shoulders. "If your intellects fail to grasp the potential of what the consortium can provide to the world, I'll be glad to explain. Science and technology have given us nearly all of the physical things by which we live. Look around you right now. How many things do you see that were produced by hand, by individual craftsmen? You are surrounded by things that didn't even exist three hundred years ago—most of them that did weren't readily available to the public even two hundred years ago."

"So what?" Grant asked. "It was a reliance on technology that brought about the nukecaust, the skydark."

"No," Snow snapped with a great deal of emphasis. "No, no, *no*. It was a reliance on politicians and the *misuse,* the misunderstanding of science by partisan fools that brought on the nukecaust. Science and technology gave humanity the tools by which humanity could avoid such catastrophes, but the tools were always in the hands of idiots. As it was, when technology was made unavailable to the nukecaust survivors, most of them died off so fast there weren't enough of them left to dig their graves."

Neither man could argue with that statement. Lakesh had told them that nearly as many people died during the skydark—the nuclear winter—as during the actual atomic exchange.

The corridor doglegged to the left, dead-ending against recessed double doors. The air vibrated with the heavy throb of machinery. Two men in khaki coveralls came to swift attention when Benedict Snow and his party approached. Snow didn't so much as nod to them. He continued talking, removing a plastic card from a pocket.

"Does it make sense to you that with nearly twenty percent of the world's land area at our disposal and an ample supply of mineral resources and fuels more than adequate to make our nation the most powerful country in the world again, that we live either under a fragmented dictatorship or worse, anarchy?"

He swiped the magnetic stripe through the lock. As the doors swung open on invisible hinges, he proclaimed, "The baronies have fallen, and today we stand at the crossroads of our destiny. The correct turn will take us to a higher level of life than has ever been experienced in world history. Any other road will lead to genocide through suicide."

Snow, Grant, Kane and the guard strode forward, past the sentries and into a vista of great machines. The walls, ceiling and floor of the chamber formed one continuous surface, making a huge hollow bubble measuring at least a hundred feet in diameter. The curving walls featured built-in shelves, but tall and deep enough to accommodate forklifts and dollies. Most of the shelves held large, metal-walled cargo containers. Elevated loading docks and platforms were connected by a series of cage-enclosed lifts and catwalks.

Conveyor belts rattled, undulating like desert sand in a windstorm, under the weight of the crates stacked atop them. Boom arms swung to and fro. At least fifty people in the khaki coveralls worked feverishly around the belts, pulling the crates off, opening them and unpacking their bubble-wrapped contents, then passing them down in bucket-brigade fashion to others at trestle tables. For every twelve workers, Kane counted one armed millennialist.

Benedict Snow gestured pridefully to the chamber, to the laborers. "The consortium has already given these outlanders marketable job skills. There's no reason why any of them should go without sufficient food, clothing, homes, medical care and other necessities that would guarantee, to all of us, security and a high standard of living from birth to death."

"And you'll give them that?" Grant inquired skeptically.

"You can see it for yourself."

"We see it," Kane remarked. "We just don't know what they're doing or why."

Snow regarded him almost pityingly. "They're performing inventory, cataloging and indexing everything in this facility. We can't very well build our new society until we know exactly what we have with which to finance it, can we?"

Snow walked toward a table where people were engaged in examining various electronic components and jotting down notations in spiral-bound notebooks. The racking, liquid cough of a man caught his attention. He turned toward a skinny balding man doubled up beside the table, hacking convulsively into his fist. When he cleared his lungs, he raised red-rimmed and watery eyes toward Snow in sudden fear.

Solicitously, Snow laid a hand against his forehead. "Oh, you're burning up. We can't have this sort of thing. You're sick. You shouldn't be working."

He turned toward a guard. "Bailey, take him out of here and have him treated at once."

The man straightened, saying hoarsely, "I can work. I haven't made my quota yet."

"Nonsense. You're not well. Go lie down. Don't worry about your quota. Bailey, take him to the break room and treat him to a lie-down."

The guard slung his subgun over his shoulder and pulled the shivering man away from the table, supporting him as they walked toward a short flight of stairs that led up to a second level.

Snow smiled after them. "That's better." Turning to the laborers, he said loudly, "He's a lucky fellow, you know. You all are."

The guard helped him up the stairs and through a door. Within a few seconds came the muffled crack of a gunshot.

"That's right," Snow continued. "A very lucky fellow. He never has to worry about making his quota again."

He strode to the end of the table. Some people, visibly shocked by the shooting, stared at him dumbstruck. Snow raised his voice. "I hope all of you paid attention. You've just seen what happens to slackers here. Nor will we tolerate disobedience. We look after you, we feed you, give you training so you can perform honest work. Now it's up to you show us the respect we deserve.

"We are not monsters or heartless tyrants, but we can be damn hard if we're pushed. You are not slaves. You won't be here much longer. Soon you'll be released and you can either go back to your wasted lives or enjoy the privilege of working toward our great civilizing mission.

"Homes and jobs will be found for you. So until then, do what is asked of you. It is for your own good and that of your future. You may even look back on this place with a certain amount of fondness, as the point in time where you actually started making a contribution to the world instead of taking from it."

Snow paused briefly. "All right, any questions? No? Carry on, then." He clapped his hands sharply and turned back toward Kane and Grant.

"Did you see how I handled that?" he asked. "I did not have that man killed needlessly. He helped make an important point."

"About what?" Grant asked, his voice frosty with disgust.

"I thought that would be obvious. Technocracy as a social design is compatible with our available resources and technology, and one that provides for the distribution of abundance. But in order for that distribution to be efficient, everyone must shoulder their fair share of the load. They'll thank me for this lesson in pragmatic acceptance of the inevitable in the future."

Casting his gaze over the expressions of barely repressed hatred on the drawn faces of the laborers, Kane quickly concluded the only way they would thank Snow, now or in the future, would be with knives in their fists.

In his egotism, Benedict Snow was blithely, serenely unaware of sitting on a powder keg of slowly seething fury. Due to his experience with the denizens of the Tartarus Pits, Kane could sense the collective energy of an uprising in the vault, the same way he sensed the approach of an electrical storm. He didn't need to look at Grant to realize he felt the same energy.

Deciding to add a bit more fuel to the hot embers of anger, Kane asked loudly, "So your workers were abducted from convoys and Outland settlements?"

"*Abducted* is an ugly term," Snow replied. "We borrowed a few months of their lives, but they will be compensated. They'll be better off for it."

A scrawny woman whirled away from the table and screamed, "What about our families? My husband and children are probably dead—"

"That woman!" Snow shouted, stabbing a finger toward her.

Two of the guards converged on her and clubbed at her with the butts of their subguns until she collapsed on the floor, curling up in a fetal position. Grant and Kane made motions to intervene, but subsided when gun barrels were poked into the sides of their heads.

"Steady on!" Snow cried. "That's enough!"

The consortium agents stepped back and after a moment, the woman shakily lifted her head. Blood streamed from a laceration at her hairline, and her left eye was surrounded by puffy, discolored flesh.

Snow stared down at her dispassionately. "Do you feel up to continuing your duties and making your quota, or would you prefer to be treated to a lie-down?"

Without a word, the woman pulled herself to her feet and returned her attention to the items scattered over the tabletop.

"Very good," Snow said approvingly. "Carry on."

He started waddling across the room, Kane and Grant walking on either side of him. Grant inquired, his voice pitched at a volume loud enough to be overhead by anyone within twenty feet, "You know you can't count on the Hell Hounds as your employment service anymore, right? We put them out of business—permanently."

Out of the corner of his eye, Kane noted several heads whipping around toward them, eyes registering happy surprise, followed almost instantly by resentment.

"Yes, so I gathered," Snow retorted with a negligent hand wave. "Catamount killed Carthew so as to keep him from revealing our whereabouts, but it turned out to be a wasted effort."

"Why?" asked Kane.

"After she learned who you were, she reasoned that I would prefer to have you—or at least one of you— brought here alive. She wasn't able to inform me of your identities until after my men had sunk the barge. It was then I decided I could use one of the three of you."

"Which one?" inquired Kane, affecting a tone of ingenuous wonder.

As they came around a conveyor belt, Benedict Snow pointed to a slender coverall-clad female figure standing before a long trestle table. She was engrossed in examining an object shaped like an oversize black egg, but frosted with a patina of diamonds.

"That one," Snow declared.

Brigid Baptiste turned her head toward them. Her sunset-colored mane was tied up in a braided bun, and so the exhaustion stamped on her face like an ivory mask was readily apparent.

"*That* girl," Snow continued, with a titter lurking at the back of his throat. "The red-haired scholarly one."

Chapter 26

"Enjoying yourself, Miss Baptiste?" Snow asked jovially.

Brigid revolved the glittering egg between thumb and forefinger. "Not particularly, no."

"Really?" Snow seemed to be genuinely disconcerted. "As a historian, I thought you would be in your element."

Brigid's eyes flicked between Kane's and Grant's faces, reacting to their contusions and abrasions. "Are you two all right?"

Kane scowled. "Don't we look like it? What's with the new rig, Baptiste?"

For a second, confusion clouded her green eyes, then she glanced down at the dun-colored coverall encasing her body and smiled ruefully. "Uniform of the day."

"Just so," Snow declared. "The uniform of a productive citizen of the new society. Conformity makes it easier for everyone to get along and cooperate with one another."

"Or to keep them in line." Brigid cast her eyes ceilingward. "Has he been proselytizing you two?"

"Damn near nonstop," Grant growled.

"What happened to Sky Dog and the others?" she asked.

"That's what we'd like to know," Kane stated, eyeing Snow challengingly. "Have you put them to work someplace else?"

The white-haired man gusted out a sigh. "We've found the noble savage can't seem to grow accustomed to performing a proper job of work, or of maintaining a regular schedule, of understanding the quota-and-reward system. Rather than waste time teaching or retraining them, we usually take care of them in a different way."

"By execution?" Brigid snapped accusingly. "You don't seem to have the same attitude toward Catamount. Maybe it's her fashion sense."

"Miss Catamount is a different matter," Snow replied stiffly, defensively. "She is a business associate. We have an understanding."

"Which is?" Grant wanted to know.

Snow acted as if he hadn't heard the query. Addressing Brigid, he declared, "You were brought to me because you were a high-ranking archivist in Cobaltville's Historical Division. I have high hopes that you will assist me in identifying some of the more esoteric items stored here." He paused and added in a tone sibilant with menace, "I trust that hope is not misplaced. What have you got there?"

Brigid smiled wanly, cupping the egg gingerly between both hands, as if it were as fragile as spun sugar.

"I believe this is some sort of gas grenade, more than likely holding a nerve or biological agent."

Benedict Snow eyed the object and her dubiously. "Rather an elaborate casing, wouldn't you say?"

"If you doubt me—" She tossed the ovoid object to him, underhanded.

Uttering a squawk of alarm, Snow fumbled to catch it, snatching the egg out of the air. His hands closed around it and the shell popped open on a hidden hinge. A tiny golden unicorn dropped out of it, clinking to the floor. Grant and Kane, who had experienced a second or two of fear themselves, grinned at the expression of befuddlement crossing the rotund man's face.

"It's called a Fabergé egg," Brigid stated, voice purring with amusement. "A collectible among the predark wealthy, a work of art. A goldsmith named Karl Fabergé made his first one way back in 1884 with an Easter egg for Czar Alexander of Russia. It became a gift for his wife, Czarina Maria. From then on it was Fabergé's job to make an Easter egg each year for Maria. Fabergé designed Easter eggs for another eleven years until Alexander III died. Then Nicholas II, Alexander's son, continued the tradition. It was agreed that the Easter gift would always have an egg shape and would hold a surprise."

A taunting smile spread across her face. "Are you surprised?"

Snow nodded and stepped forward, handing the egg back to her. "Very much so."

Then with a speed belying a man of his size and

weight, he struck her backhanded across the cheek, causing her to stagger against the table. He hissed, "How about you, Miss Baptiste? Are *you* surprised?"

Kane felt a flush of rage warming the back of his neck, but he also felt the cold touch of a gun barrel there, too.

"I don't tolerate this kind of tomfoolery in the workplace," Snow snapped. "If you wish to continue your employment—and your life—you may consider that a mild reprimand."

Brigid rubbed the side of her face and glared at Benedict Snow with emerald-hard fury. "So noted."

A harsh electronic buzz cut through the clank and clatter produced by the conveyor belt. Snow's lips twisted in annoyance and from a pocket he pulled a small trans-comm unit. Flipping up the cover, he placed it to his ear and said tersely, "Go."

He listened intently for a few seconds, then frowned. "All right, do what you can to mollify her. If she wants her damn cat, let her have her damn cat. Fetch that Sky Dog fellow, too. Tell her Miss Baptiste and I will be there in short order."

Returning the comm to his pocket, he said with a great deal of exasperation, "Miss Catamount has become troublesome. She insists I live up to my side of the arrangement right now."

"Which is what exactly?" Kane asked. "Supply her and the Lynx Soldiers with Fabergé eggs?"

Snow glanced over at him, lines of anger creasing his

face. To the guards he said, "Put these two men to work. Find uniforms for them. Miss Baptiste, you will come with me."

When Brigid showed no inclination to move, Snow closed a slab of hand around her forearm and pulled her away from the table.

Grant said, "If you want us to work, how about giving us some food first? We haven't eaten in over twenty-four hours."

"Get them protein bars," Snow order curtly as he pushed Brigid past the guards. "Let them eat while they work."

As Benedict Snow marched Brigid across the huge circular vault, the guards made unmistakable gestures with their gun barrels. Grant and Kane had no problem understanding that they were expected to join the other laborers and unload the cargo containers as they rolled along the conveyor belt.

Although they cooperated, neither man worked very hard, despite the fact the task was more monotonous than backbreaking. They were tired, hungry and thirsty and so they did as little actual work as possible, waiting for the food to arrive.

After twenty minutes, they were still waiting, so they tried to strike up conversations with their fellow laborers. They had been ordered not to speak to them, but they disobeyed the command cheerfully. However, they didn't find too many people willing to answer their questions.

Long before the work crew had been captured by the

millennialists, they were accustomed to hard lives not much better than those of serfs. They had been taught from the cradle that dreams of personal freedom were nothing but childish illusions.

The people pressed into slave labor inside the Cellar Complex had hoped that since the fall of the baronies, there would be new options and opportunities to explore. Benedict Snow and the Millennial Consortium intended to severely limit the options of personal freedom, just as the barons had done. It filled both Grant and Kane with a cold anger.

A trembling, middle-aged man with the rawboned look of an outlander whimpered, "Every couple of days they pick out one of us to make an example of. They beat us and starve us."

"Why don't you go on strike?" Grant asked, handing the man a foam-rubber-covered object that bore no resemblance to anything even remotely familiar. "A work stoppage."

The woman who had been beaten earlier whispered, "Some of us have talked about it, but we can't get everybody to go along. Some of the damn fools in here think that Mr. Snow actually means to keep his promise and let us go."

She hawked deep in her throat and spit her contempt onto the floor. "Bullshit."

"Yeah, that's pretty obvious," Kane agreed. He eyed the guard approaching on the opposite side of the conveyor belt, a pair of khaki coveralls draped over an arm.

"Maybe what everybody needs is an object lesson in labor-management relations."

The trembling man glanced over at him. "Huh?"

Kane didn't elaborate. As the guard came within earshot, he demanded, "Where's our food?"

The man tossed the coveralls across the belt toward him. "Put these on. You can wait for the slop bucket tonight like the rest of these slaggers."

Grant took one set of the coveralls and examined it, brows knitted at the bridge of his nose. "This won't fit me. It's *way* too small in the crotch."

"Put it on anyway, big man," the millennialist stated, a smirk lifting the corner of his mouth. "You heard Mr. Snow."

"Yeah, we did," Kane said, inserting a wheedling note into his voice. "We also heard Mr. Snow tell you to get us something to eat. So how about it?"

The guard scowled, then shifted his subgun to his left hand and fumbled in a coverall pocket. He fished out two paper-wrapped protein bars and leaned over the conveyor belt to hand them to Kane. As he made a motion to meet him halfway, Kane threw the coverall over the millennialist's head.

At the same instant, Grant lunged forward and with his longer reach secured a grip on the man's wrist. He yanked the unbalanced guard completely over the surface of the belt. Kane snatched the weapon from his left hand as Grant slammed the man down headfirst against the concrete floor. Bone cracked loudly.

The man lay quite still, blood slowly spreading in a dark pool around his head. Kane quickly checked the subgun, identifying it as a Calico M960. It carried a full magazine of fifty 9 mm rounds.

The laborers in the immediate vicinity gaped in openmouthed astonishment, stunned by the swift, efficient teamwork displayed by the two black-clad men as they dispatched and disarmed the guard.

Then the trembling man voiced a screaming cry of defiant jubilance: "Oh, *yeah!*"

The cry commanded the attention of two millennialists across the room. Kane put the Calico out of sight, letting it dangle at the end of his right hand, concealed by the support frame of the belt. The men seemed a little concerned that they didn't see their comrade, but not worried. They broke into a casual dogtrot.

Kane waited patiently until they were within twenty feet. One of them demanded, "Why aren't you working?"

"I've got my hands full already," Kane replied and raised the Calico. He squeezed off a short burst that blew both men off their feet, dark little dots sewed across the fronts of their coveralls.

The staccato hammering of the subgun echoed under the domed ceiling. After a long moment of silence, a cheering, yelling stampede erupted. The workers charged in a milling mass toward the doors.

A burst of automatic fire rang out from above. Kane looked up to see a millennialist standing on the edge of an overhead storage bay, shooting at the people as they sprinted for the exit. Two of them went down, slapping at wounds. Lifting the Calico to his shoulder, Kane squeezed off one shot. The man doubled over and fell, crashing down to the floor twenty feet below.

Vaulting over the conveyor belt, Grant took the sub-guns from the two dead guards and snapped four shots at a group of millennialists who worked their way around to block the doors.

The return fire was intense, bullets ricocheting off the floor and the conveyor belt in a nerve-racking cacophony. Grant stroked a short burst from his Calico in his right hand, and a millennialist jerked, lurched and fell down out of sight.

Kane triggered his own subgun, bullets pounding through a dun-colored torso. The man collapsed, blood spurting from three holes neatly grouped over his heart.

Kane shouted to Grant, "We can bet our lives there are spy-eyes in here. Snow will be sending reinforcements pretty damn quick!"

Hefting his two Calicos, Grant declared emphatically, "Then let's get out of here pretty damn quick!"

Both men sprinted toward the doors. A quartet of millennialists had regrouped, firing in the direction of Grant and Kane, their weapons chattering, muzzles flashing with little twinkles of dancing flame.

A single shot from a subgun appropriated by one of the workers drilled a hole through the jaw of one of them, punching him backward with such force his head struck the floor first. A scarlet geyser erupted from his mouth and a severed carotid artery.

Kane framed the millennialist next to him in his sights and fired a two-second burst that opened up his chest, propelling him backward in a crimson mist. The man was dead before he hit the floor. The other two ran in opposite directions, but they didn't get far before almost the entire work force of the Cellar Complex washed over them like a vengeful flood. The people buried them under pounding fists, stamping feet and makeshift clubs.

Kane and Grant pushed through the crowd to the double doors. The floor was awash with looping liquid ribbons of vermilion. Five of the laborers sprawled across it, their coveralls perforated with bullet holes and wet with fluids.

"Stand back!" Kane ordered the people. "Take some cover!"

Standing shoulder to shoulder, he and Grant opened up with full autofire at the seam between the doors. Spent cartridges arced from the smoking ejector ports and fell in a tinkling rain at their feet. Under the triple hailstorm of lead, the frames cracked, a pattern of lines running through them. Fragments struck them, but the shadow suits prevented injury. The doors shivered and the one on the left flew open.

Grant kicked it open all the way. Without pause, he and Kane raced out at the head of a horde of outraged humanity. They ran down the corridor toward the monorail platform.

As they ran, Grant panted to Kane. "Do you have anything approximating a plan?"

"No—do you?"

"I was hoping something would occur to me. Snow must have seen us on the spy-eyes by now. I feel like we're carrying targets on our asses."

Kane was almost out of breath, but he husked, "You like to fill a friend's day with sunshine, don't you?"

They turned the corner and pounded onto the platform just as a train scraped to a halt, carrying at least a dozen subgun-wielding millennialists. Kane and Grant and the laborers who had armed themselves opened fire instantly.

Bullets ricocheted off the metal of the shifter engine and struck sparks from the rail. The astonished men in the train returned fire sporadically, almost belatedly. Rolling out of the passenger cars, they stumbled over their fallen comrades or collided with those jumping from the cars. They fled down the tunnel as rounds struck all around them.

Hauling a bleeding man out of the engine, Kane sat down, examined the controls and engaged the gears. The train shivered and then began inching backward.

"Everybody who wants a lift, climb aboard!" he shouted.

The people scrambled aboard the train, filling all the seats. The ones who hadn't been able to find a berth milled uncertainly about on the platform. "We'll be back for you," Grant told them. "But right now we're in a hurry."

The train clicked on the metal railing as it picked up momentum. Within a moment it sped through the shaft. Adjacent openings and white tubes of light flitted past in blurs. The train shot like a bullet through the tunnel.

Kane felt around, found a lever and disengaged a governor relay. The train shuddered, seeming to tip over on its side as it slid around a sharp bend. There were swerving curves in the rail, but the train didn't slow as it slid along them.

Leaning forward, Grant shouted, "What the hell are you doing?"

"I thought we were in a hurry!" Kane yelled, turning toward him.

Grant saw the strange, bright fires burning in the depths of Kane's blue-gray eyes and realized his friend was in wild-man mode. He settled back, gripping the edges of the swaying car. He said nothing more to Kane as the train whipped through the tunnel.

Nothing he could say would do any good at this moment.

Chapter 27

Benedict Snow waddled into the green-grotto room, followed by Brigid Baptiste and a sentry. Brigid had visited it briefly the night before, guessing it was a central control or observation room of some sort, but she was too tired to devote much thought to why the walls were so bare.

She had been awake all night, identifying, cataloging, indexing and footnoting. Snow had expressed great delight when Catamount presented her to him, but Brigid received the unmistakable impression that both people were following individual agendas that coincided by accident. They sought different destinations by walking the same road.

When her eyes adjusted to the jade-tinted shadows, she saw Catamount, the slinking, tawny shape of Deathmaul and Sky Dog all under the apprehensive eye and gun of a coveralled guard. Sky Dog and the guard were attired identically and he appeared as exhausted as Brigid felt. Still he managed a jittery smile when he saw her.

"Where are Kane and Grant?" he asked.

"They were safe the last I saw," Brigid answered, nodding toward Snow. "He put them to work. What about the Kit Foxes?"

"Iron Horse and Laughing Badger are waiting in a cell," the shaman answered.

"Waiting for what?" Catamount snapped scornfully. "For you to rescue them?"

Sky Dog regarded her stonily, but said nothing.

Snow approached Catamount ponderously, ominously. "I had a report you were making a nuisance of yourself, young woman."

Deathmaul laid his ears flat against his head and hissed, revealing his fangs. Snow came to a halt and asked, "What was all the fuss about, then?"

"You know what it's about," Catamount retorted sharply, gesturing to the black pane of glass. "I want what you promised me. I want the *tai-me*."

"You're in no position to make demands," Snow retorted. "There are many issues yet to be decided—"

"Enough!" Catamount's cry came as loud as a whip crack. From her loincloth she whipped out a bone-handled knife and with one bound, placed the edge in the crease between Snow's double chins.

The guards snapped up their subguns, but Deathmaul whirled toward them. He snarled, belly to the ground, tail lashing. Homicidal fury glared out of his gold-green eyes.

"Steady on now, girl," Snow murmured. "Steady on. You don't want to take rash actions."

Between clenched teeth, Catamount spit, "Why not?"

Snow swallowed, taken aback by the violence of the woman's reaction. Raising a pair of conciliatory hands, he said softly, soothingly, "Calm down. I merely misspoke. I simply meant this was not the most opportune time to enter into a discussion of our arrangement. I have other, more pressing matters to attend to, like the disposal of several troublesome factors."

"Like me?" Brigid interrupted.

"And me?" Sky Dog ventured.

Snow frowned and gently pushed Catamount's knife blade away. "Yes, if you must know. Miss Baptiste, your expertise as a historian does not mitigate your well-known background as an insurrectionist of nearly mythic proportions."

The man's frown deepened. "I don't know what caused the baronies to topple and the barons themselves to vanish, but even without hard evidence, I'm certain you and your friends played a very active role in it."

Brigid didn't confirm or deny Snow's allegation, or respond to it in any way.

"Therefore," he continued, "to keep you here would be exceedingly careless and possibly earn me a written reprimand for a safety code violation."

He turned to Catamount, "As for you—"

"As for me, you arrogant swine," she broke in furiously, "you will give me what we agreed to months ago, or all your big talk of building a new society will end today, in this very room."

Snow tried to meet her infuriated, half-mad stare, then his shoulders slumped in resignation. "Very well. I shall give you my conversation piece."

Turning, he removed the remote control box from his pocket and thumbed a key. A light flashed on behind the pane of glass, illuminating the upright mummy of Towasi and striking tiny sparkling highlights from the stone attached to the post.

Brigid had seen both the cadaver and the *tai-me* the night before. Sky Dog, however, stiffened in sudden fear, drawing in his breath between his teeth. "The Owl Prophet," he whispered in horror. "The *baykok,* trapped in the Wanagi Awape Yata by the energy of the *tai-me* and the Medicine Wheel."

"Yes," said Snow in a sardonic drawl. "Trapped in the Place where Souls Wait. And Towasi has waited for a very long time."

"I care not about his filthy soul," Catamount bit out angrily.

"No, of course not." Snow pointed the remote on the wall beside the window. A dark line formed a rectangle in the surface. "A beautiful, untamed creature such as yourself. You 'care not' about anything."

The tone of Benedict Snow's voice acquired a subtle change. Although Brigid couldn't quite identify it, she felt her skin prickle.

The line on the wall expanded and became a door.

Pushing it open, he said, "All the tales of trapped souls and possession are very fanciful, rather hard for a businessman to accept."

"Possession?" Catamount retorted. "I never spoke of possession to you."

"Really?" Stepping inside the niche, he grasped the chunk of yellowish stone affixed to the timber. As he worked it free of the leather thongs, he commented mildly, "Perhaps so. You rarely spoke to me about anything and then usually in a very disrespectful manner. I would have thought your mother would have taught you better."

Catamount's lips curved in a sneer of complete contempt. "Keep your mouth shut, fat man."

"Of course, I really shouldn't be surprised." Snow pulled the *tai-me* free and stepped back into the room, casually tossing the stone from hand to hand. Catamount's eyes followed its movements as if she were hypnotized. "Your mother's manners toward her elders were execrable, as well."

Feeling her throat muscles constrict, Brigid asked, "How would you know that?"

The shadowed eye sockets of Towasi's skull suddenly flared with livid twin tongues of dancing, ectoplasmic flame. At the same time, a sly, smug leer passed over Benedict Snow's face. The lenses of his goggles reflected the flames in the sockets of the mummy skull.

Very faintly on the fringes of her hearing, Brigid heard the distant beating of a drum and a chanting voice.

As she stared at Snow, for just an instant, a fleeting microsecond, the man's white hair and rotund body rippled away, like water sluicing over a pane of dusty glass. Superimposed over him, she glimpsed a dancing figure, raising and lowering his fringed arms like a great bird about to take flight, feet stamping in time to the thudding of the drum.

In a soft, liquid whisper, Snow sang, "It is I who travel in the winds, it is I who whisper in the night, I shake the trees, I shake the earth, I trouble the waters on every land."

Snow's leer became a knowing grin. "Remember when we sang that to you as a child, Catamount?"

BRIGID'S FLESH CRAWLED. Catamount stared, face twisted in stark, horrified realization. Sky Dog blurted, "Towasi!"

Snow inclined his head toward him in appreciation. "Very good. You recognize us."

Struggling to comprehend, Brigid husked out, "You possessed Snow?"

The white-haired head wagged from side to side. "We share this vessel. When he first touched the *tai-me,* we both understood we were kindred in nature. A link was forged. We shared each other's knowledge and experiences. Our minds are intertwined. There is no real separation any longer."

The goggle-covered eyes fixed on Catamount. "Do you want to know what happened to the spirit of Nightingale Woman?"

Catamount made a motion to lunge at him, but a guard swung a gun in her direction. She checked her movement, but shrieked, "Tell me!"

Transferring the *tai-me* to his left hand, Snow wagged an admonishing finger at her. "Have a care, Miss Catamount. We've communicated with your mother—she does not approve of your lifestyle, certainly not of your mode of dress…or undress, as it were."

Snarling, Catamount snatched at the *tai-me* in his hand. Snow uttered a tittering laugh and held the stone high above his head, out of her reach. "Your mother's spirit still resides in this stone, Miss Catamount. If you wish her release, you will continue to do as we bid you."

Catamount froze, gazing at the *tai-me* with hungry, desperate eyes. Deathmaul crept forward, growling.

"The bastard is lying," Sky Dog spoke up loudly. "Don't listen to him, Catamount. Your mother's spirit is with the Grandfather. Do not heed his deceptions."

Catamount blinked back the tears brimming in her eyes. She cast a frightened glance over her shoulder at Sky Dog. "I can't take the chance—"

The buzz of Snow's trans-comm cut off whatever else she was about to say. Pursing his lips in annoyance, Snow unpocketed the comm unit and place it to his ear. "Go."

He was silent for a moment, then jerked as if he had received an electric shock. "Send reinforcements, as many as you can! Do it now!"

He dropped the trans-comm to the floor and pointed the remote at the far wall. Panels slid back, revealing a bank of monitor screens. A console of automated controls folded out and down. The three screens showed black-and-white views of the same event—a pitched gun battle in the main storage vault.

Brigid and Sky Dog exchanged amused glances when they saw Kane and Grant leading the resistance against the dun-clad millennialists.

Benedict Snow stared for a long time. It was as if he couldn't convince himself that the two men in black were actually defying him. He sucked air deeply into his lungs. "We've not come this far to be stopped by the likes of them."

He spoke almost under his breath as if he were addressing someone only he could see.

Catamount had eyes only for him; she could not have cared less about the images displayed on the screen. Enraged, she leaped at Snow. "Give me back my mother!"

A guard fired his weapon, a single cracking shot. Catamount cried out and fell into Snow's arms. He caught her, staring down in astonishment. He released her as she sank slowly to the floor. Turning toward the guard, Snow raged, "You irredeemable fool! I didn't want her dead—"

With a howl like that of a damned soul, Deathmaul sprang—not at the man who had fired, but at Benedict Snow. He screamed and went down, throwing up an arm. The cougar's fangs gleamed as they crunched into the bone and his talons sank into the man's flabby flesh.

Pivoting on a heel, Brigid ripped the subgun from the guard's hands and on a backswing, pounded the butt against the side of his head. He stumbled against the control panel, but kept himself from falling.

The second millennialist whirled toward Sky Dog, but Brigid squeezed off a triburst. The man staggered and then fell as if he had tripped over a rope at ankle level.

Deathmaul's hind claws ripped open Benedict Snow's torso from his pelvic bone to his clavicle. The man screamed in soul-deep agony. The *tai-me* fell from his hand and went clattering and rolling across the floor toward the open door to the alcove.

Sky Dog made a lunge to grab it, but the snarling panther bounded from Snow's body to intersect him, leaving the man to frantically grab at his blue-sheened entrails as they spilled onto the floor on either side of him.

The cat slid around the floor to face Sky Dog, a paw striking the *tai-me*. The stone bounced into the niche, struck a stone and then plunged into the crack in the floor. Deathmaul howled and advanced on Sky Dog, fangs bared, eyes seething with fury.

Brigid put herself between the animal and the shaman. "No!" she cried stridently, hoping to break his momentum.

Deathmaul paused, glanced toward Catamount and

the blood crawling away from her body on the floor. Then he yowled and leaped. Brigid lurched backward and fired, holding the trigger down. The great cat's body spasmed in midair, twisting in on itself, yelping in pain. Crimson strings jumped from his fur.

He fell heavily, thrashing. Lifting his head, he looked toward Catamount where she lay unmoving on the floor. Slowly, painfully, he dragged himself toward her, breath rasping in and out of his bullet-punctured lungs.

Brigid gazed at the creature, heart and mind full of remorse and horror. Deathmaul reached Catamount and his rough tongue licked her face. Then he shuddered and lay still.

Catamount raised her head, blinking in momentary confusion. Her glazed eyes fixed on Deathmaul, his face frozen in a ferocious snarl, and she laid a hand on his great head. She began sobbing like a broken-hearted child.

Brigid stepped over to Benedict Snow. He stared up at her, his eyes magnified behind their thick lenses. She saw no flicker of Towasi in them. Gasping, the eviscerated man said, "I didn't mean for it to end this way."

"No," Brigid intoned. "Evil men and spirits never do."

Sky Dog knelt beside the weeping Catamount and gently pulled her up to a sitting position. A red, raw gash gleamed on her left side. Quietly he said, "If you let me, I will heal all your wounds."

And then he kissed her.

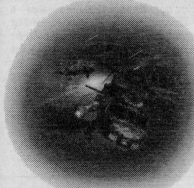

THE
DESTROYER
MINDBLOWER

An ill wind is blowing CURE off its feet...

LOOSE CANNON

When a bunch of greedy professors stole his patent idea, engineering geek Harry Kilgore got mad. And he got even. With his portable air cannon, capable of smashing anything to smithereens with the pure gravitational hammering of a 300 mph gust of wind. He can blow off rocks, bullets, poison gas, Masters of Sinanju—and, of course, all sense of ethics, morality, and the law.

Harry is stoked on the glory that nothing can stop him from doing whatever his crazy mood strikes: and right now, that means extorting billions of fun money from a Colombian drug cartel. As this maniacal geek and his supersonic air cannon leave a trail of pulverized victims in his wake, CURE must stop him before he rules the world with his mighty wind.

Available January 2006 at your favorite retailer.

DEATH LANDS®

Atlantis Reprise

GRIM UNITY

In the forested coastal region of the eastern seaboard, near the Pine Barrens of what was New Jersey, Ryan and his companions encounter a group of rebels. Having broken away from the strange, isolated community known as Atlantis, and led by the obscene and paranoid Odyssey, this small group desires to live in peace. But in a chill or be-chilled world, freedom can only be won by spilled blood. Ryan and company are willing to come to the aid of these freedom fighters, ready to wage a war against the twisted tyranny that permeates Deathlands.

In the Deathlands, even the fittest may not survive.

Available December 2005 at your favorite retailer.